"We'll make a cowboy of you yet," Kate said.

"You can try," Noah said, setting Teddie down. "Come on, short stuff. Let's see how you like this colt up close."

Teddie danced in place. He could barely contain himself as Noah opened the stall door. They held hands while Noah hunkered down and talked softly to him about the colt. Teddie threw in another fact or two, their heads close together.

Kate's throat tightened. Although she couldn't fault his being good to Teddie, she couldn't overlook the fact that Noah had been there in New York when Rob died and hadn't saved him. If only she hadn't mentioned the foal to Teddie. Should she encourage this friendship?

Dear Reader,

The most natural thing in the world for me was to write Noah Bodine's story as the latest in my Kansas Cowboys series. Personally, I don't like leaving loose ends in life or fiction—and in this case, family members. In *Mistletoe Cowboy*, I wrote about Noah's younger sister, Willow. Their middle brother, Zach, also played a role in that book. That left Noah, the eldest of the three siblings.

As the rightful heir to the WB Ranch, Noah instead left years ago to seek his fortune in New York. Now a successful CEO, he's certainly no cowboy. Yet he remained part of his close-knit family—until he accidentally skipped Willow's wedding. Can you imagine how hurt she must feel? Noah has come home to try to make amends, but I have to say good luck with that.

His life, however, is about to change. So is widowed single mom Kate Lancaster's. Despite their differences and the painful past tragedy they must resolve, I think she and Noah need each other. And while tying up the Bodines' loose ends...what if Noah is more of a cowboy than he thought?

As always, happy reading!

Leigh

Heartwarming

A Cowboy's Homecoming

—

Leigh Riker

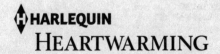

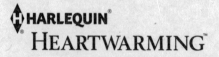

HEARTWARMING™

ISBN-13: 978-1-335-42637-6

A Cowboy's Homecoming

Recycling programs for this product may not exist in your area.

This edition published by arrangement with Harlequin Books S.A.

For questions and comments about the quality of this book, please contact us at CustomerService@Harlequin.com.

Harlequin Enterprises ULC
22 Adelaide St. West, 40th Floor
Toronto, Ontario M5H 4E3, Canada
www.Harlequin.com

Printed in U.S.A.

Leigh Riker, like so many dedicated readers, grew up with her nose in a book, and weekly trips to the local library for a new stack of stories were a favorite thing to do. This award-winning *USA TODAY* bestselling author still can't imagine a better way to spend her time than to curl up with a good romance novel—unless it is to write one! She is a member of the Authors Guild, Novelists, Inc. and Romance Writers of America. When not at the computer, she's out on the patio tending flowers, watching hummingbirds, spending time with family and friends, or, perhaps, traveling (for research purposes, of course). She loves to hear from readers. You can find Leigh on her website, leighriker.com, on Facebook at leighrikerauthor and on Twitter, @lbrwriter.

Books by Leigh Riker

Harlequin Heartwarming

Kansas Cowboys

The Reluctant Rancher
Last Chance Cowboy
Cowboy on Call
Her Cowboy Sheriff
The Rancher's Second Chance
Twins Under the Tree
The Cowboy's Secret Baby
Mistletoe Cowboy

A Heartwarming Thanksgiving
"Her Thanksgiving Soldier"
Lost and Found Family
Man of the Family
If I Loved You

Visit the Author Profile page
at Harlequin.com for more titles.

To my readers, with deep appreciation.

You are the best!

CHAPTER ONE

"I MISSED MY own sister's wedding."

Scolding himself, Noah Bodine wheeled his roll-on suitcase down the Jetway into the terminal at Kansas City International Airport. Normally, he wasn't one to engage in conversation at any stage of a trip, which provided a rare opportunity to decompress while in limbo, but he'd clearly been muttering on the plane, and the woman next to him had leaned closer to ask, "Did I hear you right?" So, out of politeness, he'd answered. Also, because she'd looked panic stricken during what had proved to be a rough flight.

After that, his seatmate hadn't said another word, even as the weather continued to deteriorate en route. But then, his explanation hadn't been pretty, or excusable. Instead of being there on Willow's special day to walk her down the aisle, Noah had left their middle brother to do the honors alone—on *Christmas*, no less. Who, other than Noah, could overlook something like that? What was he going to say to her?

Little more than a week after the wedding, here he was, headed home on a Saturday, the only open slot in his January schedule, determined to apologize to his whole family.

No matter how guilty he felt, he dreaded this brief weekend homecoming, especially with his brother, who wasn't the forgiving type.

Noah breezed through the terminal and out to the shuttle that served the car-rental agencies, suddenly wishing he'd stayed in his fifty-first-floor office overlooking Central Park. Or taken the company Gulfstream so he wouldn't have needed to make idle conversation with a stranger, but the optics of using the plane for personal business weren't any better than missing Willow's big day. Besides, his VP of Marketing for J&B Cybersecurity had flown to London last night on their jet, getting a head start on the new year and the already-troubled branch office they were opening there.

Yeah, in some circles Noah was a big deal these days, but not on the WB Ranch near Barren, Kansas, where he'd grown up. Surrounded by tough men like his dad—king of the hill there, and one reason why Noah wasn't running the spread that would have been his birthright. As the eldest son, he'd chosen the skyscrapers of New York and the career he really wanted instead. Now a driven CEO if there'd ever been one, Noah also wanted two other things—to become even more successful and, although he had a current girlfriend, to avoid any deeper romantic entanglement. He'd been in love once.

On the shuttle bus, he kept his eyes on his cell phone screen, scrolling for urgent messages. With his preferred status regarding the car, he wouldn't have to wait in line. He would be on his way in minutes. Thankful for the valuable time this saved him on such a short trip, he hoped to get on the road before the weather really closed in. It was getting bad outside the bus windows, the snow coming down in large white flakes.

At the car-rental agency, he was passing the busy counter, headed straight for the parking lot, when he did a double take and his heart picked up speed. As if he'd conjured her up, Noah looked closer at the slender, dark-haired woman standing at the head of the line, having an intense conversation with the agent. It was Kate Lancaster, all right.

Of course, his chances of running into her closer to home were good—her ranch was next to the WB—but right here in the airport? He didn't think she even traveled. Then Noah stopped thinking and came to a dead stop. He probably should have just kept walking, but he didn't.

"BUT YOU DON'T UNDERSTAND," Kate said again. "I need to get home."

Her voice had wobbled as she begged the agent at the counter. Always a poor traveler, she preferred staying home these days—to the point of being labeled neurotic by some—and now, after that harrowing flight from LaGuardia, her trip had gotten much worse. So had the weather. If only she hadn't gone to her college roommate's wedding in New York. Hadn't abandoned her four-year-old son for a few days. Kate had felt guilty the entire time.

The huge city itself had been enough to make her pulse pound. So many people, so much noise when Kate craved the relative peace and quiet of Sweetheart Ranch. Her very own plot of paradise, an hour and a half's drive at most from the spot where she was standing now.

The harried agent didn't look that sympathetic, but he said, "Sorry, miss. An hour ago, we had plenty of cars available, but this storm hit earlier than expected. Now everything we had is already on the road. I'm flat out of inventory."

Kate took another deep breath. She'd managed not to truly freak out in midair by envisioning home, counting the hours until she would be there again. The turbulence on the plane had never let up, the bar carts in the galley rattling with every pitch and roll of the airliner, and when they'd—finally!—descended through the heavy clouds that had turned from silver to lead to nearly black as the plane reached the Midwest and met the fast-moving storm, she'd prayed for a safe landing not to leave her little boy alone in the world. As they'd taxied to the terminal, Kate had watched the snow that began to fall, thick and heavy, from her window seat in coach. She gave thanks to be on firm ground again.

Through the glass sliding doors to the street now, she could see the snow-covered pavement. No wonder one of the ranch hands hadn't shown up to meet her in baggage claim, but Kate had hoped to be able to tuck Teddie in tonight, to reassure him that she wouldn't leave again—as he assumed his daddy had left him. Rob's loss still seemed like yesterday to Kate as well. On their own, she and Teddie hadn't been the same in the past year. How could they be? Widowed now, a single mom, her boy without his father…oh, and she couldn't forget their financial situation, which on a ranch could be like feast or famine. Kate struggled against fresh panic as the overhead lights flickered. Great, a power outage would send her raw nerves over the edge for sure.

She tried again to get through to the agent. "Please. There must be *some* car. I don't care if it's on its last tire. If it has a million miles on it and was headed for the scrapyard. As long as it gets me where I need to go… Would you just check again?"

She heard impatient sighs behind her in the line, the shuffling of feet, voices muttering on their cell phones, everyone apparently faced with the same problem she had. At least she stood at the front of this line. If she had any chance at all, it was here.

She was about to make a last desperate plea when, out of the corner of her eye, she spied a man nearby, openly staring at her. Kate blinked. Twice. It couldn't be. She hadn't seen Noah Bodine in years and didn't want to see him now. Or, preferably, ever. Too late, though.

"Trouble?" he asked.

She felt the burn of heat—and sudden anger—in her face. She stared up at him, which was never hard to do with any man and many women. Kate stood a mere five feet three inches tall, one of the vertically challenged in this world, and had a slight build, having inherited her mother's fine bones. Which didn't mean she was a pushover. She prided herself on being capable in her own right. Ordinarily, she had to be now, but needing assistance always felt to Kate like a failure on her part. *Noah* was the last man she would ask for help.

She didn't like anything about her former neighbor from the WB Ranch. Not his dark blond hair, smoky hazel eyes or classically handsome face. Tall, broad-shouldered and wearing an obviously expensive three-piece suit, carrying a black overcoat, he exuded confidence, and she knew all about his high-tech cybersecurity firm. Noah must be here to attend some business meeting or conference in downtown KC, and her problems weren't his. Yet, while knowing how she must feel about him, he'd paused like some knight in shining armor to see what was wrong. Hardly her savior. Because of him, Kate had lost her husband, and Teddie had lost his dad.

"No cars available," she told him. And Kate hadn't made a reservation in advance, not expecting to need one if someone from the ranch came to meet her.

"Where are you headed?" As if Noah couldn't guess.

"To Barren, of course."

"That's where I'm going too," he said.

After that there was silence, as if they'd stepped into some airlock together, shutting out the increasingly irritated voices around them. The rental agent was still clicking keys on his computer, staring at his screen. Shaking his head.

She'd apparently been wrong about some meeting. But she wasn't wrong about Noah. Eighteen months ago, his scheme to hire her husband away from Sweetheart Ranch had thrown a wrench into her life and Teddie's, put a terrible strain on Kate's marriage—live in Manhattan? No way—and for another long moment, she willed herself to turn away.

"Lady," someone said, "you're holding people up. Just take the car you reserved—"

"Hey, man," Noah chimed in as if it was his job to protect her.

Kate turned her shoulder to him. "I'll handle this." More rumblings broke out down the line, and the agent stopped studying his screen. He spoke over Kate's head, saving her the trouble of making a reply to the person behind her. "Sorry, folks. We have to close."

She glanced around, but the other agencies were going dark, too, shutting off lights and setting signs on the counters. A fresh pang of alarm ran through her. What could she do now? If she took the shuttle back to the airport, assuming it was still running, that might well be closed too. She hadn't heard a plane overhead in all the time she'd been here.

His mouth tight, Noah bent down to straighten the frequent-flier tag on his roll-on bag. Platinum level, of course. "I'm going your way," he pointed out, prompting Kate to face him. "I've got a car. I can give you a ride if you want?"

His tone had sounded hesitant. At least he must feel some shame, but she would rather hitch a ride with a stranger than get in a car with Noah Bodine.

Turn your back again. Tell him to go to—

But aching to be home, yearning with all her heart to see Teddie, to hold him in her arms and feel safe again, too, she had no other choice. She needed to get to her ranch, her refuge. Today. For her own safety, she couldn't actually flag down a stranger or walk all the way home even if she wanted to rather than occupy the same space with Noah for a single minute. The airport shuttle to outlying communities, which only went as far as Farrier, had already stopped running. Kate had checked while still in the airport. The only car available to her, it seemed, was Noah's.

"I guess I can do that," she said at last, not caring that she didn't sound gracious or grateful. *I'll have to.* In the past year, she'd learned to do whatever was necessary for her and Teddie, who needed his mother more than Kate needed to save her pride.

She just hoped that this time—unlike her husband—in the company of Noah Bodine, she would get home alive.

"You really want to know why I'm here?" Noah glanced at Kate again, seated on the passenger side of his rental car, at her glossy dark hair and accusing gray eyes. Clearly, she despised him. He took a breath before he answered her question. Kate would love this explanation. "I'm in the family doghouse again. I missed my sister's wedding."

"So everyone else must have noticed," Kate said. She obviously had. Certainly, she would have been invited too. "How was that even possible?"

She had every right to judge him—for reasons of her own. Maybe he should have kept walking when he saw her at the rental counter. Five minutes after they'd left the airport, he knew this drive would prove an even bigger challenge than his vague plan to somehow make up for what he'd done. This was his first trip home in a year…showing up at last. He could almost hear his brother say those words.

Yet despite his jet-setting lifestyle, Noah had been raised like any other western male to take care of a woman. His protective instinct was as strong as ever, but considering the rapidly worsening road conditions, maybe Kate should have refused the ride he'd offered.

He peered through the windshield. The Kansas Plains were no destination for a fun winter vacation, much less a personal guilt trip, and he'd been dead wrong about the storm. According to the weather report on his cell phone earlier in the airport's sky club, he'd hoped to be at the ranch before this blizzard arrived. It had come early. The wind howled, rocking the car from side to side, and Noah had to fight the wheel. He'd half forgotten how bad it could snow here, coming down horizontally like a train rushing straight at them, disorienting him and obliterating the landscape all around.

The wipers were having a hard time keeping up, and Kate's knuckles, hands clenched around the passenger seat cushion, were as white as the falling snow. He knew she blamed him for Rob's death, but Noah wasn't about to broach that topic. He couldn't imagine a worse scenario than getting into an argument with her—except making her cry. He had to give her credit, though, for not saying a word.

More likely, she was speechless, terrified that he might run off the road. Angry to even be in the same car with him. But Kate had seemed so determined to reach home that she'd agreed to ride with him. Go figure.

"Sorry," he muttered as the sedan slewed

again to the left. "Would have been nice if they'd put snow tires on this thing. Chains would be even better."

The words weren't out of his mouth before a semi roared past them, flinging icy slush against the driver's-side door of the sedan. Kate gave a strangled moan. Noah could barely tell where the road was in front of them now, and he'd leaned closer to the glass, trying to focus his already-burning eyes, but to avoid the big truck, he was forced to over-steer.

Just when he thought they'd made it, the car slid, and a snowdrift at the side of the four-lane highway loomed up a second before they plowed into it. The sedan shuddered to a halt, throwing Noah and Kate forward against a wall of white, but thankfully not hard enough for the air bags to deploy. Now they were stuck, other vehicles passing by too fast, someone blowing their horn as if to say *Out of the way, you fool.* Noah tried a few times to rock the car out of the drift, but the ditch he hadn't seen before he lost control kept it trapped and at a slight down-ward angle.

"You okay?" he asked Kate, who had flung

out a hand against the dashboard and was now rubbing her wrist.

She only nodded, biting her lower lip.

"Well, we can't stay here. We could get rear-ended or sideswiped," he said. "Let's get out of the car. I'll have to call for a tow truck."

He hadn't finished before someone tapped on his frosted window. Noah turned his head and saw an older man bundled in a heavy parka with its fur-trimmed hood pulled low over his face, his beard encrusted with ice. Noah rolled down the window. "Saw you hit this bank of snow," the man said, then pointed off into the distance where Noah saw nothing but pearly white. "I live up that hill. Let me see if my truck winch can help."

"Bless you," Kate murmured.

And miracle of miracles, within minutes, the farmer had managed to free them from their prison of snow. They'd been his third rescue, he said. Noah thanked him profusely and, when the man refused payment, took his contact information. He'd send something nice to show his gratitude. He didn't want to say so to Kate, but they'd been lucky not to be killed by some passing car or truck with poor visibility too.

A few miles down the road, Noah revised his opinion. Their good fortune had run out. The road had gotten even more slippery, and as they neared a highway exit, an overhead sign flashed. *Road Closed Ahead. Please exit here.* Noah eased off the gas, then managed to coast to the bottom of the exit ramp, which they'd nearly passed. He hadn't dared to slam on the brakes, or he would have lost control again. He began shaking inside.

The interstate had been rough, and he could imagine what the narrower two-lane side roads would be like.

"How are we going to get home?" Kate asked his own silent question.

Noah hated to tell her but reaching both ranches by some alternate route would be impossible. Clearly, they weren't going much farther.

"Guess we're not." At the top of the ramp, having kept his speed steady on the slight incline to not get stuck, he made a creeping turn, but the lone gas station to his right had no lights on. The small convenience store across the road looked dark too. The only glimmer in the distance on his left was a flickering neon sign that Noah struggled to read. Several letters were missing. "Let's try the Bluebird Motel over there."

Kate followed his gaze. "You mean stay the night?" she said, her tone taut. "Pull over. I'll call the ranch again. Maybe someone there can come for us in one of the trucks."

He hated to point out that no one had shown up earlier, which she'd explained to him as they walked to his car in the agency's parking lot, and no one would be using the highway now except for people like Noah and Kate still trying to get somewhere.

To ease her mind, he tried the WB, too, just in case, but his call wouldn't go through.

Kate clicked off her phone. "I can't get a signal. I was worried when no one met me at the airport, as we'd planned."

"Now we know why," he said. "Looks like we're snowbound."

CHAPTER TWO

KATE WALKED INTO the room ahead of Noah, who'd held the door for her, seeming as careful as she not to touch. She hadn't said a word while he negotiated in the office with the clerk, a bored twentysomething who'd kept one eye on the wall-mounted TV behind them, the other on the ancient computer at the check-in desk. With more stranded travelers expected, he'd been reluctant to rent them two rooms. He'd smirked when he handed Noah the keys as if he knew they were really…together.

She checked out the sorry space in the first of the rooms that unfortunately were connected and, likely, identical. Kate shivered. Also, they were cold. She saw two double beds. A small desk with one broken drawer hanging askew. Several wire hangers in the open closet that had no door. A sagging armchair in the corner. She didn't want to see the bathroom.

"I can't stay here," she said, feeling more depressed by the second.

Noah leaned against the closed door to the outside. "Do you have a better idea?"

"No," she admitted, then clamped her mouth shut.

This wasn't his fault. Other things were, but not this.

"Be glad we got two rooms," he pointed out. "Not that either one is the Ritz-Carlton."

Kate watched him slip his coat onto one of the hangers in the closet—obviously a man to whom travel and hotel stays were routine, making a home for himself wherever he landed. How were they going to get through the rest of the afternoon and night in such close quarters? This was worse than sharing his car when she could barely stand to come within ten feet of him. Which *was* his fault.

For Teddie's sake, she'd accepted the ride. And only for Teddie. Kate would do anything to safeguard him and protect her own broken heart.

Now here she was, in this cheap motel. With *Noah*. Yes, he'd rescued her at the airport, like it or not… Through the front window, she watched the snow fall in ever-bigger flakes, soundless, from a thick sky the color of milk.

"What else can we do?" he asked.

She had to agree, this must be equally awkward for him. There was no way they could make it to either ranch. Even if they reached the town first, the old road out of Barren would be impassable.

"Nothing," she finally agreed, then went into her own room and locked the door.

NOAH LEANED BACK against the bed's headboard. Night had fallen, and he could hear Kate still moving around next door. He'd seen several cars pull into the parking lot after theirs, then a few more that promptly left again. The sign outside the window now said *No Rooms*. Where could those other people have gone instead? He felt guilty for taking up these two rooms, yet Kate would never have shared one with him.

His stomach growled. He needed food. He hadn't eaten before his flight, or on the plane, but the Bluebird had no on-site restaurant, and the nearby convenience store was no longer open. Obviously, he wasn't going to eat now. Plus, nothing in this place seemed to work. At first his room had been freezing, but he'd fiddled with the knobs on the ancient heating unit until, finally, he'd felt a slightly warmer blast of air. Now it rattled and banged and clicked through each cycle. He'd hoped to at least find hot coffee in what passed for the lobby, but right after Noah checked in, the clerk had closed up and gone home before five o'clock. The whole world seemed to have shut down.

Noah rose from the bed to rap on the connecting door. "You awake?"

"Of course." He could almost hear her teeth chatter. "It's frigid in here, and I can't seem to get any heat."

Noah offered to work his questionable magic on her unit, and Kate, looking reluctant, let him in. Her eyes never met his. When he finally managed to produce the same feeble flow of warmth into her room, too, he headed back to the adjoining door, but to his surprise Kate stopped him with a single word. "Hungry?"

"Starving but there's no—"

She held up two packs of crackers stuffed with orange cheese. Another pair were in her other hand. "This is me saying thank you with the only things I had in my bag. I'm afraid you'll have to wash these down with water, though. The only vending machine I saw—"

"Was in the front office, which is locked. We're on our own."

She hovered near the open doorway, clearly waiting for him to go back to his room.

Noah said, "I heard a plow a little while ago." But who was he kidding? "Getting to Barren tonight after all might be possible—or not." But then he'd have to navigate the likely more slippery, narrower road out of town to the WB. The gates to Kate's place, where he'd have to drop her off first, were a mile farther than that, and if he remembered right, the driveway to Sweetheart Ranch was more of a rutted track. His rental car would never make it up even that small slope. If he did get in, he might not get out. When she didn't respond, having probably reached the same conclusion, he said, "Dumb idea, huh?" Noah paused. "Do you think you *can* sleep yet?" It was still early.

In answer, Kate rolled her eyes.

"Neither can I," he said. "Mind if I, uh, hang here with you for a while?"

"Would I seem rude if I said yes—I do mind?" She gestured at the bed, then sighed. "Have a seat."

She went into the bathroom and came out with water in two plastic cups. Keeping her distance, she settled onto the sagging armchair to open her crackers, still looking uneasy. Yet he'd sensed that, like him, she didn't want to be alone. Noah couldn't blame her. Their surroundings were nothing to crow about, the utter quiet of the falling snow isolated them like two survivors and he knew she must be worried about her little boy. Enough that even Noah's company had become tolerable. She turned on the TV, but the small screen was snowy like the weather outside, and Kate shut it off. Neither of them said much until he could no longer stand the silence. This wouldn't work. He waved a cracker in the air. "Thanks for dinner. Hard to believe places like this still exist."

"At least we're sort of warm and dry," she pointed out. "I mean, what if the car broke down? Or ran off the road again? I should have tried to get a room near the airport. Then there'd be people around and an open restaurant, even a Wi-Fi signal."

"By then the hotels would have been filled. Didn't you see all those people with their cell phones out? Calling ahead soon after we touched down?"

"This weekend was the first time I'd been on a plane in years. I don't know the drill." She paused. "I really am thankful for your help—at the airport too."

To Noah, her tone sounded grudging. "Not sure how much help," he said. "Look where we are now."

"We could have still been in that snow-drift. Frozen."

"True." He tilted his head, recalling her positive outlook years ago—before Noah had enticed Rob Lancaster to join J&B in New York. Before she'd learned to hate him. "You always look at the glass half-full?"

"I try—with more success some days than others. Anyway, we gave it a shot." He could hear the frown in her voice, see it on her face. Not as brave as she must want him to think. "My real concern tonight is Teddie. He's home with my aunt who lives with us now, but he'll wonder why I didn't read him a story as I promised to do when I got home. They'll be worried."

Noah knew about Teddie only from Rob, who, for those six months together on Noah's home turf, had often bragged about his über-smart kid, showing him pictures every time Kate texted new ones from the ranch. Teddie riding his bike with the training wheels or trying to throw a lasso at a makeshift "steer" the cowhands had devised for him. Teddie, his face smeared with birthday cake, grinning above the candles. "How old is he now?"

"Four," she said with a quick smile that seemed to light the dim room, which had only a lone lamp on the nightstand, before she sobered.

"He must really miss you."

"Yes, and I miss him. He's my...heart." The word was almost a whisper.

Noah tried to imagine being a parent but couldn't. He didn't even have nieces or nephews to spoil, though he soon might. Willow and her guy wanted a family, she'd told him during one of their rare phone conversations not long before the wedding. After that call, *how* could he have forgotten the event was on *Christmas Day*? Well, not forgotten. He'd had his tickets, a limo scheduled to LaGuardia. He'd sent the gift ahead. But then, there'd been the latest of a series of crises with the new branch office in London, and to deal with that mess, he'd had to fly east instead of west.

"I'm not sure my sister's missing me now,"

he said as if to continue their talk in the car. "Or that she'll be glad to see me. I know my brother won't."

"I don't see much of Willow or Zach these days," she said. "I kind of stick to myself, but she and I used to do things with the same group of girls now and then. She's a great person."

"So is Zach, just not with me. Especially about the wedding."

"And you'll apologize," she said as if to prompt him.

"Yeah, like that will cover it." He had some serious explaining to do but not to Kate. No matter how pretty her brief smile had been.

She must have decided not to pursue that subject. She told him about the wedding she'd attended in New York, then said, "I'm curious. Years ago, before you were in business, why didn't you stay in Kansas? Your dad wanted you to run the WB, didn't he?"

"You have to ask? You knew him." Noah's father had passed away a year ago, shortly before her husband died. "We didn't see eye to eye on a lot of things, particularly that." And after years of watching their relationship grow increasingly contentious, Noah had finally bailed, unable to make headway with his domineering father. The darkened room, the stillness, the heavy snow drifting past outside, seemed to shut him behind a curtain with Kate in which confidences seemed natural. Even between two people who were far from being friends. "He groomed me from the time I could walk, but I'm no cowboy. In fact, horses and I have never been friends."

"I love to ride," she said. "I love everything about my ranch."

Another bone of contention between them, then.

"I punch keys on a computer all day, not cows. I don't much like cows either."

Silence again. That didn't impress her. Not that he was trying to.

Noah sure wouldn't tell her that, after her husband's death, the company's IPO had been one of the best in tech history. In his awkward angle against the headboard, his neck burned, and his shoulder hurt. His right hand had fallen asleep. He changed position, shook out his fingers to get the blood moving. His stomach rumbled again. He told himself he was only making idle small talk with Kate because she'd shared her crackers with him, but the snack hadn't been enough to satisfy his hunger.

"It's hard," she admitted, "running the ranch by myself, but I do have cowhands to help, and I love that Sweetheart Ranch is still mine." He could hear the pride in her voice, tinged with sorrow because Rob was no longer part of that. "One day I'll turn it over to Teddie. He can't wait," she said. "I got him a pony for his fourth birthday, and I have to pry him out of the saddle. You should see him r—"

She broke off. For a long moment, she studied her hands in her lap. Rob would never see his son ride or graduate from college or get married. Noah felt guilty all over again for bringing Rob on board with him at J&B. The unforeseen consequences had proven dire.

"I know it's not easy, Kate. I know how much you loved Rob, how he loved you and Teddie. In New York he talked about you all the time." He wouldn't have brought up the painful subject, but it was Kate who had, by inference, and so it needed to be addressed.

"He never should have been there," she said.

Kate had jumped up from her chair and was standing by the connecting door. He didn't know how to make her understand about the attack that had taken Rob's life, wasn't sure about it himself. Instead, he simply said, "Listen. About what happened— I'm sorry," before his throat tightened, and he couldn't go on. The words seemed inadequate. "Kate…"

When she didn't respond, Noah got up, then walked past her into his room. They were like proverbial ships passing in the night. For this one night. In the morning, he'd get her home and, considering his short stay, he might not see her again.

He wished that didn't matter. Yet it still did.

Rob had been his friend. And he'd married Kate—the only woman Noah had ever loved.

CHAPTER THREE

"Mommy!" Teddie flew into Kate's arms the next day as soon as she got through the door, nearly knocking her over, and she gathered him in, her heart bursting with relief to be home. Bandit, their dog, leaped and jumped around their legs, barking his own welcome.

"Arf!" The Australian shepherd, as active as Teddie was, all but shattered her eardrum with his joyous greeting. He pawed at Kate's jeans.

"Get down," she said with a pat on Bandit's head, but found it hard to speak.

Kate held her son closer. Teddie was a bundle of love wrapped in that small, warm body, his blond hair so like his father's sweeping against her cheek, his eyes dancing. The best gift she'd ever gotten. How unfair that he, like Kate, would never have a sister or brother, as Noah Bodine did—even if Noah wasn't getting along with his family at the moment.

Honestly, she felt almost sorry for him having to face his brother's wrath and Willow's disappointment. She'd had the impression that, in contrast to her eagerness to get home, Noah didn't feel the same way. He'd seemed to be stalling that morning, insisting they stay at the motel until check-out time. Why not play it safe, he'd said, until the roads were cleared? Having slept late, they'd eaten a breakfast of microwaved egg sandwiches at the little convenience store, where Noah had ordered a third cup of coffee, perusing the local newspaper (*First Blizzard Shuts Down State*) at the only table while he ate his second doughnut. She couldn't blame him for not wanting to rush to the WB, and the drive along snowy roads from the Bluebird Motel hadn't been easy, but at least the storm had ended.

Teddie tipped his head to gaze up at her with his father's blue eyes made larger by the thick, black-framed glasses he'd worn since he was eighteen months old. "Where did you go?" Then, without a pause, he asked, "Did you see my daddy?"

Kate stomped snow from her boots, then gentled her voice. "Bunny, you know I didn't." To her sorrow, this message never seemed to get through. "We've talked about that and I know it makes you sad, but he wasn't in New York. Sweetie, he can't be with us anymore."

Kate drew away and straightened, clasping his hand. So delicate, so fragile. She would die herself rather than hurt him, yet he couldn't continue to believe, to hope, that Rob would come home. Teddie's pediatrician claimed that wasn't good for his health. She'd made a mistake last year in not telling Teddie the truth right away... She'd thought he was too young to grasp the concept of death. After that mistake, his mind had been set.

Her eyes filled. "I missed you, baby." Diversion at Teddie's age was always her best friend. "What did you do while I was away?"

"Before the snow, I rode Spencer."

"Of course, you did," she said, blinking to clear the tears that had threatened to fall. At least she and Teddie weren't talking about Rob now. His loss had brought Kate to her knees, and she missed him dreadfully, too, but Teddie was still crouching, emotionally, in some mental corner, hoping every night to see his dad again. She hadn't been able to convince him otherwise. "I hope Spencer took good care of you."

"He's always good." Teddie sent her a chiding look. "You know that, Mommy."

He was the pony's constant protector, his defender whenever need be.

Kate's aunt Meg, wearing jeans and a green long-sleeved Henley shirt, appeared in the kitchen doorway at the other end of the entry hall, wiping her hands on a dish towel. "I'm not surprised you were delayed. I was worried. How were the roads today?"

"Pretty bad." She'd managed to call earlier but would detail her misadventure with Noah later. She couldn't stop the remembrance, however, of last night in the Bluebird Motel with her worst enemy, never mind that they'd managed to hold a civil conversation without Kate's anger erupting. Barely. She couldn't believe they'd actually dared to talk about Rob.

Kate had learned early in her life about loss. She'd been a little girl, not much older than Teddie was now, when her mother had abandoned the family. Years later, just as Kate reached adulthood with the beloved father who'd raised her, he'd been killed in a tractor accident. More recently, she'd lost her husband and Teddie his dad. There would be no more losses in their lives, if she had her way.

Meg's brown hair looked mussed rather than tidy, but she flashed a bright smile. "If this boy could sleep with that horse, he would."

"He'd fit in my bed with me," Teddie agreed, nodding. "He would."

She shot Meg a look. "I'm sorry I didn't get home last night." Kate angled her head toward Teddie. "We've established that Spencer behaved himself." She tried a teasing tone. "What about my boy here?" she asked Meg.

Her aunt's blue gaze looked weary yet warm. "Teddie is an angel."

Which was pretty much true, though he could be exhausting at times. Kate had to smile, but had she taken advantage of her aunt? Meg, who was only seven years older than Kate, had moved in with them not long after Rob's death—and her own divorce. Having an on-site babysitter was a blessing, but Kate, who was thirty, worried about her. She treasured her companionship, but Meg had a tendency to sacrifice herself for others when she should be making a new life for herself. "Thanks for watching him again."

Meg smiled. "Always my pleasure. Good to have you home, Kate."

"Well, then." She clapped her hands, setting Bandit off again. The dog raced around the hall, skidding on the floor, tail wagging a mile a minute. "Let's celebrate. How does some ice cream sound, Teddie?"

His eyes lit up. "Chocolate chip?"

Meg had already turned back into the kitchen and was heading for the refrigerator. "I bought a half gallon before the snow started."

"One scoop for me," Kate called after her. "I ate way too much at the wedding reception on Friday night, and the breakfast buffet on Saturday before I left the hotel looked too scrumptious to resist."

She'd eaten more yesterday than Noah had, he'd told her. Offering him the cheese crackers she'd bought in LaGuardia for Teddie, Kate had taken pity on him—not something she cared to repeat.

Sitting across from Teddie at the table, she felt herself begin to unwind. She was home. *I'm no cowboy*, Noah had said, but Kate was, or rather, a genuine cow*girl*. There were a few other women ranchers in the area like her, yet it was still a man's world. And even her friend Nell Ransom had her husband's help on the big NLS Ranch. Kate couldn't afford to miss a day of work. Sweetheart's survival was up to her now.

A fresh pang of sorrow went through her for Teddie and herself. Clearly, she needed some distraction to help her forget last night and seeing Noah briefly as a human being instead of the monster who'd let her husband die.

She'd take Teddie riding tomorrow, hoping to forget for an hour or three her constant worries about her son's well-being and her own still-shattered heart.

"WELL. IT'S ABOUT time you got here."

Noah had knocked, then turned the front doorknob at the WB's main house—his home, once, which was rarely locked—when Zach appeared, his gaze widened in surprise. Or was that shock? Noah was in for it now, as expected. He'd hoped his mother would come to the door instead, but no. Not his luck.

Leaning against the living room door frame, arms crossed, his brother looked him over. His tone stayed mild. "How many of those fancy suits do you own?"

"Enough to get the job done," Noah drawled.

He never stepped foot on this ranch without his accent changing from city to country, which irritated him. From the next room, he could hear the drone of some game on TV, probably basketball, and a shuffling sound from someone who'd shifted perhaps on the sofa. He knew his mother didn't care for sports. So who could be watching? Willow, most likely. "Could I bring my bag in before you start on me?"

Zach didn't blink. His hair honey colored, his eyes that serious hazel, he wore his usual jeans with a plain white T-shirt. Zach was in his sock feet. "You already blew off Willow's wedding. Why turn up now? The damage was done on Christmas Day," he said, then, "No, actually the night before, when you didn't show up for the rehearsal dinner."

Noah flicked snow off his sleeves. "I'd, uh, planned to come of course but—"

"Save your excuses for Willow." Zach paused. "Oh, no, wait. She's not here. She's on her honeymoon."

Noah's stomach sank. He'd figured Willow would be put out with him, too, deeply hurt, but she was a far more forgiving sort than Zach. "Honeymoon? Last time we spoke, I thought she and Cody were postponing any trip until they got their new training business started."

"They did and Cody changed her mind." Zach paused. "You probably won't be here by the time they get home, looking all tanned and happy after their Caribbean cruise." He turned his back on Noah. "As far as I'm concerned, if this is another of your drive-by visits like the one for Dad's funeral, you should have saved yourself the airfare. This family hasn't been a priority since you graduated from college. And took off for greener pastures."

Noah had felt he had little choice then but wasn't about to explain himself yet. He'd dropped Kate earlier at Sweetheart Ranch, then hightailed it back into town. Lunch at the café; a snowy walk down Main Street, where most of the shops never seemed to change; a burger at Rowdy's bar, lingering there over a beer before he finally drove out of Barren to the WB well after sunset. Working up his nerve.

"Zach," a woman's voice called, "take it easy."

Noah glanced toward the other room, then back to Zach.

"Mom's watching a game?" He'd hoped to be rescued, yet that didn't sound like her.

"No, she went into town yesterday, but once this storm hit, she stayed there with friends. Avoiding the drive home in all this snow. Why? Did you expect her to be here to greet you when you didn't bother to give anybody a heads-up about this royal visit?"

The woman who'd spoken before came out to the hall, her sock feet gliding across the polished wooden floor. In jeans and a flowy top, she had auburn hair that tumbled down her back, her eyes a bright blue. Familiar, like her voice. This seemed to be his week for running into people he used to know.

Cass Moran laid a hand on Zach's spine. "Excuse this one. Your mother tried to teach him manners, but obviously she failed. It's good to see you, Noah."

As with Kate, Noah hadn't seen Cass in years, and the last time he'd heard, she was in California, working as an event planner in Malibu. Now she looked at ease in his family's house.

She held up one hand to show him a sparkling diamond. Noah had missed something else, all right.

"You're engaged?"

"See what I mean?" Zach said to indicate Noah had proved his point.

"I realize I have a lot of apologizing to do. But on my way to the WB, I got stuck yesterday in that blizzard. You must know the roads were closed. Couldn't get a phone signal to tell you I was even coming." Unlike Kate, he hadn't called the ranch this morning. Coward. "I have to say, the snow made me glad I left Kansas back in the day, which I'm sure won't surprise you."

"You could have called before that."

"This trip happened fast. In New York, I meant to call but got tied up, then barely caught my flight." Better not to mention his crowded schedule, this narrow window of opportunity. But what could he have said anyway, or say now, that wouldn't make his brother angrier with him than he already was? Maybe it was a good thing he'd chopped a day off his trip because of the storm. In fact, he might leave tomorrow instead of on Tuesday.

"He was probably afraid of the very reception he's getting," Cass murmured. Then she took Zach by one well-muscled arm and gave Noah a sympathetic look. "I know exactly how that feels. My family's not warm and fuzzy—or, they weren't. There's always hope," she added. Apparently, the Moran's longtime rift had been healed. "Come on, mister. You'll miss the end of the game. You can talk to Noah in the morning."

And vent your fury, but she didn't need to say that.

Just before they disappeared into the living room, Noah spoke again. Yeah, he felt remorseful about his sister's wedding, but he wouldn't let Zach steamroll him either. "By the way," he said in that same drawling tone, "your driveway needs plowing. In my rental car, I almost got stuck."

Zach stopped. Noah should have kept his mouth shut, but to his surprise Zach turned back, then suddenly grinned and they were brothers again, if not on good terms, needling each other as they used to do at the drop of a Stetson. Neither had ever been able to resist the challenge. The back-and-forth had been easier between them then, not loaded with Noah's perceived betrayal of the family by moving east, leaving Zach responsible for the WB.

"I plowed at lunchtime," Zach said, "but if you want to give it another pass, knock yourself out. I'd change those fancy clothes first."

"I'd rather pay some kid from town to plow."

"Bet you would." Zach studied him. "City boy."

Noah blew out a breath. "Don't try to tell me you don't like running this ranch, Zach. I've never figured out why you cared that I left. You were born in a saddle. I wasn't. So who better to take over than you?" Besides, more important, Zach had mostly gotten along with their overbearing father. He'd avoided all those escalating arguments.

"I didn't say I don't like it." Zach rubbed his neck. "But, after watching it snow all night and having you suddenly appear in the flesh, I got to thinking. Winter's not my favorite season, but other than minor chores and catching up on stuff after summer, it's not that busy. Yep, I believe we should."

Noah's pulse skipped. "Should what?"

"Trade places," Zach said mildly. "For me, explore the world beyond the WB. Like you. I mean, I haven't had a break in over a year. Not that you would know, but this whole ranch got taken over by Willow's wedding plans from July straight through New Year's."

Cass murmured, "It was a humdinger of

an event. Maybe the best I've ever done."
She paused. "What are you saying, Zach?"

His grin broadened. "Seems to me, remembering Willow's honeymoon and all, it's time for a vacation of our own. And Noah's here."

"Oh, now, wait," he said. "You don't think I—"

"Can manage the ranch?" Zach shook his head. "Guess you'll have to figure that out. You've got a lot to make up for, might as well start there. Or maybe you just can't hack it?"

"Zach, I have a business to run. I have meetings next week in New York…" He didn't go on. He also had a big social event to attend with Margot, his girlfriend, who wouldn't be happy if he wasn't there to escort her. Recently, she didn't seem happy most of the time, and he needed to think more about that. Have a serious talk with her. Maybe he should head out the door and back to the airport right now, but the light in Zach's eyes told him he'd already lost this round.

Noah tried again anyway. "Listen. I left here fifteen years ago. Dad practically threw me out. 'Leave now,' he said, 'and you're no son of mine.'" Which had only added to Noah's constant sense of failure. He'd been gone that very night, determined to prove himself. *I'll show you.*

"Tough," Zach said, "and still he left you part of this ranch. Maybe it's time you earned that. It's your turn now, *brother*. First thing tomorrow, Cass and I are leaving on a little road trip." She looked so surprised that Noah guessed Zach's decision really had been made on the spur-of-the-moment. It was also payback, Noah felt certain, for him missing the wedding and a lot of other things. Noah could hardly deny that. He didn't speak before Zach added, "I'm leaving the WB in your hands."

As it should have been in the first place, but Zach didn't say that, or add *capable hands*.

"Try not to mess it up," he added.

He left Noah gaping after him in the entry hall.

THE NEXT MORNING, all bundled up, Kate and Teddie rode across the far pasture under the pretext of looking for newborn calves, although in early January even those first births should still be weeks off. The snow was deep in places where they had to pick their way, nearly swept bare in others by the wind, which held a bitter chill that made Kate hunker deeper into her parka, but the big sky was that brilliant, cloudless azure blue she loved. The brisk, clear air felt sharp enough to cut. They rode for sheer pleasure, Kate on her buckskin mare, Lady, and Teddie on Spencer, his black-and-white Welsh pony churning through the snow on chunky legs.

"Mommy! Look!" Teddie pointed at the sky. "Is that an eagle?"

"A hawk, honey, probably a red tail."

"Is he hunting for his food?"

"I bet he is," she said, reaching over to ruffle her son's hair. Her memory of New York, all that traffic and bustle and ear-shattering noise, was truly behind her now. Like Noah Bodine and the Bluebird Motel. On Sweetheart Ranch, she had peace and quiet, safety and the feeling that nothing could hurt her. She had her best memories of Rob here. She never wanted to leave, not even for another weekend. After a good night's sleep, she'd awakened to Teddie and Bandit bending over her, her son's hands cupping her cheeks, the dog drooling on the bedspread, both wanting their breakfast. Kate had been grinning before her feet hit the floor.

For a few more minutes, they rode on, Teddie frequently finding some new object of interest—a flock of doves, an icicle hanging from a branch, a lone puffy white cloud that looked to him like one of his favorite superheroes. Kate couldn't see the similarity, but it made Teddie happy. And thus, her too.

"What's that?" he suddenly asked. Ever on the lookout for adventure, he motioned toward the horizon, where Kate saw movement along the edge of her property. She squinted into the sun. A large cougar? Or a bear? Kate had a milder version of Teddie's nearsightedness, but she could see that whatever the blur in the distance might be, it was moving at a good speed. She reached around to touch the shotgun she always carried in a scabbard behind her saddle, making sure it was still there. Then, a few yards on, she made out the shape of the galloping horse.

A rider-less horse, she noted. This wasn't some escapee from the barn or a paddock where someone had left a gate open. Fully saddled, it had obviously tossed its rider. The reins trailed, which could easily cause a stumble, a fall that might lead to a disastrous injury. Even when the horse wasn't hers, she might then have to use the shotgun, as any rancher would, to put the animal out of its misery. But in front of her child?

"Wait here, Teddie," she said, then spurred Lady, already knowing he would ignore the order and follow her. Teddie couldn't keep up, but he tried, and as he fell behind, Kate urged her mare forward in the snow. The horse with no rider had picked up its pace, too, its saddle askew, in danger of coming off and spooking the animal more than it already appeared to be. "Teddie!" she called back. "Don't come any closer." The runaway, she saw, was not a gelding and could be dangerous although few ranchers she knew rode stallions.

How had this horse gotten away? And where was its rider? Oh, wait. Obviously, it had come from the WB. The range on that end was open to Kate's in places, and for years the two ranches had often shared grazing land. Then she recognized the big, sleek black that belonged to Zach Bodine. Surprising that he'd let him get away. Zach was a superb rider, not that every person she knew hadn't been thrown at some point, including herself. Turning her head, she glanced back to make sure Teddie had stopped. His eyes were wide as the stallion drew closer, tossing its head.

Teddie shouted, "Be careful, Mommy!"

Kate had feared the horse might run her down or change course toward Teddie. Instead, breathing hard, he downshifted into a high-stepping trot like a Tennessee Walker, finally sliding to a halt in the snow. As if he'd been lost and was happy to be found. "Whoa, easy," she said, holding out one hand.

Thank goodness, the stallion took only a lazy interest in her pretty mare, sidling up to them, sniffing the air, until Kate was able to reach for his bridle. If she remembered right, Zach called him Midnight. "There," she murmured in a soothing tone, using his name several times to show him she was a friend. "What got you so lathered up, huh?" He looked like he'd been running free for a while, white foam flying from his mouth.

She eyed Midnight for any signs of trouble. Kate had never spent time with this horse, didn't know what to expect of him. She'd seen other horses without their riders, had caught a few of them herself. She'd also seen several people get badly injured.

As the animal quieted down, his sides still heaving, she told Teddie, "Stay behind me,

Bunny, but we need to go find his owner."
Zach could be hurt.

She took Midnight's reins to lead him, and the horse snorted. His eyes had calmed, though, no longer rolling to show the whites. "I think he scared himself," she told Teddie.

"Like Bandit does sometimes?" Their dog usually came with them, but Kate had thought the snow too deep and left him at home.

"Barking at shadows, yes," she said, trying to keep things light so Teddie wouldn't fret. Praying they weren't about to run into a desperate situation.

They were halfway to the WB that adjoined Kate's land when Teddie cried out.

"There's a man! He can't walk right!"

Following his pointing finger, Kate saw not Zach but Noah Bodine, who had crested a small rise and was stumping toward them through the snow. Despite his tentative gait, he cut quite a figure, backlit by the morning sun, a battered Stetson on his head, and wearing worn jeans with a navy blue shirt under his unzipped winter jacket. She preferred that look to his three-piece suit, like an ID badge from New York announcing a life she wouldn't have on a silver platter—

but which Rob had wanted enough to leave her. Kate drew up close to Noah. "What happened?"

He looked up at her from the ground. "Obvious, isn't it? I just ruined a good pair of boots in this snow. Or do you want to hear me say it?" He didn't quite smile. "My first time on a horse in a while and I had to pick this one." He reached out to stroke the side of Midnight's muscular neck. "Guess I got my comeuppance."

Kate remembered Willow telling her how competitive her two brothers could be. "You were trying to show Zach you could handle anything?"

"I suppose I was," he admitted.

"Really?" As soon as a person got comfortable around a horse, complacent, you were asking for trouble. He should know that. "You win the Hubris Award of the day." Then she glanced at his leg. "Are you actually hurt?"

"Mostly my masculine pride. I may have sprained my ankle."

Teddie was watching them, as if pleased by this latest adventure, but so far—for once—he hadn't said a word. Kate hesitated, knowing she should make introductions yet reluctant to do so; she didn't want her son, trying to clear his fogged glasses with one mittened hand, to know Noah Bodine. If, while Rob had worked for him, she'd mentioned him by name to Teddie, it had been only once or twice. She hoped he wouldn't remember.

Teddie made up his own mind. "Hi," he said, pushing his glasses back on his face, then edging Spencer too close to the stallion. "I'm Theodore Robert Lancaster. Who are you?"

"Noah," he said, offering his ungloved hand. "Your, um, neighbor."

"I'm a better rider than you," Teddie pointed out.

Kate said, "Honey, don't be rude."

"No, he's right," Noah agreed as the two shook hands. He sighed. "My brother took off this morning with his fiancée for somewhere, anywhere, I imagine, that left me to work the WB until my sister gets home."

"I can't picture that," she said, not setting a good example for Teddie.

Noah looked offended or pretended to be. His eyes held a glint of amusement. "Why not?" He hooked a thumb toward the WB. "My only mistake was choosing this guy instead of Willow's mare. I may be out of practice, but if I have to—which it seems I must—I can still do some ranching."

"Apparently not," she murmured with a look that said he was on foot and his horse had crossed the range without him. "Maybe you should stick with one of the ATVs."

The stallion nudged Noah in the stomach as if to apologize for throwing him. Noah stroked one hand down its nose. "You don't know me very well, do you?"

His question seemed loaded, and she and Noah had had all the cozy conversation they were going to have in this lifetime the other night. Then, as if they were the only two people left in the snowy world, talk had been acceptable as long as they stuck to safe topics. She'd wanted to reach home as soon as possible more than she'd needed to shut him out. But she wasn't about to remind him now of Rob's loss with Teddie sitting here on his pony. "I think I know you well enough," she finally said. "I am surprised, though, that you agreed to stay."

"Zach didn't give me much choice. And he did have a point. I had all night to think about that. I left the WB to him years ago. I left him to deal with Dad then, and I've even kept away since Dad died. Can't tell you how many birthdays, Christmases, summers I've missed, visiting the family, so a few days shouldn't have to matter. Won't be long," he added. "Then there's my mom. I wouldn't leave her to cope with the ranch alone."

"Are you mad, Mommy? You look mad." Teddie was frowning at her. "Why? I think he likes us."

"I do," Noah said, looking at Teddie, not her, as if the two of them had already forged a friendship. As if, right now, Noah needed a friend. "While I'm here, if it's all right with your mother, maybe you'll come visit some-day, short stuff. My mom's always ready for company."

"Can I, Mommy?"

"We'll see." Kate blinked. Was Noah bait-ing her? She had her own opinion of him, which, after all, hadn't changed. She'd hoped he was passing through when now, it seemed, he would be here at least for a short time. She hoped Willow would return soon. "Teddie, come on. Aunt Meg will be waiting. We need to drive into town."

He turned in his tiny saddle. "No, we don't. She already got groceries."

"I said, let's go. Please don't argue." She

handed Noah his reins. "Can you ride? I mean are you okay to ride home."

"I'm sure not walking all the way back," he said, massaging his leg again. "I'll *manage*."

With a light touch of the reins against Lady's neck, Kate turned her mare toward home. In the opposite direction. Although Noah was an attractive guy, and there was nothing sweeter to her than a man who was kind to a child—her child, in this case— she couldn't overlook Noah's part in Rob's death. She didn't want him here now, and Kate vowed to keep her distance from him.

"I'm glad you're okay," she heard Teddie say and glanced back. He was still sitting there on his pony, petting Spencer and staring at Noah with a little smile, which Noah returned.

"Thanks. Nice to meet you." He and Teddie were on their best behavior when Kate wanted to spur her horse and hightail it back to the barn—as if a faster pace were possible in the snow. Her son watched Noah shift his lopsided saddle, tighten the cinch, then flip the reins he held over Midnight's head into place. With a soft grunt and the creak of leather, a jingle of brass, he climbed into the saddle.

Kate stopped her horse. Had he been saving his pride until she was out of sight? Maybe he was hurt worse than he'd claimed. Should she accompany him to the WB— In that, he might be like Rob, who'd never wanted to show any weakness. But why worry about Noah Bodine? She would not, Kate told herself. Still, she didn't go on until she saw that he was able to ride.

Then she trotted on a short way, hoping Teddie would catch up so she didn't have to go back for him, wishing she'd stayed home this morning in her nice, warm house. She needed to avoid any further chance meetings with Noah.

She was about to use her best Mom voice when Teddie finally started toward her.

They were nearly home, trotting into the barnyard, before he spoke again. "Why don't you like Noah?"

"I don't need to like him, Bunny. He isn't staying here. He lives far away."

He gazed up at her, owlishly. "Where you went to the wedding?"

"Close enough," she hedged, ruffling his hair again. "Now, Mr. Twenty Questions, how about we make some lunch?"

But Teddie wasn't done. He rarely was, and

Kate had been fielding questions from the time he said his first words, her little boy whose pediatrician had recently called him a genius—and meant that literally. Way beyond a four-year-old's normal innate interest in the world, Teddie's acute mind never stopped working. He saw everything. At the moment, he saw too much, and his curiosity knew no limits. Neither did his firm conviction that, one day, Rob would walk through their front door.

Kate's hands tightened on her reins at his next question, which she'd dreaded. She heard some variation of Teddie's fantasy every day.

"Mommy. Does Noah know where my daddy lives?"

Kate couldn't come up with an answer. There was none that would satisfy Teddie, except to have his dad home again. In her mind, the issue was very different. Kate missed Rob, at least most of what they'd had together, but she already knew—and accepted—that he wouldn't ever hold her again, kiss her or talk about planning the rest of their family. Never roll around on the living room floor with Teddie while he tickled him and Teddie roared with laughter.

Why, in the midst of that sad reality, had Noah come back into her life? Whether he wore a suit or a pair of jeans, and no matter how good he looked, she definitely needed to avoid him. Not only for her son's sake.

CHAPTER FOUR

"GOOD HEAVENS. WHAT happened to you?" Noah's mother had rushed into the kitchen as soon as he'd opened the back door and limped into the house. He hadn't seen her when he arrived last night while she was staying in town.

"Midnight happened," he said. "Nobody warned me that Zach's horse can be a killer."

"Why on earth did you try to ride him?" She pulled out a chair. "Here. Sit down before you fall down."

Noah didn't argue. The ride home after he'd met up with Kate and her son had been slow torture. At least the stallion had shown him some mercy, but Noah hadn't trusted him not to throw him again. He'd left the also-tired horse in the barn with one of the hands to be cooled down and groomed. By then, Noah had been gasping, defenseless against the pain that now radiated from his ankle and up his leg. It certainly wasn't numb any longer.

"If I'd known you were coming, Noah, I would have stayed home." Her still-blond hair flying, she bustled around the room, taking a bag of peas from the freezer, grabbing a clean towel from a drawer and clucking her tongue the whole time.

Jean Bodine was the WB's matriarch, the glue that had always held this ranch, and their family, together. As she lifted his throbbing ankle and slapped the improvised ice bag on it, he managed, "Hey, Mom. Good to see you too."

She stepped back, hands on her hips. "Why *didn't* you tell us you were coming?"

"Zach asked the same question."

"Yes, and it's a good one. Noah Andrew Bodine, we haven't seen you since—"

"I know, Dad's funeral." He said it for her because any mention of his father must still be more painful for her than his hurting ankle was to Noah. He could see tears in her eyes.

"Then not to turn up for Willow's wedding—"

"Inexcusable." He tried to explain his unexpected trip to London at exactly the wrong time for Willow. "I hope you can forgive me."

Her eyes, a softer hazel than his or Zach's, softened. "You know I do." She leaned over to hug him, and he could feel the beat of her heart against him. "How could I not forgive my firstborn son? It's wonderful to have you home."

"Thanks, but Zach didn't share your opinion."

"No, he wouldn't. Is that why he and Cass took off before dawn?"

"Partly. I think he really wanted to stick me with the WB until Willow gets back."

She gave him a wistful smile. "Wait till you see her with Cody. I've never known Willow to be this happy—even when she and Cody were together before. Maybe their breakup—and his determination to reform his wild ways—produced more good than even I'd hoped."

He grinned. "And you're already looking for that first grandchild, aren't you?"

"Guilty." She ruffled his hair. "So, you're managing the ranch after all."

"For a few days. Willow's cruise gets back to Miami next Sunday, right?"

So, he'd spend a week all told on the WB

again, then go back to his real life, to J&B and that talk with Margot about their relationship. Far away from Kate Lancaster and her cute little boy, if not his own memories of Rob lying on the pavement in New York, bleeding. If it weren't for Noah, she believed her husband would still be alive. He couldn't say she was totally wrong.

"Willow sent me a text from the ship," Jean said. "She doesn't know you're here."

"Did you tell her?"

"No, until I got home this morning, I hadn't seen you yet, and I couldn't know how you wanted to handle this—she really wanted you here for the wedding, Noah."

He tried again to explain, which only ended up sounding as if he put business before his sister's happiness. Without intending to, he actually had. That apology would be the hardest of all to make.

"I do hope you weren't inadvertently punishing Willow, staying away because of the break with your father years ago."

"Not that I'm aware of, and I am sorry, Mom."

"Well, I imagine Zach made this family's disappointment clear enough." She turned away, and Noah saw her dab at her eyes.

"You missed a beautiful wedding. If only Dad could have walked her down that aisle, danced with her…"

With a fresh twinge of guilt, he touched her shoulder. "Hey. I'm sure he was there in spirit. He always doted on Willow." So had Noah. He waited until his mom turned back. "How could *he* miss that?"

She managed a laugh. "Can you just see him? His chest all puffed out, his eyes, so blue, and sparkling?"

"Complaining the whole time about the cost of the thing."

"Yes, he would have." Then she sobered. "Noah, I wish you and he had made peace before he died. He did love you so."

Noah couldn't call that love. "Not that he ever let it show."

"I know he could be difficult, but please try to understand. His fondest dream——"

Noah had a bitter taste in his mouth. "Was to see me take over this ranch." That was all that had mattered to his dad. So why, after their final argument, had he willed a part of the WB to Noah? *Maybe it's time you earned that*, Zach had said.

Their mom hesitated. "And I know that wasn't the right choice for you."

The words were like a punch to the heart. She'd forgiven him twice today, which he didn't deserve, and he hadn't spent time with her like this, just the two of them talking, in the past fifteen years except for the one visit she'd made solo to see him in New York after he'd first met Margot. His father had stayed home.

As if she'd read his mind, she said, "I wouldn't trade the WB for that city if someone tried to force me, but I'm proud of you, honey. You've made such a success of that company you started on a shoestring, and that's only the beginning."

"I started J&B in part with an investment from you."

"A small one."

His father would have been livid.

"You never told him, did you?"

She shook her head. "I should have. We had no other secrets from each other, but I'm still glad I could help you out. You were living then in that tiny studio apartment in the old building above the subway, remember, existing on noodles and oatmeal—"

Noah murmured, "I could afford a fast-food burger occasionally."

"Now you're in that gorgeous high-rise

condo with its own elevator that opens right into your entryway. Didn't Margot help you with the interior design?"

"She did." Uh-oh. Here it comes.

"How is she? I enjoyed my visit with you both before your father took ill."

He hadn't taken sick. He'd dropped dead of a sudden heart attack without warning. And his mom's tone had been dry as it always was whenever she mentioned Margot.

"You enjoyed that visit?"

She glanced away. "Yes, of course. You showed me Rockefeller Center, Times Square, the Chrysler and Empire State buildings, and I'll never forget that glorious dinner we had at… What was the name of the restaurant?"

"Gramercy Tavern."

"Where you told me the wait time for reservations could be three months, yet we just walked in as we would at the Bon Appetit or the café here—and they fell all over themselves to seat us right away."

"Margot and I go there quite a bit." Thanks to her father's influence.

A short silence told Noah his mother wouldn't ask the real question. *Are you going to marry her?* He knew his mother didn't like Margot, but she was too polite to say so, which said more than any words might. "Yes, we're still seeing each other, Mom, but the launch of the new London office takes up most of my time right now."

The change of subject apparently suited them both.

"So, this morning," his mother said, returning to the original subject, "after Midnight threw you, then ran off, how did you get that horse back? He has such a mind of his own."

"He took a nice tour of the WB, then on to Sweetheart Ranch—where Kate Lancaster managed to stop him."

She smiled. There'd been a time when his mom had hoped Kate might keep him here. "Ah. She's an excellent horsewoman, a good rancher, too, and there you were on foot like some greenhorn. That must have been humiliating."

"It was," he admitted, "but she was relatively nice about it. I met her son."

His mom's face brightened. "Oh, isn't Theodore the sweetest thing?"

"Kate doesn't have the same opinion of me, obviously." Jean knew why.

"Rob's death was not your fault, Noah."

"Couldn't prove that by her." Which only

added to the sense of failure that his father had instilled in him. "Anyway, we got by this morning—" he hesitated "—just as we did the night before I came…home." He told her briefly about their impromptu stay at the Bluebird. "I would have been here on Saturday if not for that storm."

"My goodness," his mother said. "It's like the hand of Fate."

Noah shifted, which made his ankle throb even harder. "Mom, you can forget your daydreams of me with Kate. She picked Rob instead. And she does blame me for what happened."

"Time heals all wounds. You wait long enough—she may change her mind."

"I'VE DEFINITELY DECIDED," Meg told Kate the next morning. "I'm changing my name."

"Why?" Kate kissed Teddie, who sat at the kitchen table, on top of his head. She poured herself a first cup of coffee. "What's wrong with McClaren?"

"Everything." Meg immediately dreaded the rest of this conversation and wished she hadn't brought up the subject. The topic of her ex-husband always made her stomach hurt, yet Kate was usually a good sounding board. Now, she didn't seem to agree.

"By the way, he who shall not be named called again last night."

"Who called?" Teddie piped up, his mouth full of cereal.

Meg made a zipping motion across her lips. "Little pitchers," she murmured.

She marched from the center island to the counter and began washing up her breakfast dishes by hand. Their dishwasher had broken down a few days ago, and the repairman couldn't fit them into his schedule until next week.

"Who called?" Teddie asked again, and Meg turned back, a dripping bowl in hand, to see Kate's reaction. Even Bandit, lying at Teddie's feet, looked interested. "Uncle Mac?"

"Yes." Kate wiped Teddie's mouth with a napkin. "If you're finished, sweetie, you may be excused. Go up and make your bed. Then we'll go down to the barn."

"And I can saddle Spencer? Are we taking another snow ride?"

"Not this morning." After the season's first blizzard, a warmish day was turning the snow into slippery slush, and Meg knew

Kate wouldn't risk injury to her son or the horses. "I need to talk to Gabe."

"And tell him what to do?" Teddie asked.

Gabe Morgan was the ranch foreman. Meg avoided him as much as she could. Men in general were not her favorite thing these days, even if Gabe had never been anything but nice to her. He was, however, inclined to turn up wherever Meg happened to be. Which made her uneasy.

Kate said with exaggerated patience, "Yes, we'll go over today's chores, then you can help me clean tack, including Spencer's saddle. It got pretty dirty on our last ride."

"Then later, we'll go visit Noah? I never get to see people, Mommy, or make new friends. Please, can we?"

Kate's features arranged themselves into a blank mask. "No," she said.

Teddie's mouth set. "But he asked me to come over."

"He was only being polite."

"He *told* me—"

"Not without my permission. That was your assumption, Bunny." Teddie looked adorably perplexed. Chances were he didn't know the meaning of the word, but Kate plowed on in full mommy mode. She didn't look at Meg, probably for fear of seeing the smile she was trying to hide. "And you, young man, should call him Mr. Bodine. The same goes for Mr. Morgan."

His mouth looking mulish, Teddie slipped from his chair, then stomped off in his cowboy boots toward the front hall, Bandit at his heels.

"That boy has your obstinacy, Kate."

She groaned. "I know."

Meg saw her opening to escape any further discussion of her ex. "But I'm curious. What do *you* call 'Mr. Bodine'?" This conversation had been put on hold after the blizzard when Kate had returned from the Bluebird Motel.

"I'd rather not call him anything. With luck, he'll be on his way to New York in a few days. In the meantime, I don't intend to see him again." She brushed off her hands as if to rid herself of Noah, who was an old friend of Meg's.

"The poor guy gave you a ride home in the storm, and you repay him with the cold shoulder?"

"You know the reason."

Meg lifted her eyebrows. "How is he? You promised me a full recap of your stay in that motel. Was he a gentleman—"

"Of course. He's…fine. If he had tried anything—and why would I think he'd want to?—he'd be missing an arm today." Kate told Meg the barest details of the overnight she'd spent in the stellar Mr. Bodine's company. "We passed the time, that's all. I could hardly do otherwise when, as you said, he was bringing me home."

Meg gave in to the smile she'd been holding back. "Still. I think you're being unfair." She had known Noah from girlhood and couldn't say a bad word about him. Even Teddie must agree. Meg could hear him banging around in his room upstairs.

"*I'm* being unfair?" Kate shook her head. "Noah Bodine is a near-stranger to me at this point, but *you* refuse to even answer the phone when Mac, the man you married, calls?"

"I don't need to hear what he has to say. We're divorced. I don't have to care what he thinks, what he's doing or who he's doing it with." The last words just slipped out. "I mean it, Kate. Changing my name seems the sensible next thing to do. What could be better for my sanity than a clean and final break?"

"Seriously," Kate said. "Do you have any

idea how many other changes that will lead to? Credit cards, car registration, passport? But never mind that. Talk to the man, Meg. You don't even know what he wants." She waited a beat that put Meg on high alert. "What's unfair is for you to expect me to answer his calls. I can't bear that sad note in his voice."

"Thanks for sharing," Meg muttered, then went back to washing dishes.

She didn't need a man in her life now.

Especially Jonathan "Mac" McClaren.

GRITTING HIS TEETH with every step, Noah hobbled to answer the door at the WB. Both of the local docs had assured him, as did an X-ray, that he hadn't broken his ankle, but he did have a wicked sprain that had kept him off his feet ever since he'd taken Midnight for a ride three days ago—or rather, Zach's horse had taken him.

Today his mom had gone out somewhere. Alone in the house, he opened the door to find Hadley Smith standing there. Noah hadn't expected company when for the past few days he'd been trying to catch up remotely on J&B business from the sofa.

"Hey, Noah." A big man with dark hair

and serious deep blue eyes, Hadley tipped his hat.

What a surprise. Noah hadn't seen him in years. Even when Noah had lived on the WB, his friendship with Hadley, who'd been a foster kid at Clara McMann's ranch then, had never been more than casual, Noah, at thirty-seven, being older by a few years. They'd never even been in the same grade at school.

"Hadley. Come on in," he said, wondering about the purpose of his visit.

"Thought I'd stop by, see how you're doing." The WB wasn't far from Clara's ranch, which was partly Hadley's now, Noah's mother had said. Hadley grinned. "Heard about the spill you took. Word gets around."

"Small towns, huh?"

"You may have forgotten, but there's never a lack of information." Hadley removed his hat, left his snowy boots at the door, then took the chair Noah offered him. Noah settled again onto the sofa. It had become his daybed, littered with books, his laptop and food wrappers. A half-finished milkshake sat on the end table. "Someone keeping you fed?" Hadley asked.

"My mom, of course." Having her fuss over him again seemed oh-so-familiar and, at the moment, especially welcome. "I'm supposed to be in charge of the WB, but so far I've had to rely on the foreman." Which wasn't going that well.

Hadley frowned. "On your own, then, with Cody and Willow away on their honeymoon, Zach off somewhere with Cass. The latter case sure sounds like a setup."

"Yeah, I messed up about the wedding." And around Barren, everyone knew everything instantly, which could be either an endearing sign that people did care or an invasion of privacy. Noah saw it now as the latter. "Paying my penance till the newlyweds get back."

Hadley toyed with the hat in his hands. "Zach told me he wasn't confident his foreman would work out."

"Wilkins hasn't been especially helpful. He could have tipped me off that Zach's stallion wasn't the best choice to take out after the blizzard, but he didn't. Which is one reason I ended up on this couch. I was already mad because Zach left me holding the bag here."

Hadley snorted. "That's a shock."

Again, there were no secrets. "Well, all those family issues have sure gotten worse.

My fault. But you're right. I wouldn't have chosen this—another bit of information to pass on."

Hadley stiffened. "I'm not one of the gossips."

"Sorry." For a few minutes they spoke instead about Hadley's family, then J&B. Noah said, "I know I always talked about getting off this ranch, but I never thought I'd end up back east. At the moment, my partner and I are launching a new office in London, which has been nothing but trouble. I need to be there soon or in our New York headquarters."

"Noah." Hadley leaned forward and crossed his forearms on his knee. "I don't know how to say this, but I've heard, of course, about you and Rob Lancaster's widow."

He groaned. "Then everyone knows she and I spent a night together in that storm."

"Word gets around," Hadley repeated. "I was real close to her and Rob when he was… still at Sweetheart Ranch. Since he's been gone—passed, I mean—even though she never asked me to, I've tried to watch out for her."

"We had two rooms that night. We talked. That's all. People can spin that any which way they want."

"Doesn't help her."

Noah tensed. The movement sent a spark of agony through his injured ankle. "Then maybe I should give one of those local gossips a call—set the record straight. That why you're really here now?"

"Nobody sent me, if that's what you mean. I told you, I care about Kate. But everyone knows you'll leave this town again. She'll still be here. She's pretty vulnerable, Noah."

"You're making a mountain out of a molehill about a woman I used to know." *The woman I loved and lost*, which he wasn't about to reveal. "I would never do anything to hurt Kate. I probably won't see her again before I go."

"Might be the best decision."

Noah rubbed his throbbing ankle. He couldn't disagree, but could Hadley know about his past feelings for Kate? Even Noah wasn't sure what they ought to be now. Years had passed since he'd lost her to Rob. Noah had been best man at their wedding. And then, he'd destroyed their three-way friendship with his offer for Rob to join J&B. Noah had done enough, not that he was in any position to do otherwise right now.

Hadley stood, shifted his weight from one foot to the other.

"I've never been the talkative type. Didn't intend to step over any lines." He half smiled. "Couldn't stop myself, though. I'm counting on you—a lot of men in Barren are, I suspect—to recall your roots and be as protective of her as any of us, including me, would be."

"Message received."

Noah struggled up from the sofa, even though Hadley had motioned him to stay seated, then limped beside the other man to the door. Hadley put on his boots. Noah had no reason to be angry with him when he had just cautioned himself to be careful with Kate. Nothing good could come from his trying to be part of her life again. Yet he seemed to have put her in a bad position in this town, which bothered him.

"You're concerned about Kate," Noah said. "I understand. I am too."

"Wouldn't hurt for you to make that call to one of those women who run the town grapevine." In the open doorway, Hadley tipped his hat as if in apology. "And those WB cowhands of Zach's know you're laid up. With your temporary status here, I doubt they'll respect the boundaries they would observe with him. Think I'll wander on down to the barn—check things out for you before I go."

"Thanks, Hadley."

"On my way in, I noticed they hadn't put fresh hay out for the cattle. Those steers were milling around, bawling to beat the band. I'll put the fear of God in those cowboys, if I have to. And I'll talk to Wilkins."

Noah thanked him again. He stood in the door taking in the fresh air, watching Hadley cross the front lawn then head for the barn.

Hadley's visit had been part warning, yes; part insistence on helping, maybe; but also… friendship? Noah wasn't sure. He took his pulsing ankle back to the sofa, unable to decide if, after his longtime absence from the WB, he was welcome in Barren. Or, merely suspect.

Did anybody trust him?

He knew Kate Lancaster didn't.

CHAPTER FIVE

KATE ENTERED EARL'S HARDWARE on Main Street the next day with a mental list of supplies she needed to order. She'd been a rancher all her life, but she was still getting used to running things without Rob, who'd often handled this chore.

At the front register, she saw a tall man chatting with Earl. Her steps faltered. Kate would know that form, that voice, anywhere. Noah Bodine.

Recalling her vow to keep her distance, she pivoted on her boot heel, then turned the corner into an aisle. And ran smack into Bernice Caldwell, the biggest gossip in Stewart County. Kate received the sort of pitying look she'd become accustomed to in the past year from many people. "Oh, you poor thing. How are you holding up? And that sweet little boy of yours?"

"We're fine, Bernice." Fighting an urge to groan, Kate added, "And you?"

"I was perfectly well, thank you very much—until my Barney moved out."

Bernice shifted her packages from one arm to the other. Her grown son had always lived with her, perhaps too intimidated by the woman to dare leaving home.

"I knew he'd resigned—" Kate began.

"Can you believe? Vice president of Loans at the Barren Cattlemen's Bank, one of the most prestigious positions in this town, but he'd rather become a trainee at some brokerage firm in Kansas City." She patted her brown hair. "He has broken my heart."

"I'm sorry to hear that." Kate gave a silent cheer for Barney Caldwell. Finally, he'd gotten out from under his mother's thumb. "I'm sure you miss him terribly."

Bernice's brown eyes welled with tears. "For now. I expect him to come running back any day. He has standing in this community. What on earth could be better than that? Certainly not living in a strange city far from his own people. A trainee," she repeated with a sniff.

Kate didn't comment. She wished Barney every success. At least now he was on neutral ground, while the rest of Barren's population still had to deal with Bernice, who, at this very moment, must have some agenda. She always did.

Bernice squared her shoulders. "I don't mean to pry into your business, but there have been a few whispers about—" she hesitated "—our recent blizzard. Staying overnight with Noah Bodine didn't look good for your reputation, Kate, and so soon after poor Rob died. That man was your husband's friend. And to move in on his grieving widow…" She let out a breath. "I thought I should say something."

Kate refused to explain. "I appreciate your concern, but there's nothing to worry about."

It also wasn't the end of this, she felt sure. Bernice couldn't wait to spread that gossip, adding her own interpretation to what was already out there.

"Well, my own cross is mine to bear," she said, then touched Kate's arm. "Do take care of yourself, and give that boy of yours a hug from me. I don't know how you cope with your loss." Unless it was to fall into Noah Bodine's presumably waiting arms.

Bernice hadn't left before Kate heard a thumping sound behind her. Please, not another well-meaning person with sympathy in their eyes. She turned, but it was Noah himself, limping. He leveled a look at Bernice before he spoke, his voice coolly authoritative. "Mrs. Caldwell, let me assure you, if it hadn't been for that storm, Mrs. Lancaster would have been safely home long before dark—reading a story to her little boy at bedtime. Would you have preferred her to drive alone, perhaps ending up stranded? The roads were bad. I'd offered her a ride—only that—but, after a slight mishap in the snow, we had no choice except to stop overnight. Speaking of which, I stayed in my room and she stayed in hers. Period." Which was a slight exaggeration, though Kate wouldn't say so. "I'd appreciate your silence on the matter."

Bernice sniffed again but said nothing. She stalked off toward the store's entrance.

"Sorry," Noah said to Kate. "I overheard and had to say something."

Kate, feeling the heat in her cheeks, sighed. "She is not alone."

"One good reason why I'm living in New York."

"And why I come into town as seldom as possible. You didn't have to defend me, Noah."

"Yes," he said, "I did."

Kate had kept her cool during her conversation with Bernice, but she was now on the verge of a familiar panic attack. Maybe she wouldn't order those supplies today. The ranch had enough for another week or so—

Noah said, "Bernice Caldwell may not let you off the hook, but I hope I was persuasive."

"Thank you." Remembering her promise to herself, Kate tried to step around him. "Now I have to go. I need to get back to Sweetheart Ranch."

Noah stopped her with a light touch on her arm. "Kate. Why care what anyone in Barren has to say? We both know nothing inappropriate happened at the Bluebird."

"And in time, the talk will die down. There's always another news flash."

"Yeah, but I don't know how you take it."

"Because Barren really is a great place to live, to raise a family." Not that he would know. Noah had left the WB before the ink had dried on his college degree. He'd spent his last two summers interning in Denver then LA, and by then he'd already been gone most of the year, much to Rob's dismay. And, she supposed, Noah's father's. She eased back from his hold. "I really have to go."

She glanced at his leg. "I hope you're feeling better."

"Some, thanks." He seemed to want to linger. "I'm glad I got to meet your son the other day. He's a good kid."

"He is," she said, heart thumping, but the last thing she needed was a touchy-feely talk with Noah, even after he'd dealt with Bernice. Her mental list forgotten, Kate strode down the aisle, then out the front door. On the sidewalk, she spied a dark-haired woman coming toward her. It was her friend Lizzie Barnes— no, Maguire, now that she'd remarried.

Lizzie waved. "Wait up, pal." Her green eyes sparkling, she hugged Kate. "You'd think in such a small town, we'd run into each other all the time. I haven't seen you in ages."

For a few minutes, they chatted about Teddie, then Lizzie's second husband and her children from her first marriage, plus the baby she and Dallas now had together. "Hannah's not a year old yet and almost walking. I swear, she moves faster than all three of my others combined. Dallas has spent the past week sticking protective covers over all the outlets in our house and putting locks on the cabinet doors. I can't get into anything these days—but, even still crawling, she's like a wizard."

Kate laughed but envied Lizzie. Oh, how she would have loved a sister or brother for Teddie. She worried that because they spent so much time together, he would become spoiled. He still wasn't talking to her after Kate had refused to let him visit Noah.

"I have a bone to pick with you," Lizzie said next, not looking angry at all. She nudged Kate in the side. "We've had several Girls' Night Out meetings where you were noticeably absent, and we keep asking each other when you're going to break your fast, as it were, and join us again."

Kate glanced behind her. "I keep meaning to, but something always comes up."

"We all have other commitments, but those get-togethers keep us sane. Really, get off that ranch the next time." She softened her tone. "We miss you, babe. Oh, and when you do come, bring wine." Lizzie peered past Kate's shoulder and across the street. "Why do you keep looking over there?"

"I just encountered Bernice," Kate said, "who's probably staring at us right now from the emporium. She oozed sympathy for my loss, as she always does, then couldn't resist mentioning that I stayed at a motel with Noah Bodine."

"How fun," Lizzie murmured.

"I haven't recovered yet—about her, I mean. That woman makes me paranoid, and then, to put the icing on the cake, I ran into Noah again here." He was still inside the store.

Lizzie raised her eyebrows. "That man has a lot to offer."

"Not to me. Please, Lizzie, don't be like Bernice."

"Sorry, you know I won't take part in any gossip. I had enough of that myself."

Before she'd married Dallas, Lizzie's ex had shamed her in front of the whole town when he was the one who'd committed adultery. She still disliked being in the public eye, if not as much as Kate did now about her sad widowhood.

Lizzie caught her gaze. "You're not mad?"

"No. I'll try to make the next meeting. I just need to get…home."

Without another word, in full panic mode now, she hurried off. Away from Noah.

Back to her comfort space, the safety she so badly needed at Sweetheart Ranch.

Away from the pain.

EVEN IN WINTER'S slow season, there were chores to be done, and Noah was on a horse again—Willow's mare, this time, not Midnight—riding fence that afternoon with one of the WB's cowhands. They picked their way through the now-muddy field. That first blizzard was gone, but in retrospect Noah preferred the snow.

"You sure you want to do this?" Flicking dark hair off his face, Calvin Stern gave him the side-eye. "I can manage by myself."

"I'm fine. Just a bit sore still, that's all." An understatement. His ankle didn't agree.

"Spending today in the saddle won't help. By tonight—"

"I said I'm okay." Noah didn't know Calvin well, and he shouldn't have used that sharp tone, but Hadley Smith had been right. None of the hands, especially Wilkins, seemed to respect Noah's ability to take over from Zach or to do a decent job. Sure, as a cowboy, Noah was rusty. Who wouldn't be after so many years off the ranch? But this area of the country was one in which manly men still ruled. And Noah had his pride. "I may have done a fool thing taking Midnight out, but I learned my lesson. Who hasn't?"

A few years ago, in a different way, Calvin had gotten into some trouble when he and two other young cowboys stole cattle from another ranch. They'd been let off easy, and Calvin, who'd worked for others before he'd been hired at the WB, was, by all reports, a devoted family man now with a wife and son. Reformed, people said, and that was enough for Noah too.

"What's that over there?" He pointed toward the far corner of the fence line between the WB and Sweetheart Ranch.

"Looks like trouble."

"Let's ride," Noah said and bumped Silver in the sides with his heels.

They cantered across the sloppy field. Noah spied Kate's boy on the other side of the fence, on his knees in the mud, sobbing, and alarm swept through him. Teddie's pony, wild-eyed, pranced in place, or tried to. He was obviously hurt.

Reaching the boy, Noah slid off his horse. "How did this happen, Teddie?"

He raised tear-streaked eyes to Noah. "I wanted to visit you."

Calvin dismounted too. Nearby, part of the fence wire lay, beaten down, almost to the ground. "Looks like they tried to jump this gap."

"Jump it?"

Teddie shuddered with another sob. "We almost did, N—I mean, Mr. Bodine. But his legs are too short, and Spencer couldn't make it."

Calvin was on his knees now, running his hands over the pony. "Hope he didn't break—" He glanced at Teddie, whose eyes couldn't get any wider behind the thick lenses of his black-framed glasses.

Taking his cue, Noah led the boy away from the scene. "Let's leave Mr. Stern to check Spencer out." He hunkered down to meet Teddie's gaze. "Does your mother know you're out here by yourself?"

Teddie looked down at the mud. "Maybe."

"Tell the truth." He couldn't imagine Kate letting her boy take off on his own.

"I forgot to tell her."

"Theodore Robert Lancaster." Even Noah knew that was a lie. He'd been a kid once, bent upon every adventure that crossed his path. He still was. He also remembered his father's wrath whenever he'd strayed. "I'm flattered that you decided to come visit, but—just taking a guess here—I bet your mother is worried sick by now."

"Noah." Calvin had straightened beside

the horse. "Think we're okay, but I'm going to call the vet. He'll prob'ly want to see this pony."

"You stay with him, then. I'll take Teddie home—borrow Kate's trailer rig."

Calvin lifted Teddie up onto Willow's mare, then Noah mounted with only slight difficulty. Holding the boy close across his lap, he picked up the reins.

On the ten-minute ride to Sweetheart Ranch's barnyard, Noah could practically feel the remorse coming off Teddie in waves, and by the time they reached the house, he was trembling. As soon as Noah stopped the horse, Kate flew out the back door.

"Teddie! I was so frightened. Where have you been?" But he didn't answer.

Noah handed her son down to her. "He took a little ride to the WB."

"A ride? On your own?" Fresh fear flashed in her eyes. "Where's Spencer?"

Teddie gestured behind them. "Out there."

Kate met Noah's eyes, as if begging him not to say that something terrible had occurred. "It's okay," he said. "The pony misstepped but—"

She glanced at Teddie's muddy clothes. "Doing what?"

"Um, jumping the fence," he said.

"*'Jumping'?*" she echoed. "You were jumping, Teddie?"

Noah leaned on his saddle horn. "Spencer's... He'll likely be fine. One of the WB hands has called the vet."

She turned on Teddie. "How many times have I told you? You are not to leave this yard without permission. You certainly aren't allowed to start jumping that pony. Do I need to take him away from you?"

"Please, Mommy. Don't. I won't do it again."

"And what did we say about bothering Mr. Bodine?"

"He's good, Kate. I don't min—"

"Teddie, go into the house." She waited, all but tapping her foot, until Teddie slunk off, his head down and with more dry sobs. Then she whirled to face Noah. "I don't care whether you mind or not. Teddie is my child, and I make those decisions."

Noah's mouth tightened. "Which I imagine is a blanket one, meaning no."

She glared at him. "How can that possibly matter to you?"

Her tone made Willow's mare, Silver, shift her weight, ears flat against her skull. "It matters because I think you're being way too hard on that kid right now." The door had banged shut behind Teddie. "If you don't want him to visit, I get that. I'm only here till Willow gets back—yadda yadda. However…"

"Don't 'however' me. You know nothing about my situation, except for the fact that because of you, my husband isn't here any longer."

Trying not to flinch, Noah climbed off the mare. He looped her reins around the rail in front of the barn. "Forget your opinion of me. We're wasting time." He shot a look at the darkening sky. More snow was predicted, and the temperature was already dropping. "Let's hitch up your trailer. Then I'll drive out to pick up the pony, and you can punish that boy more than he's already punished himself—I won't have to see it."

"*I'll* drive the rig. Teddie will wait with Meg until I get back."

"One of the WB Gators mired in the mud earlier. What if you get stuck?"

"I'll unstick myself."

Noah shook his head. "You are one stubborn—"

She jabbed a finger at his chest. "Don't you dare make some sexist remark."

Noah threw up both hands. "Wouldn't dream of it."

For a long moment, they stood there, as if squaring off for a showdown at the OK Corral. Then, finally, Kate sighed. "All right. Maybe I can use the help." She looked him over, ending at his ankle. "That is, if you're up to it."

THAT EVENING, KATE was back in her happy place—one of them. In the kitchen, rather than the barn after dusk, she removed the lid from her biggest pot and inhaled what had turned out to be an enticing aroma, if she did say so herself. Usually cooking chores were part of Meg's duties, but in the dead of winter, Kate had more time on her hands, and nothing was better on a cold, possibly snowy night again than a hearty beef stew simmered to perfection. Fond memories of the years with her dad when, by necessity, she'd learned to cook followed her from stove to table. So did her set-to earlier with Noah.

Trying to block that out, she assessed the four place settings of her mom's best china. An ivory damask tablecloth that had belonged to Kate's grandmother. The crystal water glasses Mom—no, call her Ellie—had brought from her family home in Chicago, determined as a bride to become a rancher's wife. That hadn't worked out, but at least she'd left these legacy items behind. Along with Kate's father. And Kate. Five was too young to lose your mother. Anytime was, really, another reason she felt so protective of her son.

Meg swept into the kitchen, her face flushed from her shower, her hair in wet tangles around her face. "Wow, what's the occasion?"

"There's no occasion—well, except to celebrate Spencer being all right. I also think it's good for Teddie to work on being socialized, to learn his manners." And know that his place, and hers, would always be at Sweetheart Ranch.

"You mean which fork to use? Where those beautiful water glasses go at each place?"

Kate heard a disapproving note in Meg's voice. Definitely not on board with this. "Have I done something wrong?"

"Sorry, the table looks lovely, but it reminds me of Chicago. I don't miss that other life I had there." Meg straightened a fork. "I definitely don't miss having that man in my life—*man* in his case being a loose term."

"Whoa." A deep male voice spoke from the back door as it opened. "Should I just back out now? Before the shooting starts?"

A gust of wind following him inside, Gabe Morgan shut the door, stamped his boots on the mat, then shrugged out of his fleece-lined jacket. Tall and rangy, the ranch foreman had hair the rich color of mink and warm amber-brown eyes. Meg glanced at the four plates then sent Kate a startled look that clearly said, *What is he doing here?* Gabe didn't often eat with their little, improvised family. "I'm glad you could join us," Kate said, taking a sudden interest in the napkins she'd set by each plate. "There's beer in the fridge."

He helped himself, appearing right at home. The silence was unnerving. Another look from Meg. *You invited him?*

Kate didn't understand her obvious objection. *What?*

Meg ran a distracted hand through her messy hair. For a woman who had turned away from her former life and sworn off men, she seemed very much aware of how she must look at the moment. No makeup, either, which Meg, blessed with dewy skin and a pretty face, didn't need. Kate held her gaze. *I understand, sort of, about Mac. But Gabe?*

Meg stirred the stew in the pot, lingering over the steam that rose into the air. Her tense shoulders told the story. *Because he's here.*

Kate cleared her throat. "We're ready to eat. I'll call Teddie."

Unfortunately, her son wasn't speaking to her again. After she'd left him with Meg to take Spencer to the vet, his "punishment" had been banishment to his room until dinner.

Meg beat her to the hallway. "No, I'll get Teddie. Back in a sec." And she disappeared.

"Kate, what's her problem?" At the table, Gabe pushed his beer bottle back and forth on the ivory cloth. "You know, every time I see that woman, she turns to ice. What did I do?"

"You were born male. Sorry, Gabe, but Meg's still…grieving, I guess you'd say, about her divorce. She tends to be prickly around men."

"No kidding. She didn't divorce me, though. The other morning, she came down to the barn, looking for Teddie. I was dropping bales from the hay loft. When I said hey, she just stood there looking up at me. Then she spun on her heel and marched off."

"Um, where was Teddie at the time?"

"In Spencer's stall." Gabe lifted one eyebrow. "Feeding that pony treats he doesn't need. You ever wonder why his barrel gets as wide as the oak version, look no further."

Kate smiled. Talking to her foreman was always a treat in itself.

"How's Spencer now?" he asked.

"Like nothing ever happened. Well, not quite. The vet said there was no break and that the pony had strained a ligament, so we'll watch that while he heals. He'll need to be under close supervision. Kind of like Teddie."

"Guess not riding his pony is punishment enough for trying to take that fence."

"I'm being punished too," Kate said. "He didn't like me telling him afterward to sit on his bed and think about what worse injury could have happened to Spencer instead."

"You're a good mom, Kate."

"Thanks." She liked Gabe's easy manner, his way with her son, and she welcomed this reprieve from the memories that had been dogging her around the kitchen tonight. She'd been on the verge of remembering Rob, seated at this same table, teasing Teddie and Kate as they all caught up on their day. "I knew he was sneaking treats. I keep telling him ponies don't like candy."

"According to Teddie, this one does." Gabe cocked an ear toward the hall. "It's taking your aunt a long time to call him. My stomach's growling. Mind if I start eating? I may be working late tonight. That sky looks ready to let loose again."

"I hope not." Kate hastily ladled stew into a large serving bowl, then set it on the table. "Help yourself," she told Gabe, but his attention stayed on the kitchen doorway.

Kate heard firm footsteps and then a sudden clattering of little ones before Teddie burst into the room and scrambled onto his chair. "Hi, Gabe!"

"Hi, yourself, squirt." The two exchanged high fives before Gabe began to eat. "Wait till you taste your mama's stew."

Teddie wrinkled his nose. "I don't like my food all mushed up together."

Kate sighed. He wouldn't look at her. Beyond the silent treatment for her, Teddie was at the stage when he had definite opinions about everything.

"Eat," she said and slid into her own chair. "Meg?"

Her aunt still stood on the kitchen's threshold. Kate glanced at her with raised eyebrows. There was no reason to treat the ranch foreman this way—or was there?

Gabe shot out of his seat to hold Meg's chair.

"Thank you," she said and reached for the bowl of stew. She refused to look at him.

"Welcome." He frowned at Kate instead as he sat back down. "Pass me the bread?"

She couldn't miss the defeated tone of his voice, but Meg clearly tried to. For the rest of the meal, she kept her gaze on her plate or on Teddie, engaging him in silly conversation, her cheeks flushed but no longer from the steam in her shower. Was she uncomfortable around Gabe because she didn't like him for some reason, or because she did but didn't want to?

Kate took another look. Meg had blow-dried her hair into a silky curtain of brown with gold highlights. She'd put on a dash of lipstick. Ah, so the sparks Kate had seen in Gabe whenever her aunt was nearby weren't one-sided.

Still, progress. Maybe Kate had been wrong,

and Meg was farther along the road to making a new life for herself without Mac than Kate had imagined. There might as well be one of them who could put the past behind her.

Kate managed to wait before speaking until after dinner when Gabe had gone with Teddie to the living room. He'd promised to show her son how to play a new video game, and although Teddie was too young, with his intelligence it wasn't long before he'd mastered the game and beaten Gabe. Their roars of victory and protest made both women, who were washing dishes, smile.

"He's a good one, Meg."

Her shoulders stiffened again. "I adore Teddie, but be prepared. Before he's in his teens, he'll probably graduate from college."

"I meant Gabe Morgan."

Meg glanced over her shoulder. "You hardly know anything about him, Kate. He may have that smile, but he also has the devil in his eyes." Her gaze widened. "I hope you aren't trying to matchmake here. I'm too old for him."

"Nonsense. You're still in your thirties, a young woman—"

"—who feels like she's a hundred years old. No way," she muttered. "The last thing

I need is another Peter Pan like Mac who never grew up. And he was gone so much I felt more like a widow than a wife."

Kate's gaze fell.

Meg had turned pale. "I'm sorry. You know I didn't mean that about being a widow."

But the memories of loss had kicked in again. Kate's mother, driving away—not a rancher's wife after all—abandoning Kate and her dad. The two of them, holding each other up, the years softening the loss but never completely. Then Rob had taken the job with Noah and flown to New York— leaving her too. Forever. "I'm glad you've never known how that feels."

Meg hugged Kate close, and without words their near argument ended, replaced by regret. Still. Kate couldn't put her aunt's feelings out of her mind. She also knew Meg had sometimes felt abandoned by her parents years ago whenever they had to be away from home for work. Until she dealt with Mac, she would probably keep holding Gabe, or any other man, off despite an attraction she might feel.

Which only made a newer memory pop into Kate's mind. She shook her head to clear it of Noah.

"I need to put Teddie to bed," she said, because *he* was her life now.

"Kate, I can tuck him in—"

Obviously, Meg had hoped to avoid Gabe, but he was already coming back into the kitchen, Teddie perched on his shoulders. He set Teddie down, gave him another complicated high five, then headed straight for his coat on the hook beside the back door.

"Thanks for dinner, ladies."

With Meg there, Kate resisted the urge to say *Come again*.

"Have a good night, Gabe. Let's hope the snow holds off."

She hadn't asked him to dinner with any intention other than to feed him, but, considering Meg's attitude, perhaps that hadn't been the best idea she'd ever had.

CHAPTER SIX

IN THE WB'S OFFICE, Noah tossed his pen onto the desktop. He couldn't seem to concentrate. Did Kate regret the tense words they'd said to each other before? He did, for sure. And yet…he'd been right. She'd needed help with Spencer, which he'd been happy to provide. He'd liked feeling useful again, rather than inept, around the ranch.

But man, that drive to the vet clinic had been weird. Neither of them had spoken, Kate obviously fretting about Spencer's welfare, her brow furrowed, her hands wringing in her lap. Noah's grip had stayed tight on the wheel. After the diagnosis, she'd almost leaned against him in apparent relief before she thought better of that. On the way home, they'd repeated the same silent journey.

A rap at the door brought his head up. "Yeah, come in."

Jed Wilkins, the WB's foreman, stepped inside. "Got a minute?"

Noah welcomed the interruption. While he'd been nursing his sprained ankle, he'd only seen the man or spoken to him a few times. "Sure. What's up?"

Noah should have added *now*. He had a dozen calls from his office in New York that he needed to return and another crisis brewing in London, plus something on the ranch always seemed to require constant attention. His shoulders felt so tight, he thought they might snap.

"Weather report says that storm's moving in."

Noah searched his memory banks for the routine his dad had always followed at such times. But wasn't the ranch already prepared? Before he could speak, the foreman did.

"I'll handle it." Wilkins was all darkness to Noah, hair and eyes, with a grim personality and voice to match. "Just wanted to let you know we might lose some cattle. Snow's one thing, but the temperature's been droppin' since noon." He propped both hands on his hips. "The boys will bring in as many of last spring's calves as they can round up and some pregnant cows, but there may not be enough room in the barns. Told your brother we need another one."

Noah might not recall his ranching days with utter clarity, but as an executive, he often made quick decisions. "Let's get some estimates, then."

The foreman shook his head. "I'll wait till Zach gets back. Or Willow."

Her cruise would end tomorrow, but Noah, who'd been nominally in charge for a week, was here now.

"Do we have a problem, Wilkins?"

He looked puzzled. "Problem?"

"If you already knew what has to be done, if you're going to wait for my sister or brother to show up, why even tell me?" Unless he wanted to remind Noah of his temporary status, his creaky skills. On the range, Calvin Stern had displayed a similar, if milder, attitude.

Wilkins shifted. "Zach claimed you're running things, that's why."

"But it seems people here believe I'm not." Noah rose from his chair, putting him on a level with Wilkins. "I am, however, doing my best while he's gone. So why don't we agree to try to work together anyway? No sense making things more difficult than they are."

Wilkins stared at him. "I'm not the only one who thinks you should have stayed in the big city. Pardon me—pardon us—if we all have a hard time seeing you as one of the Bodines."

Noah returned the steely glare. "I am one of the Bodines." Wilkins didn't have to like that, either, but he could respect Noah's place—or leave.

"I owed you an update on the storm coming in. You got it." Wilkins tipped his hat, then left the office. "Doesn't mean the hands or I have to like this."

And now Noah knew for sure. The men didn't respect him, just as Hadley had said. They didn't particularly want him here any more than Noah wanted to stay.

He also knew, all over again, why he'd left. His father's overbearing manner, his own need to lead a different life—for himself. He hadn't forgotten that last quarrel or his dad's final ultimatum. *Leave now and you're no son of mine.* Noah was still trying to prove himself, if not to the family patriarch, then maybe to the rest of his family. Was that partly why he'd agreed to stay? Yet how could he manage the WB, even for this brief time, when every man on this spread seemed to not only disrespect him but ignore his authority? It was going to be a long few days waiting for Willow to get home.

"YOU MUST THINK I'm a terrible person." Meg paced the living room again, not daring to look at Kate, who'd just taken her to task for her treatment of Gabe at dinner.

On her next circuit of the room, Kate caught her forearm. "You're not an awful person, but what has that man ever done to you?" She paused. "I wasn't going to mention this, but I did happen to notice that your overreaction to Gabe might be due to an attraction that you're trying to suppress?"

Meg's pulse skipped a beat. "Don't be ridiculous. Gabe feeds horses, rides fence, herds cattle and the cowboys on this ranch—and that's all he is, your employee. To me, he's like…a piece of furniture."

"Hmm."

"That didn't sound good, did it, and I don't want to seem mean, but Teddie says you weren't 'very nice' to Noah Bodine either."

"Teddie didn't see us then. I'd sent him to the house. He's only trying to get back at me for making him sit in his room."

"And because you took Spencer away from him?"

"He said that? Not true," Kate said. "That pony needs stall rest until his leg heals."

Meg pulled away from Kate's grasp. She couldn't help grinning. "Kind of like Noah?"

Kate didn't answer that reference to his sprained ankle before the landline phone rang on the end table. She grabbed it, then, seeing the screen, mouthed the words *It's Mac again*.

Meg took a step backward. Her eyes must have been as big as dinner plates.

"No." She shook her head. "I can't." The phone kept ringing. She hated to put Kate on the spot again, and she knew how awkward that must be for her, but Meg would rather talk to Gabe Morgan. "Tell him I'm already asleep."

"It's only eight o'clock."

"Answer," she said. "Then make any excuse you like. Please."

Kate rolled her eyes. She rarely denied Meg anything and finally accepted the call. "Hi, Mac." A brief silence. "No, I'm sorry, but um, she's not here."

Their conversation was mercifully brief, but after it ended, Kate looked furious.

"Honestly, Meg. He sounds worse every

time he calls. Mac must have a reason. I get the impression he regrets the divorce."

"Just as he 'regretted' every one of our arguments when we still had them until, finally, there was just silence left. We had no real marriage, Kate. By the end, I was a convenience, that's all. He counted on me to 'keep the home fires burning' while he flew off to one country after another." Mac was a commercial airline pilot. "His schedule varied all the time, and he rarely missed an opportunity to take another colleague's slot. He loved flying more than he did me." to her dismay, her voice had cracked. "He wasn't even home when I lost the *baby* he claimed he'd wanted too. But did he, really? Kate, I was like—"

"A piece of furniture?"

Meg put her head in her hands. She wished she hadn't mentioned her painful miscarriage. "Mac makes me crazy. We were never right for each other like you and Rob were."

"We had our issues too," Kate reminded her.

"Well. Mac and I don't have them anymore, and I'm fine with that."

"Are you?" Looking disappointed in her, and sad herself, Kate set the phone back in its cradle. "I will not answer again for you. Whatever is or isn't with you and Mac, is between the two of you—not with me in the middle. And here I thought I saw something new with Gabe."

"You didn't." She tried to change the subject. "And according to Teddie, who did see this part, you wore your 'mad face' with Noah. Are you sure that wasn't out of all proportion to the event? Something to think about."

"All right, he and I did have words, but Teddie exaggerates. He has this fixation about visiting Noah, which I don't understand. And I won't have Noah override me as Teddie's mother. Whatever decisions I make are not his concern. Besides, there's no point. I have no interest in Noah. He was a friend once, but he's not a friend now. I won't mention Gabe again if you'll stop bringing up Noah Bodine."

"I'll try." But Meg had to smile.

Kate swatted her arm. "Try harder." Then she couldn't resist having the last word. "The next time Mac calls—and he will—you'd better answer. If you don't, he told me he'll be coming to see you."

THE NEXT MORNING Kate glanced out the kitchen window and saw Noah Bodine's truck—or rather, one of the WB's pickups—rolling up the drive. Her talk with Meg had made her wonder. Had she been unfair to him? Still, even after she'd made a bargain with Meg, and for her own good, Kate should maintain her vow to keep him at a distance. What was he doing here now?

Bandit was barking in the yard, and she went out the back door to silence him.

"Hey, Kate." Noah climbed down from the truck. "I'm not here to say goodbye, which you were probably hoping to hear. But I did want to tell you this—I can't blame you for wanting to parent Teddie as you see fit. I wasn't trying to step in your way. But I could sure identify with his take on things, punishing himself more than you ever could. I was the same way years ago, full of self-recrimination every time I tangled with my dad. I wasn't criticizing you. I just understood Teddie's emotions."

Kate hesitated. She had come on pretty strong yesterday. What harm could there be in apologizing now? That didn't mean she had to scrap her promise to herself to avoid him. "Well. I may have overreacted about the pony."

The words, which might have sounded grudging, weren't out of her mouth before Teddie banged out the kitchen door and down the steps. "Mr. Bodine, you should see Spencer! He feels so much better."

Noah glanced at Kate as if to challenge her. "I would like to see him. Lead the way."

Kate reluctantly followed, and in the barn the three of them stood at Spencer's stall. The pony did look good. He'd stopped sulking by the rear window and was eating his grain.

"He drank all his water too," Teddie pointed out. "Maybe I can ride him now?"

"Teddie, he has to stay right here until Dr. Crane checks him over."

"When will that be?"

"Soon," she said, being deliberately vague.

"Can I go in his stall? Spencer wants me to brush him."

Remembering that her foreman had told her Teddie had already been inside, Kate looked at Noah. "I guess you may, as long as I'm nearby—or Gabe."

"Yay!" Teddie grabbed the nearest brush, then slid the door's bolt back. As he groomed Spencer, interrupted by numerous pats on his neck and kisses on his nose, Kate and Noah stood there in the aisle until suddenly Teddie said, "Can I tell N—Mr. Bodine about my new book?"

"Yes." But Kate pitied him. "Prepare yourself, Noah."

For the next ten minutes, her son rattled off dozens of statistics about the planets, his newest interest. He knew all about Mars and Venus, their distance from the earth, their composition and how many moons there were. "Did you know we'll have a man on Mars soon? Maybe I'll be an astronaut and go there."

The figures swirled in Kate's head, but Noah kept nodding, his gaze keen on Teddie.

"You're an astronomy fan too?" she asked.

"Sure am. Takes one to know one."

Kate lowered her voice. "Teddie's also into dragons, cars and airplanes. I can't keep up with him sometimes."

"You have a very bright little boy there."

"We make a weekly trip to the library in Barren, but there are never enough books in the house to suit Teddie."

"That's a good thing. He wants to learn." Noah hesitated. "If you like, he can visit the library at the WB. Most of my books from childhood are still on those shelves."

"You were a 'brain' too?"

"You probably won't remember because we weren't in school together, but yeah, not something that's easy to live down with other kids. My folks eventually put me in a special gifted program. I got bored with public school. I think Dad hoped I'd learn so much that I'd get interested in ranching, too, then follow in his footsteps."

Teddie had stopped reciting numbers and facts. He lifted his head from Spencer's side. "Mommy, doesn't he look good?"

"Beautiful," Kate said with a smile.

Teddie looked disgusted. "Spencer's not beautiful. He's a boy. He can't make baby ponies but—"

Noah caught her eye, and they both smiled. Kate said, "Too much information, Bunny. If you're done here, let's make lunch."

"Can N—Mr. Bodine eat with us?"

Noah ruffled Teddie's hair and saved Kate from having to answer. "Thanks for the invitation, but I have chores to do, short stuff. Better get back to them." They walked out of the barn to his truck, where Noah bent down to Teddie's level, then laid a hand on her son's shoulder. "Mind your mother. I still do mine—or else." He lingered another moment. "By the way, have you ever seen a meteor shower?" Teddie said he hadn't. "You missed some earlier this month," Noah told him, "but the Lyrids will streak past in April, and next summer the Perseids will be on display. Maybe your mom will let you stay up to watch them." He gave Teddie the coming dates, then got into his truck.

He was gone before Kate could thank him. She almost wished he had stayed for lunch.

CHAPTER SEVEN

NOAH FILLED THE last water bucket, then carried it to Midnight's stall and hung it on the hook inside. The horse eyed him as if thinking whether to start kicking, revenge for their one ride after the first blizzard, but Noah should be the one seeking payback after getting dumped. Kind of like Zach about the WB. With a pat on the stallion's neck, which made Midnight shy, Noah slipped out into the aisle—and ran into Wilkins.

The foreman's tone was grudging. "Thanks for helpin'."

The comment didn't sit well with Noah. *Helping?* "Thought I'd made myself clear. You work for this ranch—meaning me, at the moment." That afternoon, after he'd left Kate's, the two of them and Calvin Stern had counted head, rescued a balky steer from the dry wash near Sweetheart Ranch and herded a few more heifers toward the safety of the barn for tonight. "I wasn't 'helping' this afternoon. I was leading the way." That latest storm system had stalled out last night, but the snow was almost here now. Looked to be a long winter. Noah hoped Willow, whose cruise ended tomorrow, might be home the day after.

By Tuesday—after he'd made his apology to her—he'd be on a plane to LaGuardia. Even with Noah's attempt to work remotely, things were already slipping through the cracks at J&B. Yet oddly, and in spite of that, he wasn't as eager now to get back as he'd expected to be. The realization unsettled him.

And at Sweetheart Ranch today Teddie had been glad to see him, but Kate not so much, although she had managed to apologize. He'd felt tempted to accept her son's invitation to lunch, but he could tell Kate hoped he'd say no. So, instead, he'd returned to the WB, where Wilkins never missed an opportunity to remind him that Noah didn't belong here.

Noah even agreed. He would never succeed on the WB. But for now, "Wilkins, tell the new guy at the ag store that last delivery had some mold."

"I've ordered more hay—and made the complaint. Probably a onetime mishap. When the load comes, I'll make sure it's better quality." Wilkins gazed at him. "Anything else?"

Evening feeding was finished, the horses bedded down, blankets on against the growing cold, a monitor set up at the house for one pregnant mare on stall watch. She wasn't due yet but had shown signs of preparing for birth. Noah hoped that wouldn't happen. He looked forward to spending the evening in front of the TV. Tomorrow being Sunday, and the end of the cruise, couldn't come soon enough.

"Nothing else," he finally told Wilkins, who left the barn without further comment.

Unlike his work at J&B, which needed his presence, Noah was out of his element on the WB. He still didn't understand why Zach was so angry with him for leaving when Zach seemed to run the ranch with ease. He'd made it even more profitable than their father had.

If Noah had stayed, by now the ranch might have filed for bankruptcy. Not that he'd let anyone else point that out. This wasn't his arena in which to truly prove himself, yet even at J&B, and without his dad around, Noah still felt the impact of his disapproval. "Have a good night," he called to Calvin, who was in the feed room, measuring out doses of medications for the next morning. "See you all at five a.m."

In New York, too, Noah got up early—sometimes even spent the night on the sofa in his office—but this was ridiculous, day after day working in the dark, the cold and snow, until his fingers and toes went numb. Why was Kate, a woman alone now, so all-fired bent on keeping Sweetheart Ranch for Teddie? If she sold their land, his college would be paid for. She'd have the funds then to provide extra education for Teddie, the stimulation he needed. She'd have time to focus on her own needs, but he wouldn't dare to mention that.

In spite of his exhaustion, Noah couldn't sleep that night. In fact, he'd no sooner closed his eyes at last when the foal monitor went off. On his feet in the next second, he pulled on the clothes and jacket he'd worn that day.

Between the alarm sounding and his reaching the barn, to his relief the mare had delivered her premature foal without help, which Noah suspected in his case would have been minimal anyway. But at midnight he was on his own. It being Saturday, Wilkins had gone with the other hands into Barren for a few beers at Rowdy's. Calvin was home with his wife and baby.

Noah hunkered down beside the too-still foal in the stall bedding. The mother hadn't nudged it at all and was standing in the farthest corner, clearly spent.

"She's rejecting that foal," Noah's mother said, startling him as she opened the stall door. "It happens, but I'm never pleased when it does."

"Mom. Sorry I woke you."

"You mean practically falling down the stairs in those boots? Of course not." She knelt down next to him beside the foal. "Poor baby."

"You think he won't make it?" The newborn was a colt, its hide wet from birth and a darker bay than its dam. It had a broad white strip down its face and a pair of blinking brown eyes that seemed to beg Noah to save it.

Jean laid a hand on his arm. "I'll call the vet."

Noah's gut clenched. Did she mean for advice or to put the foal down before it had any chance at all? When his mother came back, the news wasn't great. The WB's vet had gone to Topeka on another emergency, and Noah thought of calling Wilkins, then just as quickly decided against it.

"Mom, you must know what to do in cases like this."

Her tone softened. "I run the house. Zach's responsible for the rest of the ranch. That's our agreement, just as it was with your father. My heart goes out to this baby—" she glanced at the mare in the corner "—but for now, we'll just have to hope his mama decides to take care of him."

Noah stroked the tiny colt's side, its flesh quivering. He hadn't felt this helpless, so alone with a problem, except for the day he'd finally packed his bags, then left the ranch for the last time as his father's favored son. They'd barely spoken for the rest of his dad's life. It had been a long time since Noah had even seen a newborn colt, and then his father had still been in charge. Now Noah had another choice to make about this helpless little being. Call a different vet from another town? Or wait to see what happened?

As he wrestled with the options, he heard a sudden sound.

"Look, Mom." The foal had nickered feebly. "I think he wants us to try. That's a good sign, isn't it?" He took a breath. "Call Kate. She'll know what else to do, won't she?"

"Yes. I imagine she will."

KATE KNELT DOWN in the stall bedding. "Gosh, he's awfully small. Winter foals are often less vigorous. Has he tried to stand?"

"Not that I've seen," Noah murmured, grateful that she'd answered his call so quickly.

Frowning, she ran her hands over the colt. "We should try to get him up. I wish Doc Crane could be here. I've delivered my share of foals, but this boy, in addition to his size, isn't as alert as I'd like to see either. He may be exhausted from birth—his mama appears to be—but he should stand within the first two hours of life."

With a bit of prodding, and a coaxing tone, she managed to help the foal to its feet. "I was right. His legs are weak. See how he's down in the pasterns and fetlocks?"

Noah glanced at his mother. She looked as uncertain as he felt.

"Can't say that I do," he admitted.

"His legs will probably straighten out soon, and I can't see any obvious defects, but I wonder why his mom isn't taking to him as she should."

Noah shrugged. "I don't know this horse— or any of the others on the WB."

"Except for Midnight," Kate couldn't resist saying, tongue in cheek.

Jean thought for a moment. "I do know Zach was concerned about this mare. Before he and Cass left, he told Wilkins to keep a close watch during the day and to keep the monitor on in the off-hours." That duty had fallen to Noah tonight. "I believe this was her first foal. She may simply not know what's expected of her yet or even realize that she gave birth."

"Rejection is more common then," Kate said. "Let's hope it's temporary. Her ears aren't flattened. I don't think she'll hurt this little guy, but she's not curious about him either." Kate guided the colt closer to the bay mare. The foal was still standing but wobbly, his legs splayed out to hold him upright. He nickered again, as if to ask his mother for permission to come near. "He needs to nurse."

"I don't think we have any other nursing moms on the WB right now," Jean said.

Kate encouraged the foal to take up the

proper position, but his dam sidestepped out of reach. Kate bit her lip. "Hold him, Noah. I want to take a closer look at this mare."

"You think she's sick?"

"It's possible she's only feeling a 'let down' response to her milk coming in, which can be uncomfortable…" She bent to examine the horse. "Ah," Kate said, straightening. "It appears your foreman wasn't watching her as closely as he was supposed to. She's inflamed and must feel quite tender, which probably explains her reluctance to let her baby nurse. I suspect she has a fever."

Noah didn't like the sound of that. "Doc may not come before tomorrow to prescribe medication."

But Jean remembered Zach keeping some antibiotics on hand and offered to look in the feed room, leaving Kate alone with Noah.

"Thanks for coming over," he said, "but this doesn't look good."

She kept her gaze on the foal, which had lain down near its mother yet not close enough to get kicked.

"We're not done yet," Kate murmured. "This colt still needs to nurse. It's vital to get colostrum into him—with the antibodies his mama should pass on to him. For tonight, you're going to have to milk her."

"Me?" And get booted into the stall boards?

"I don't see anyone else here in charge of the WB. Do you?"

Noah thought of asking Kate to stay, but as soon as she'd arrived, she'd claimed she needed to get home, and she'd already sacrificed a night's sleep to help him.

"Once you get this mare treated," Kate added, "I imagine she'll accept her baby. If not, after the vet sees him, give me a call. I have one mare who might act as a surrogate mom."

"Thanks again, Kate."

She arched an eyebrow as if to prompt Noah, who had no choice but to take his cue.

"Show me what I need to do."

A COUPLE OF hours later, Noah went to the house, kicked off his boots inside the kitchen door, then rummaged through the refrigerator. After all the excitement in the barn, he'd managed, ham-handed, to get a few ounces of milk from the mare—who certainly wasn't his friend—and he'd given the colt a bottle. Knowing he wouldn't sleep now, he popped open a beer, tore into a bag of corn chips, then collapsed on the living room sofa with the TV remote. He hadn't started to channel surf before he remembered a call he should have made. His partner, Brent, had labor issues in London; the office manager they'd hired had abruptly quit after a contract dispute. Yawning, Noah had just dealt with that when he noticed a missed call from Margot. He glanced at his watch. It was almost five, six o'clock in New York. Better call her back, or she'd be peeved again.

"Hey, baby," she purred, having answered on the first ring. Margot was an early riser. Noah conjured up an image of her, that rich dark red hair, her brown eyes.

"Hi. What's up?"

"Does something have to be 'up' for you to return my calls?"

Already peeved, then. Noah raked a hand through his hair, which felt gritty. He needed a shower. The last thing he wanted was a confrontation, never his strong suit. "Sorry I didn't phone before. I've been too busy to do anything but drop my weary bones onto this sofa every night. I'd forgotten how rough this kind of work could be."

And how capable Kate had been tonight. Which wouldn't impress Margot.

"There must be staff there, Noah." Margot hired people for everything. He could imagine Wilkins's reaction to being called staff. "You work too hard. Sometimes you forget to have a life beyond J&B—and now, it seems, taking care of a bunch of smelly cows and horses." She took an audible breath. "You forget about me."

"Margot, Willow's cruise ends today." He was counting the hours. Milking the mare had been enough for him. "That's good news, isn't it?"

Margot paused. "I could fly out for the last day or so you'll be there—if I didn't end up sitting in the house by myself while you play cowboy?"

"Hardly." But at least she imagined he could.

Her voice perked up. "You could tour me around, then we could fly home together. Wouldn't that be fun?"

"I wouldn't want you to be disappointed." The WB was far from the home where Margot had grown up, the pampered only child of wealthy parents in Greenwich, Connecticut, who'd indulged her every whim. They still did. Her dad was one of the original investors in Noah's firm, which was how he had met Margot. He was always trying to play catch-up, as he had with his own father, a role he didn't relish any more than he did "playing cowboy" on this ranch. He studied the room. "My folks' house is comfortable, but it's part of a working spread, without the sort of elegance you're used to."

Even her three-bedroom apartment in Manhattan, which Margot owned, had been done to the nines, including expensive artwork on the walls. Noah always feared sitting down and ruining some pricey piece of white furniture. At least in the barn, he didn't have that worry.

"I'll be back before you know it," he said. "Besides, it's freezing cold here."

"I suppose you're right. But I do miss you."

A short silence followed while she waited for him to say he missed her, too, but Noah couldn't. Finally, she said, "Hurry back. There was another party at the Plaza last night, one of Mother's charities. I had to make an appearance, so I went by myself, and everyone wanted to know where you were. This is where you belong, Noah— where *we* belong." As if he needed the reminder. Then: "With J&B doing so well, there's no limit to where we can go."

Noah straightened. She was about to broach the topic of an engagement. Margot had begun to slip that possibility into every conversation, and he couldn't blame her. They'd been seeing each other for almost two years now. She'd been the first woman he'd taken a serious interest in since he'd left the WB. At first, he and Margot had rubbed along with no conflicts, but lately... He owed her a commitment but couldn't seem to make one. He'd liked things the way they were. He didn't relish the tough conversation they needed to have—but not tonight.

When his cell phone dinged again with another text, he breathed a sigh of relief. "Sorry, don't mean to cut you off, but I have to take this other call."

Without waiting for her objection, Noah hung up with a promise to phone tomorrow. Then he looked at the incoming text from Zach, who said nothing about when he was coming home, and the bottom of Noah's empty stomach dropped out. Just heard from Willow/Cody. Spending extra days in Miami after cruise. Zach had added a smiley face emoji and the words—Stay put, buddy.

Noah wasn't going anywhere.

CHAPTER EIGHT

KATE HADN'T PLANNED to return to the WB, but at breakfast she'd told Teddie a new foal had been born overnight, and after that there'd been no choice but to get in the truck. Now, as they drove through the ranch gates, the tires making fresh tracks in the snow that had finally fallen, she wished she'd explained her morning yawns a different way. "Remember, we can't stay long," she cautioned him, meeting Teddie's gaze in her rearview mirror.

He drummed his legs against the car seat and wriggled with impatience.

"I read all about baby horses in my book from the library," he said.

As she pulled up at the barn, Kate just hoped the foal had stayed alive and they weren't walking into a sad situation. She'd called the WB first, of course, but something might have changed since then. "I want you to stay here until I see if it's all right for you to meet the baby."

Perhaps because of Kate's tone, Teddie went on alert. "Is he sick?"

"No, but...please stay in the truck."

Too tired to think of a better explanation, she reached for a bag on the floor, then hopped out just as Noah appeared in the barn doorway. He lifted a hand in greeting. "Sorry to be a pest," she began, "but your neighbors are wondering how the new arrival is doing."

"Same as when we spoke." Noah glanced over at Teddie, and the two exchanged waves. "The colt looks better. But he's still wobbly, and his mama doesn't want much to do with him."

"Have you managed to give him more colostrum?"

Noah rubbed the back of his neck. "Yeah, and that's always fun. Good news—the vet's coming at noon to see its mama. Over the phone, he agreed with your diagnosis of infection."

"In the meantime, I've brought you a present." Kate handed him the bag. "The mare I mentioned donated lunch." She paused. "And if you don't mind, Teddie is beside himself. Is it still all right if he sees the colt?"

"Sure." Noah motioned for Teddie to join them, and her son unbuckled his seat restraints, then tumbled out of the truck.

"Hi, N—Mr. Bodine!" Teddie flung himself at Noah's legs. "Congrat'lations. You have a new baby! I bet he's prettier than even the ones in my book." Teddie started to reel off every statistic he'd read about newborn foals.

Noah grinned over Kate's head. "He definitely has enthusiasm."

"That's my boy." She trailed them into the barn, blinking against the change of light.

At the stall, Noah lifted Teddie so he could see inside. "Well, what do you think?"

"He's…so…*cute*," Teddie all but whispered, an arm around Noah's neck. "Can I touch him myself?"

"If your mom says okay."

Kate peeked into the stall. The mare was standing in the corner, as she had last night, the foal on the opposite side, as if he knew better than to approach her. "I'm worried she hasn't taken to him yet. They should have bonded, or at least be bonding by now."

"I think she's feeling worse than last night," Noah said. "I couldn't have done that milking without you."

"You'd have figured it out. The WB will make a cowboy of you yet."

"It can try," he said, setting Teddie down. "Come on, short stuff. Let's see how you like this boy up close."

Teddie could barely contain himself until Noah opened the stall door. Noah talked softly to him about the colt and Teddie threw in another fact or two, their heads close together.

Kate's throat tightened. Although she couldn't fault his being good to Teddie, she couldn't overlook the fact that Noah had been there in New York when Rob died but hadn't saved him. She couldn't forget her own renewed promise to avoid him. Why encourage this fledgling friendship with her son? If only she hadn't mentioned the foal to Teddie…

"Mommy, he likes me! I wish he could be mine."

Noah's eyes met hers. "I can't give him to you, Teddie. I would if I could, but the colt belongs to the WB. How about this instead? Since Zach's not here, I don't see any reason why you can't name this colt."

"I can?" He turned to Kate.

"You certainly may." She had to blink. For another few minutes, she stood outside the stall while her son ran through a dozen choices with Noah. They didn't reach a conclusion, but she hadn't seen Teddie this happy since he'd been given Spencer for his birthday.

At last, Teddie burst out of the stall. "I'll think some more, N—Mr. Bodine. Is it okay if I name him tomorrow? I want to pick exactly the right one."

"No problem." Noah touched Kate's shoulder. "This boy of yours has the absolute best ideas. I've never heard such good choices for a colt." Like Twinkle Star and then Thumper, after the rabbit in his book about Bambi. Noah grinned at Teddie. "It'll be hard to narrow them all down."

"Leave it to me," Teddie said, adjusting his glasses.

Then, being the active child that he was, he skipped out to the barnyard, talking to himself. Kate heard more names being bandied about and couldn't help laughing.

Noah did too. "You're going to have a very talkative afternoon."

"I know. Thank you, Noah, for being so kind. That meant the world to Teddie."

"He sure knows a lot about foals."

"About everything," she said, admitting, "I

hope I'm up to the challenge of homeschooling him."

Noah stepped back. "You're not sending Teddie to public school?"

"He can already read—as you may have guessed. In fact, he can pass standardized tests through fourth grade. I didn't want him to feel 'different,' to be in classes with kids much older than Teddie."

"True. But what about a gifted program like the one my parents found for me? In Farrier?"

"Barren doesn't have one, and taking him to Farrier every day—I looked online—just isn't feasible. We're not eligible for the school bus route there either."

"Then all I have to say is, good luck. Being a teacher, along with running your ranch, won't be easy."

"Meg has promised to help."

Noah walked her to the truck. "Let me know if there's anything I can do."

Kate had one hand on the door handle, an eye on Teddie, who was chasing one of the ranch dogs around the yard. "That would be…helpful, *if* you were staying." Which she didn't want him to do.

"Guess this word hasn't gotten around

yet." Noah took a breath. "Zach texted me—after you left. My sister and her new husband have extended their honeymoon. I was told to 'stay put.'"

Kate's spirits sank. Despite their necessary proximity in this very barn the night before, she didn't want Noah here. How could she let Teddie get close to another man when he'd taken Rob's death so hard? And, most of the time, still did? Keeping Teddie away from Noah, however, wouldn't be possible either. For now, he was staying at the WB. Way too near to Sweetheart Ranch. And also, her.

NOAH HADN'T EXPECTED the news to thrill Kate. She didn't want him to stay for even another day. Yet here he was, in the ranch office again, thanks to Zach—and Willow. He would try to contact his sister, which hadn't seemed critical when she was on the ship, but now he needed to clarify her schedule—not get the word second hand from Zach. He couldn't blame his sister for wanting more of a honeymoon, but for how much longer? He couldn't stay forever.

His mother rapped at the open door, her brow furrowed. "Were you planning to eat dinner tonight—or roll right through at that desk to breakfast? Noah, you work too hard."

"That's what Margot says."

Jean's lips pressed tight. "Perhaps one thing on which we can agree."

No news there. Jean Bodine was fiercely protective of her brood. She thought Margot was "uppity" and not right for him and had some hidden agenda that would end up hurting Noah. "Mom, I do neglect her, and with the new London office in the works, how can I not?" Which didn't help his need to discuss their relationship. "Trying now to run the company from here, see to the WB, deal with that new foal—"

"I just checked on him. That mare still doesn't seem like the best mother."

"No, that title's reserved. For you." Noah tried a smile that he wasn't sure reached his eyes. He felt dog-tired after a night without sleep, the hours he'd spent today with the colt and his latest conversation with Kate. Plus, he had a ton of New York business waiting before he even thought of bed tonight. Then there was Margot. How could he tell the woman he'd dated for nearly two years that he had doubts? "I mean that, Mom. Thanks for putting up with me."

"I know you don't really want to be here."
She studied her hands. "I've also heard that
you and Wilkins don't get along."

"As a kid, I saw Dad lock horns plenty of
times with various foremen. Why think I'd
be any different? I spend more energy trying to steer clear of Wilkins than I do actually getting anything done."

"You've done very well with that foal."

"Kate brought some milk for him today,
which helps, but I'm still worried."

Jean smiled. "You're taking an interest.
That's a good thing—from my viewpoint."

"As long as you remember this is only a
visit."

"I know that too."

"And that still hurts you." Noah toyed
with a stack of papers on the desk. "I'm
sorry, Mom. But you've seen for yourself
that I don't fit in here. I mean, what kind of
rancher falls off his horse the first day? We
may still lose that foal, and in case you've
forgotten, Kate doesn't want me around."

But Jean disagreed. "She came last night,
brought the colt a bottle this morning, didn't
she?"

"Not for my sake. She's a compassionate
person, and she's loved animals since she

was that annoying kid who followed Zach and me around years ago."

"She never had a brother of her own." Jean paused and he sensed what was coming. "How irritating is she now? She's a lovely girl." Better for him than Margot, but she hadn't said that.

"Here we go again," he muttered.

"I'm just saying."

"Yeah, and then what happened? Did you miss this part? She married Rob." That still hurt Noah too. "Now I'm the convenient scapegoat for her loss."

"You're using that as an excuse. I suggest you talk to her. You're both young, with your lives ahead of you. That boy of hers could use a strong male influence in his life." She grinned. "Not to mention, Teddie reminds me of you. Smart as a whip—"

"Kate plans to homeschool him." That had been troubling him since this morning.

"Yes, I've heard that. I assume you think that's a mistake. So do I."

"Remember how I drove you and Dad crazy? None of us would have been satisfied with a homeschool experience. It's not the right choice, either for Teddie or her, even with Meg's help."

"Maybe you could convince her to try another solution?"

"I suggested the program I went to. I doubt I could convince her of anything." Not just about Teddie, and certainly not about Noah's part in Rob's death. He'd tried that once during the blizzard.

"If you don't still have feelings for her—"

"Mom. What kind of relationship could we have with me in New York and her glued to Sweetheart Ranch? Besides, I'm with Margot." For the time being.

"I am an excellent judge of character, Noah. Consider this—you've been 'with Margot' for some time, yet I haven't seen a diamond ring. Doesn't that tell you something?"

"Not everyone jumps right into marriage." Like Kate had with Rob.

Noah squirmed in his seat. He'd brought his doubts about the future Margot had planned for them with him, but he wasn't about to share that with his mother. Margot deserved to know first. "I realize I can be too focused on details at times, but…"

"You'll what? Propose eventually to a woman you don't seem desperate to marry? You should have been here when Cody was trying to win Willow over. Now *that* was determination. I only want you to be as happy as they are, darling."

He scowled at the paper mess in front of him on the desk. If the London launch—and J&B's acquisition of a small start-up company they were looking at—ever happened, it would be a miracle.

"Mom. Cut me some slack. Juggling two full-time jobs—one physical, the other mental—isn't easy, and they couldn't be more different."

"I'm sure you'll manage." Jean stepped back from the doorway. "If you aren't in bed by ten o'clock, I'll be back." She would too.

Shaking his head, Noah went back to his paperwork. His normally rightful place.

Too bad he couldn't seem to get a handle—temporarily—on the ranch. Those accounts were waiting for him too. Another all-nighter maybe when he couldn't forget that morning visit from Teddie. And Kate.

Or, no matter what he'd told his mother, the talk he needed to have with Margot.

"I MEAN IT, KATE. Don't answer that."

Still focused on her earlier visit to the WB, Kate had nearly forgotten her promise not to pick up Mac McClaren's next call, and obviously Meg felt she needed a reminder. Another shrill ring seemed to split the night and threatened to wake Teddie. Kate handed her aunt the phone. "Do it."

Meg's eyes held Kate's as if to say *whatever happens, this will be your fault.* She jabbed a button on the landline's handset. "Yes, Mac?" she said, her voice cool.

His voice filled the room. "Finally. I was getting tired of talking to your niece."

"I suppose you also got frustrated calling my cell, leaving those messages I never intended to respond to. By the way, I've put you on speaker. Kate's right here."

"Ah," he said, "the Sweetheart Ranch version of 'this conversation may be recorded.'"

"Did you not get the papers from my lawyer? We're divorced. My half of our assets— or the portion that has been liquidated—is in my account at the Barren Cattlemen's Bank. I fail to understand what other business we might need to conduct. Or is this about selling the house? You have two minutes."

"I should have followed my first instinct— to get in the car and come see you."

Her voice hardened. "Don't you dare."

"This isn't about the house." Mac was still

living there, dragging his feet about a sale. He laughed a little. "Funny, I just pictured you standing on the front porch there with a rifle in hand."

"Shotgun," she corrected him. "The image is correct. If you show up here, I won't be responsible for my actions."

Kate kept sending her hand signals to tone it down.

"Megan, all I want is to talk. Why do you keep throwing up roadblocks?" He paused, then softened his tone. "Hey, Kate. How's everything? I bet Teddie's half-grown by now."

She had to smile. "He is. Growing too fast. Nice talking to you, Mac."

She arched an eyebrow at Meg, then started to leave the room. Meg snagged her arm. *Stay here.*

Kate glared at her. *I refuse to eavesdrop on your private conversation.*

Meg made a praying-hands motion. *Please.*

Kate stopped walking. She couldn't ignore her aunt's plea. Meg had been invaluable after Rob died, and her generous offer to move in and help with Teddie was a debt Kate could never repay. In addition, they were friends, the best Kate had. Meg needed her support. What else could she do then but nod? She sank down on the sofa, crossed her arms and tried not to listen to the call. Their divorce had made her sad.

"You still there, Meg?" Mac asked.

"Yes. But your two minutes are up."

"Don't," he said, probably knowing her finger was poised above the end-call button.

"Quickly, then. Say what you need to say."

Kate stuck both index fingers in her ears and silently intoned the Pledge of Allegiance to turn off her thoughts. Part of her understood Meg's reluctance to give Mac any further place in her life. Because of Rob, the rest of her didn't.

She was still reciting the pledge when Meg hung up.

Kate rose to hug her. "How bad was it? You look like you're about to cry."

Meg's mouth quivered. "He hasn't sold the house because he thinks our divorce was a mistake. Can you believe that?"

"Yes," Kate murmured.

Meg looked away. "After all he put me through? I don't want to 'try again.' You may not remember, but when we were going through that—when *I* was—Mac was flying to Shanghai, Paris, somewhere… While I was trying to recover from losing *my* baby, grieving, Mac had to sign the final decree from our lawyers via some online app. He just tried to tell me he thought that might not be legal."

"Is it?"

"I don't know! Why wouldn't it be?" Meg threw up her hands. "Now he's obviously looked around—and finally noticed I wasn't there to make his life easier. That's all."

"Is it?" Kate repeated.

Meg ignored her. "I had enough drama then to last the rest of my life. Maybe someday I'll meet a guy who actually puts me first."

Kate couldn't keep the sorrowful note from her voice. "I thought Rob did, but then he chose New York over me and Teddie." *And I lost him.* "Come on," she said, "let's see if Teddie's really asleep or hiding my iPad under the covers to read a book of names for that horse."

"Which reminds me. You never said how today went at the WB?"

"Teddie hasn't stopped talking about that foal since we hit our front door." She trailed Meg up the stairs.

"I meant Noah." Oh, no.

"Hush," was all Kate said.

CHAPTER NINE

THAT WEEK, MEG'S great-nephew was into horses all the way. The following morning, in the snow that had again covered the yard, she took Teddie down to the barn. Meg hoped to clear her head after the phone call Kate had forced her to take from her ex last night. Just hearing Mac's voice had brought back too many memories—not all of them bad. To Meg, that seemed worse than being able to blame Mac for their divorce. She'd looked into the process for changing her name but hadn't done so yet and silently ordered herself to get moving.

"Morning," said a male voice from the nearby tack room. Gabe Morgan.

She should have known he'd be here; the barn was his workspace. She tried to hold on to Teddie's hand, but he wrenched free and raced down the aisle to his pony's stall.

"Don't open that door," she told him.

Holding a worn bridle, Gabe came into

the aisle. "Teddie and I have an agreement. He asked my permission to see that pony— and I watch over him. I knew he was coming. He's okay."

"Well, I'm here now." Meg focused on a split board in a stall across the way. "You can get back to whatever you were doing."

Instead, Gabe leaned against a post. "I'm doing just fine, *thanks*. And *I* run this barn. Meaning I make such decisions."

"I know what you meant." She didn't have to like it. Meg started down the aisle, then glanced back over her shoulder. "Kate said to remind you, the farrier's coming today."

"On my calendar already." He didn't quite smile. "Don't open that door," he repeated in a drawl.

Mocking her? Meg bristled. "I should tell you that I have a low tolerance for bossy men."

"You're pretty bossy yourself."

His lazy tone irritated Meg. She turned back. "Oh, mister. You have no idea."

He studied his boots. "I'm curious. What's your ex's name?"

"Jon McClaren." Once upon a time, she'd written his name on notepads like a schoolgirl, adding her own, of course. *Megan*

McClaren. Meg and Jonathan McClaren.
"Why?"

She feared she knew what was coming, just as she should have known her relationship with Mac wouldn't work out. As for Gabe Morgan...

"No reason...except I kind of feel sorry for the guy. He really missed out—that bossiness aside," he added.

What did that mean? Was Gabe coming on to her? Kate thought he was attracted to Meg. Farther down the aisle, Teddie was talking to Spencer, telling him the names he'd come up with for the new foal at the WB. His sweet voice reminded her she wasn't here to spar with Gabe. Or to fend off any advances. "Really. Don't you have work to do?"

"The men are out spreading hay for the cattle after that latest storm, rounding up strays. I'm here waiting for the farrier." He held up the bridle. "Mending tack. Not that I need to justify my time."

"Not to me," she agreed, with a look toward the tack room.

Gabe jingled the bridle in his hands. Strong hands with sturdy wrists. As if she would welcome being cared for, protected by him. By anyone. And why would she want him to? Meg had learned the hard way with Mac, and as a child, that she had only herself to rely on. From the minute she'd met Kate's foreman, she'd tried to maintain distance. Sure, he was good-looking, but Kate was wrong. Meg would never throw herself at another man as she had so trustingly done with Mac—at least, not anytime soon. Besides, she always had the impression that inside, Gabe was laughing at her.

He wasn't laughing now. When Meg started down the aisle again, he came after her. "Wait." His dark eyes looked somber. "Seems to me we got off here on the wrong foot. I get that you're unhappy with your ex. Maybe you have the right to be. I don't know him, though he must be pretty dumb to have let you go." There was no way he could have known about her past, but Meg had wondered more than once about his. An air of mystery seemed to follow Gabe. Even Kate didn't know that much about him. "But you're not doing yourself any good wearing that chip on your shoulder."

"Only with you," she murmured.

"Kate warned me earlier you might be touchy this morning, but you do understand your breakup has nothing to do with me?"

Meg stilled. Had Kate told him about Mac's call? About her insecurities? As a girl, she'd often spent time at Sweetheart Ranch because, whenever her parents had been deployed, she couldn't stay home at Fort Riley alone. She'd bonded then with Kate, who had been motherless, too, in a very real way.

Teddie had poked his head out of Spencer's stall and was staring at them.

"Nothing has anything to do with you," she told Gabe.

"You sure about that? You seem to reserve a special animosity toward me. I keep wondering why." He cleared his throat. "I don't know how long you'll be staying here—how long I might last either—but at least try not to hate me, especially when Teddie's watching."

Meg turned her back, strode along the aisle to Spencer's stall, then laid a shaking hand on Teddie's head.

He peered up at her through his glasses. "I think Spencer's almost all better. Gabe said I could give him a carrot. Did you bring 'em?"

"I forgot."

A hand reached around her. Strong, masculine. "Here. Take the bag."

She passed it to Teddie, fearing she

couldn't speak. As always, Gabe's presence had unsettled her. "Let your pony have his treat, then meet me at the door." She brushed past Gabe, then marched to the barn entrance, feeling his gaze on her the whole way.

SURROUNDED BY PRINTOUTS from his New York office, Noah shifted the phone from one ear to the other and cringed. It was as if his partner were leaning over the desk in the WB's office rather than calling from London.

"What were we thinking?" Brent Jeffries's bass voice boomed. "I've hired three office managers so far. One of them crashed our new computer system and lost critical data. I mean, really? At J&B Cybersecurity? The second took two hours for lunch every day, and the newest was more concerned about his girlfriend losing her job than with his own." Brent took a breath. "I fired him before I called. And don't get me started on our VP of Security."

Noah held the phone away from his ear. "Go ahead and rant. I understand and I apologize. I should have handled that. I'd be there if I could."

"Well, it *was* your turn to fly to the UK, not mine."

"Two trips since New Year's is a lot, Brent. Breathe," Noah said. "We'll get through this, and before you know it—"

"*'We'll'* get through this?" He snorted. "Strange, but I haven't seen you in New York or London lately. I hope you're enjoying being a Kansas cowboy again in all that snow."

"Can't say I am." Noah glanced at the pile of papers on the desk. Ranch accounts, invoices, emails from other ranchers wanting to breed cattle from one of the WB's bulls. Oh, and the pending Prentice Security deal. He and Brent were trying to buy that small start-up firm to give them a broader reach into military contracts. His head had already been spinning over both jobs when Brent phoned.

For a brief moment, Noah half wished he hadn't partnered with Brent, thus the company name J&B. The guy was a bona fide genius, but his people skills weren't that great, and he had a quick temper—like Noah's dad. Then there was his too-loud voice. Ditto. Noah and Brent had started the business together. But what if Rob had later worked out? His personality had been more laid back, and they'd been such close friends they almost read each other's minds. Except about Kate, he hoped. Maybe, in time, he would have bought out Brent's stake, then partnered instead with Rob. Kate might have changed her mind by then and moved to New York. If so, would Rob still be alive? Instead, now he had to smooth Brent's ruffled feathers.

And, as he'd told his mother, try to manage two jobs when tonight his mind kept straying to Kate and Teddie at the barn yesterday. He hadn't slept any better last night, but Noah should focus on business—at the moment, two of them.

"We'll be okay. Let me make a few calls, see if I can tap into some contacts I made when we were looking for venture capital. I met some pretty talented people with experience. Maybe one of them would be interested in heading the London office for us if we beef up the salary. Let me think about a security person too."

"Gee, then I could actually sleep in my own bed for more than two nights running?"

Noah smiled a little. "I wouldn't go that far. But I feel your pain. The mattress in my old room here at the WB should have been replaced long ago." If he were staying, that would be another priority. Plus, he'd love to update the security on this office computer, which had holes like a sieve, and replace Wilkins. "Seriously, if my sister hadn't decided to tour Miami after her cruise, she'd probably be home by now—and I'd be back in Manhattan tomorrow."

"Which would make Margot happy."

Noah started at the mention of her. He hadn't talked to Margot since that last phone call, and frankly he'd been so caught up in the operation of the WB while placating Brent that he hadn't even thought about her. "You've spoken to her?"

"Indirectly. She called before this last trip of mine."

"Why?"

Brent hesitated. "For one thing, your admin told me she didn't sound pleased."

That was nothing new. "Yeah, but what did she actually want?"

Brent cleared his throat. "I'm not supposed to say."

Noah had a bad feeling. "Spill it, Brent."

He sighed. "Margot wanted to know if Daphne had booked your trip home yet. She needed the details."

Noah ran a hand over his hair. "I told her myself. I don't know when I'll be flying back. I texted Willow to see when she and Cody are actually coming home, but she hasn't answered." Willow must be livid about the wedding. He hadn't heard anything more from Zach, either, who might not alert him anyway. And why hadn't Daphne told him about Margot's call? Her dad may have helped to bankroll the firm, but it wasn't as if she was Noah's wife.

"With that call Margot stepped over a boundary between our personal lives and business."

Brent said, "I may be out of line here, too, but from what Daphne said, your girlfriend strikes me as awfully high maintenance."

Noah liked a lot of things about Margot— her smile, her boundless enthusiasm, her elegant style and even her patience, though that had become increasingly limited where he was concerned…but not her intrusion into his professional life.

"Am I right?" Brent asked because Noah hadn't answered.

"I guess that comes with the territory. Her father *is* one of the most important, wealthiest men in the city, so I suppose her expectations of the high life and, above all, my devoted attention, seem natural to her."

"Speaking of intentions…"

"I said 'attention.'" Noah swiveled the desk chair back and forth. Brent was tweaking him now, and maybe he deserved it for sticking his partner with a large chunk of J&B business in his absence, but Noah wasn't about to take the bait.

Brent said, "Margot did ask if you'd made any recent trips to Tiffany, Cartier or Harry Winston."

"She what?" Brent had finally diverted him from J&B, New York and even Kate. "I'll talk to her," Noah said.

"Can you get me that okay on the Prentice deal first? I have lawyers breathing down my neck, eager to finalize the agreement."

Noah studied his computer screen. "I'm looking at it now. You'll have it by tomorrow morning, guaranteed."

"Make that stat," Brent muttered. "Please."

A second later, Noah was staring at his dead phone. He would definitely have that talk with Margot.

And torn between J&B and the ranch, he faced yet another sleepless night.

ONE OF KATE'S favorite moments in the day was putting Teddie to bed. There was nothing better than the feel of his warm, cuddly body next to hers as they read—or rather, reread—*Janie Wants to Be a Cowgirl*. The now-tattered book had been handed down from other children in town and was always a Teddie pleaser.

"Again, Mommy." He snuggled closer, knocking his glasses askew.

Kate straightened them, then tapped a finger on his nose. "Don't you get tired of hearing the same story, Bunny?" He hadn't seemed to be quite paying attention tonight.

"I like Janie." Bandit lay beside him on the bed, with Teddie idly petting him. "Her horse isn't as nice as Spencer, but she gets to ride him anywhere she wants. Anytime."

This was another dig at Kate. Ever since Noah had fallen off his brother's horse, Teddie had been negotiating with her daily to ride over and visit him. That she'd taken him to meet the new foal had failed to dull the edge of his demands, in fact, had made things worse. Kate flipped to the first page of the book, then started the story again.

"Mommy." After a few sentences that Teddie could have read himself, he covered the page. "Do you think the baby horse is okay?"

Kate was curious herself. The vet hadn't

been there yesterday while she and Teddie were at the WB, and she hadn't heard anything since then. Was the mare better and the foal now able to nurse? "Mr. Bodine is taking good care of him."

"But he might need help."

"Nice try," Kate murmured.

Teddie nodded. "I could fill his water bucket. I can give him carrots like Spencer. I can—"

"Teddie, I told you we'd see the newborn colt, but that was a onetime offer."

"Why?"

Kate didn't want to fall back on her usual answer. *Because I said so.* This was one of the times when she missed Rob most. They'd always taken turns settling Teddie for the night, and she could almost hear the deep rumble of his voice as he'd read to their son. She'd enjoyed that as much as her own storytelling duty. Now, she read to Teddie every night unless Meg offered. "I don't—you shouldn't get attached to him."

"To N—Mr. Bodine?"

"No, the foal. Yes, you can name him but, Teddie Bear, that will be the end of it."

"Not if the baby wants me to come over." Teddie peered up at her through his glasses.

"Yes, he does, Mommy. I know he does. Mr. Bodine does too."

"You have no way of knowing that."

"Uh-huh. When we left yesterday, he said he'd see me next time."

"That was a figure of speech." Kate rephrased that. "He was—"

"Being polite again?"

"Yes, I'm glad you remember that." She gently pried his hand from the page of the book. "Now, young man, it's time for you to sleep."

Teddie's tone turned into a whine. "But why can't I help? You always say we need more help here. I bet Mr. Bodine does too." Teddie squirmed. "I bet he misses his brother."

"I'm sure he does, and his sister." He must be praying hourly for Willow's return.

Teddie plucked at the bed cover. "I miss Daddy, and I want him to come home, so maybe that's how Mr. Bodine feels too."

Kate took a shaken breath. "Oh, sweetie."

"I bet he feels bad because you don't like him. But I do." Teddie nodded again, his glasses slipping down his nose. He pushed them up. "I like him a lot."

Were her misgivings about Noah that obvious? Apparently, they were.

Kate had liked him fine before he'd lured
her husband to the big city. It would be too
easy now to revisit their happier past when,
in earlier years, the three of them had been
friends. But with Rob missing from that trio,
how happy could that memory be?

And where could it possibly lead?

Kate and Noah couldn't be more different.
She was a country girl; he was now a city
boy. As far as she knew, Noah was a confirmed bachelor; she was a single mom, with
Teddie's welfare uppermost in her mind. She
didn't want to go anywhere. Kate preferred
being "cooped up" at home; but Noah was
chafing to get back to his bigger world. The
world he'd held out to Rob like a carrot on
a stick, far from Sweetheart Ranch and her.

"Mr. Bodine won't be here much longer,"
she warned Teddie. Or was she reminding
herself? Even after the news that Willow had
extended her honeymoon, that must mean
only a few extra days. "If you get to know
him better, think how sad you'll feel when
he leaves."

Teddie's lower lip trembled. "Like I did
when Daddy left. I'm still sad." Now Teddie

was softly crying, leaning against her, the tears soaking Kate's shirt. She'd said exactly the wrong thing. Gabe had claimed she was a good mother, but how true was that? It had been days since Teddie had last cried, and she'd hoped he was beginning to deal better with his grief. To accept.

Kate held him close until, at last, his sobs became shudders, then a sigh.

"Teddie, Daddy didn't want to leave us."

"Then neither will Mr. Bodine, right?"

"That's not the same." Kate silently prayed that he wouldn't take this discussion any further. She couldn't take another mention of the daddy he missed with all his heart. The next thought stabbed like a knife through her mind. Did Teddie see Noah as a stand-in for his father? That could only lead to more heartbreak. She closed the book and laid it on his nightstand. She wiped his tears, then kissed the top of his head.

Teddie's mouth had set. "Yes, it is the same."

Kate had no answer for that. "Time to close your eyes, Teddie Bear." She rose from the bed, tucked the covers around him, slipped off his glasses and leaned down to kiss him goodnight. "Sleep well."

He yawned, his eyes at half-mast. "Tomorrow I need to tell what the baby horse's name will be. So we have to go back, Mommy."

Kate decided, as she left the room without responding, that if Teddie—like Noah so long ago—didn't want to be a rancher after all, he would make a fine lawyer.

CHAPTER TEN

ANOTHER TRIP TO the WB proved unnecessary.

"Mom, he's here!" The next morning, Teddie raced out of the house. "Noah!"

"Stay away from that truck," Kate called after him, her heart already in her throat. After Noah's call earlier that morning, she'd been expecting him, but his arrival was a surprise for Teddie. Noah had asked if they might try putting the mare and foal with hers, as she'd first suggested. She'd been half-inclined to reject the plan now, but for the colt's sake, in the hope of a closer bond with the mother and better nursing for him, she hadn't.

With Bandit barking, Kate hurried outside as the WB's pickup, towing a two-horse trailer, pulled up at the barn. Noah climbed down from the truck and tipped his hat. "Morning." In boots, jeans and a shearling-lined jacket, he didn't seem like a New York CEO.

"You're looking quite the cowboy today, Mr. Bodine." She sent Teddie a pointed look to remind him of the proper form of address.

Noah grinned then went around the rear of the trailer, Teddie dogging his heels and chattering away. When he saw the foal inside, he let out a shout that made the mare dance too.

"Careful," Noah said, a hand on Teddie's shoulder. "These two rode with no trouble, but we don't want something to happen to them now."

"What would happen?"

"Teddie," Kate put in, "we don't make sudden movements near the horses, just like with Spencer or Lady."

Teddie dug the toe of his boot into the dirt. "Sorry."

Kate wouldn't scold him further. He was a quick learner but also sensitive. She thought of the night before, when he'd cried again over his father and defended Noah. She watched Noah pull down the ramp, then coax the mare out of the trailer. Wherever she went, the colt would follow. At least, that's how it usually worked.

"So, there's been no real bonding?" she

asked, recalling their earlier conversation today.

Noah handed her the mare's lead rope. "I kept hoping she'd get accustomed to him, and that mastitis has greatly improved. She does allow him to nurse, but afterward she turns away and still ignores him." He shook his head. "I'm thinking maybe Zach should sell her once this colt is a bit stronger. Wilkins tells me she's not the best cow pony, and if I were running the WB permanently, I'd be more than reluctant to breed her again."

Kate led the mare into the barn, Noah behind with the foal, which seemed stronger yet not as much as she would like to see.

"I can't imagine rejecting my own child, but then I'm not inside her head. She may win Mother of the Year next time, who knows?" Kate saw the open stall door at the end of the aisle. Gabe had been wise to separate their guests in that quieter spot. "It's possible she thinks your little guy is too small to survive and she's keeping her distance, not to get attached." Just as Kate had advised Teddie to minimize his contact with Noah.

"Not *my* guy," he said. "He belongs to the WB."

No surprise. Noah might look the part of

a cowboy, with his cream-colored Stetson set just right and wearing a red plaid shirt with his jacket, but he wasn't. He'd made his choice. That he'd pushed it on Rob, too, was a definite sore spot for Kate. She watched Noah urge the foal into the big stall.

"The vet gave him a thorough exam," he said. "His only problems seem to be size, his early arrival—and that his mama wants little to do with him."

"We'll let them settle in before we introduce them to my mare and her filly."

"Who, Mommy?" Teddie had stayed outside the stall but peered around the door frame, his eyes fixed on the foal.

"Miss Sarah and her daughter, Janie." Teddie had insisted on using the name of his favorite character in the cowgirl book. "I think they'll be good teachers for these two."

"Are they going to play together?"

"Let's hope." The WB's mare stood placidly in the corner by the window. "My mare has had three foals," she told Noah, "so she's pretty experienced. Let's cross our fingers that this works."

Satisfied that the WB's mare had sampled the water in her bucket and the colt was now lying safely against the wall to nap, she

turned toward the barn entrance and saw that
Teddie had reached for Noah's hand. "Bunny,
let's go up to the house. It's almost lunchtime."

He dug in his boot heels. "But N—Mr.
Bodine and I have to name the baby."

Teddie started to reel off his latest choices,
and Noah had grasped his hand as if that was
the most natural thing in the world.

"We do," Noah agreed, practically daring
her to say no. "Besides, I'm going to stick
around until you feel it's a good time to put
your visitor out in the field with—who is
it?—Sarah—"

"And Janie," Teddie said. Then he was off
on another tangent, telling Noah all about his
favorite story. A smile played over Noah's
face, lighting his eyes as he glanced at Kate.

Feeling torn, she stood for another moment, watching her son, his hand tucked
trustingly into Noah's, happiness written all
over him. What a picture they made—the
sort of image she cherished of Rob with Teddie. She would never have envisioned Noah
playing surrogate dad, as she'd feared, just
as he'd appeared to be a cowboy this morning... Kate marched toward the doors. She
needed to nip this in the bud before Teddie

came to depend on Noah more than he already did. "Come on, Teddie Bear."

He didn't seem to hear. Or didn't want to, more likely.

She was about to make a stronger case when Meg walked into the barn.

"I thought I saw your truck. Hi, Noah. Nice to see you." She glanced at Kate, then at him again. "Kate, I came to tell you lunch is ready." Another look at Noah. "Please join us."

"Yay!" Teddie cried. "We can name the baby while we eat."

"Brownie or Spencer Junior..." With his mouth full, at the kitchen table Teddie continued to rattle off names for the WB's foal.

"Swallow before you talk," Kate said.

He gulped down his food. "Or, hey, maybe Lollipop—"

Noah couldn't stop smiling. He cut into his chicken pot pie. "Sounds like a girl's name to me."

He knew practically nothing about kids, no more than he seemed to know about women, especially Margot, yet Teddie brightened his day just by being...Teddie.

Meg caught his eye. "Sorry you accepted our invitation?"

Her invitation, not from Kate, who picked at her meal. The question didn't require an answer.

"How about something more boyish," Noah suggested.

Teddie beamed. "You mean like me? Or Seth? He's my friend, but I don't get to play with him very often—unless he comes here with his new dad. Did you know kids can have more than one daddy?" He looked at Noah as if he were being given a test.

"Uh, yeah, I did know that." And he noticed Kate was frowning.

Meg explained, "Seth is a bit older than Teddie, so he's usually in school."

The conversation ping-ponged between Teddie's talk of names for the colt and Meg filling Noah in on everything that had happened in Barren since he'd left the last time, after his father's funeral. Teddie finally won out.

And... Lancelot it was. Noah had gone through a similar knights-and-dragons phase as a boy. Apparently, Teddie's interest in astronomy had been shelved for now. Noah was still grinning to himself after lunch when he followed Kate back down to the barn. He wondered how Zach would react to Teddie's name choice as he told Kate, "Meg's pot pies and salad were terrific—if not the kind of rancher's meal the WB has at noon. Mom always lays out the heavy protein and carbs."

Kate took a moment to answer. "Meg's a great cook, too, but we don't feed our hands every day. Thus, today's lighter meal. Whenever we do, she makes fried chicken for them instead, or a roast. Stick-to-your-ribs food— like Jean's." She glanced at him. "You could have refused, gone home to eat."

Noah stopped smiling. "I wasn't complaining. It was kind of Meg to invite me."

"That's one way to put it," Kate murmured, as if she had a bone to pick with Meg too.

He didn't want to examine that. Most likely, it involved him. "I enjoyed talking with her during lunch while you seemed so intent upon not talking."

Her gaze fell. "I figured she and Teddie could carry the conversation. I didn't mean to make you feel unwelcome."

She'd sure made him feel that way, though. "Then what did you mean, Kate?"

"My mind was on other things." She led the way into the barn, to the stall near the end, and took a lead rope from the hook by the door. "I'll take the mare. You bring the foal."

"Yes, ma'am."

She didn't react to his dry tone. For the time it took them to walk the horses into the nearest pasture where her mare and filly were waiting, he knew he should let it go. Finish settling this pair from the WB, then hightail it back to his family's ranch and hope Willow had answered his text by now about her return.

"In the open air, with room to run," Kate said, "the horses should be fine."

"I appreciate you doing the WB this favor. I hope this won't be too much of a burden. Of course, I'll pay for their board."

Kate closed the gate. "I won't take your money."

Noah's irritation grew. He was being dismissed. "Why not?"

She studied the horses. The two mares were nosing each other in greeting. The filly danced up to the colt's side, her tail swishing. "Because it's no trouble to add the WB's two temporarily to my herd, and if you're lucky, a miracle may happen with Lancelot's mom."

His mouth tightened. "I'd still like to pay my share."

"Your share? Then perhaps I haven't been clear." She turned to lean back against the fence, shaded her eyes against the sun and squinted up at him. "You're going to force me, aren't you? Make me spell it out, as I've tried to do before?"

"Guess I am."

"I don't want to deal with *you*, Noah. As soon as Willow drives through the gates onto the WB, you will pack your bags, then get the…heck out of Dodge—or rather, Barren."

"I see. Which really bothers you most? Me not leaving soon enough to please you? Or the implied part about New York?" Noah couldn't avoid this subject any longer. "I live in constant fear with you of accidentally mentioning Rob again. I did not cause his death, Kate. I only wish I could have sav—"

"Then who was it who offered him that job in your cybersecurity firm?"

"Me," he admitted, then looked at the ground. "Rob and I talked a lot by phone when he was still here at Sweetheart Ranch. I knew you were having financial troubles then. I also knew that he—" He broke off. "Scratch that. Our conversations were between us, as the close friends we always were…" He couldn't go on.

"Until you convinced him to leave here."

Noah sighed. "I expected Rob to bring you and Teddie with him."

"Really? I was supposed to turn my back on this ranch, uproot my son and destroy the only *security* he has? Move to a huge city that shreds my nerves—give up Teddie's heritage?"

"That's not true. You could have kept the ranch, leased it to someone or left your foreman in charge. Once Rob grew into the job there, I would have promoted him, later made him a partner if he wanted to be. You and Teddie would have had financial stability—"

"Except that Rob's life ended on the street!"

"I wasn't responsible for that attack. Some knife-wielding guy out of his mind was. If it gives you any comfort, I see that same scene in my head every day. I wake up sweating."

"You wake up alive." Her voice shook. "My husband is still dead, and Teddie no longer has a father! Just last night, he cried again, which still happens more often than I can bear. Obviously, he likes you—too much—which can only hurt him eventually. For me, that's a dangerous combination."

His stomach lurched. "You're right about one thing. Teddie and I took to each other from the start. He reminds me of myself at his age and while I was growing up. I can see that he needs more of a mental challenge than he's been getting. Social stimulation too. He needs to explore the larger world beyond the gates of Sweetheart Ranch."

"That's all fine, but not everyone has your view of New York."

He decided to just go for it. "I happen to like the city, the museums, restaurants, the constant bustle. The opportunities. If not there, maybe—for Teddie's sake—you might consider seeing different places yourself. And frankly, I think you should reconsider your plan to homeschool him, maybe take another look at that special gifted program offered in Farrier—the same one I went to years ago."

"I can't afford such a fancy program, and I don't want Teddie spending that much time away from home. I understand, believe me, that he has taken to you, but you can have no real place in his life. I won't have him regard you as some kind of superhero when tomorrow, for all I know, you may be gone.

I won't let you co-opt my son, and you certainly won't be Rob's replacement!"

Noah hoped the flash of hurt didn't show
in his eyes.

But, wait. Was this only about Teddie? Had
Kate seen Noah's attraction to her? When
he wouldn't acknowledge it himself? He
sure wouldn't do so now. His voice sounded
hoarse. "I was only trying to help. I get a real
kick out of your kid, Kate, but from what I
just heard, I know when to back off." He gestured toward the WB fence in the distance.
"From now on, for the rest of the brief time
I'm here, I'll stay on my side of the line. You
and Teddie should stay on yours."

What was Kate so afraid of? Not just him
regarding Teddie. It seemed obvious that she
only left Sweetheart Ranch when she absolutely had to. Teddie had said during lunch
that he only saw Seth when his friend came
to the ranch. Kate had locked herself and
Teddie inside its gates.

To Noah, that seemed no healthier than her
resentment of him.

"Noah," Kate began as if she knew she'd
said too much again.

"No, I understand." He glanced at the
field, where the two mares were wandering

across the snow-covered grass as if holding a friendly conversation, and the colt and filly were lying on a bare patch of ground in the shade of a cottonwood tree. Noah turned toward the truck. "Thanks for keeping the mare and…Lancelot."

Sweetheart Ranch was an idyllic setting, and he couldn't blame Kate for wanting whatever peace she found here.

Sadly, though, to Noah, it wasn't a life.

KATE HADN'T BEEN able to forget her after-lunch argument with Noah. "In the end, I tried to back pedal a bit," she told Meg that night, "but he was already upset."

"You think?"

Meg had a point. "I meant what I said, though. I won't have Teddie holding Noah's hand, looking up to him—"

Meg glanced up from the book she'd been pretending to read. "How could that be a bad thing? You and I see every day how Teddie misses Rob. He had a good dad, but now he's gone. In those last six months, I know you had troubles before Rob—"

"It's hard enough carrying on without him." Kate suppressed another sad memory of her husband. Many of their talks then had been by phone. "Please don't remind me about those disagreements. And now, while I'm still grieving, Noah had to come along—"

"Why despise him for what happened? Whenever I'd come to visit as a kid, I loved watching you with those two guys. The laughter, the pranks they played on you, the earnest conversations you all had… Why not remember those good times instead?" Meg stuck a bookmark in the page where she'd stopped reading. "It seems to me, Noah's still on your mind. Take lunch today. You didn't say two words, but I saw you steal a few glances at him. I saw him do the same to you. Maybe there's something more here that *you're* trying to overlook. How sure are you that he's nothing to you now except a constant reminder of Rob's loss?"

This wasn't going well at all. Kate went on the offensive. "You're a fine one to talk. You say you're over Mac—but are you, really?"

For an instant, Meg looked shocked. "You heard me on the phone."

"When you sounded more scared of your feelings than of him."

"Kate. Don't think I failed to notice how neatly you just tried to change the subject again. You may not be wild about the choice Noah made to leave Barren, but you can't deny he's made a life for himself in New York. Noah isn't Rob, but he seems just as solid in his way, steady—"

Kate said in a harsher tone than she intended, "Meg, I'm not looking for another relationship any more than you say you are."

Meg picked up her book, then set it aside. "But what's the real harm in him being friends with Teddie? Those two looked so sweet at the table today. Noah didn't ignore Teddie, he paid close attention to what he was saying. He let him pick that colt's name even when Zach will probably have a fit that it doesn't suit the WB. Noah seems to understand your boy who can, let's face it, be a challenge to other less-brilliant people."

"True, Teddie's like the brainy kids at school who were set apart from the rest of the class when all they wanted was to belong." Was that why Noah had pushed her about Teddie and the gifted program? Because, years ago, he'd been one of those kids himself?

"Is that why you want to homeschool Teddie?" Meg asked.

"Partly, yes."

"But you can't wrap him in cotton, Kate."

"That's what Noah tried to tell me. I don't want to keep Teddie from having friends. He's so happy when Seth comes to play, and of course he should have the best schooling he can get, but how could I drive him to Farrier every morning for school? Even if I could afford that program? Send him off with a backpack and his lunch? Worry about him the whole time he was gone?"

Meg gazed at her. "All parents worry," she said gently.

Kate swallowed hard. "Yes, but I already watched Rob leave for New York after his last visit home. We quarreled up to the minute he slammed the door of his car, then shot down this same driveway. I never saw him alive again."

"Which was a tragedy. My heart breaks for you, but that doesn't mean you can't ever be happy again—with someone else. Maybe not right now, maybe not with Noah, but you shouldn't deny yourself that happiness. You shouldn't keep Teddie from having a normal kid's life, either, Kate."

Her heart was beating like a steel drum, and for a moment she couldn't speak. When she did, Kate could guess how absolutely neurotic she must sound. "But what if... something happened to him too?"

CHAPTER ELEVEN

"KATE LANCASTER. Is it really you?" Jean Bodine had rushed from the house to meet her as soon as Kate came up the WB's driveway the next morning and got out of the truck. She wrapped Kate in a bear hug. "You've actually left that ranch again?"

"Not often," Kate admitted, remembering the night the colt was born. She hadn't hesitated to help then but, "Sweetheart takes up all my time. With Rob gone..." She looped an arm around Jean's waist as they walked toward the porch. "Anyway, I'm here on a mission."

"Ooh, that sounds interesting."

"I doubt Noah will think so." Last night's talk with Meg had preyed on her mind until Kate had to set out for the WB. She had treated Noah badly and felt rightfully ashamed of herself.

I was only trying to help, he'd said. She would have driven straight to the barn, where he must be this time of day, but clearly Jean wanted to visit, and Kate had spent the short trip between her ranch and the WB trying to think what to say to him. She still didn't know.

"Ah," Jean murmured, leading the way inside, "now I know why he was like a bear with a thorn in his paw at breakfast. And that scowl…"

"My fault."

After Jean had poured coffee for them, they sat in the living room. The air smelled of furniture polish and showed Jean's pride in her home. Kate said, "I came to apologize, but that's between me and Noah. All I can tell you is that I let my resentments get out of hand. Obviously, I have issues to resolve."

Jean sent her a sympathetic look. "Darling, in your situation, who wouldn't?"

Like Meg, Jean had been a rock after Rob died. She'd taken care of Teddie whenever Kate needed her. She'd been like a mother to Kate, or rather, like a mother should be. Kate glanced around the room, which was a cozy blend of old and new. "I don't think I've seen some of this furniture before—except, of course, for that lovely étagère in the corner, which was your grandmother's, right?"

"Yes, and hers before her."

"The color on the walls is different too."

"A much-needed update for this room. Cass and I worked like dogs to get ready for Willow's wedding. But you weren't at the reception here, were you?"

Kate shook her head. "I couldn't come, Jean. I'm not a party person these days—if I ever was. I went to the church, though. The wedding was so beautiful. Willow looked exquisite."

"And Cody? I've never seen a man so eager to tie the knot."

"They're good together, aren't they?"

"We all had our misgivings at first about Cody, but yes. I think they'll be just fine. Thank goodness," she added. "Now I have a brief reprieve before we start to plan Cass and Zach's summer wedding." She paused. "That will leave only Noah on the loose."

"Maybe he doesn't want to get married."

Jean wrinkled her nose. "He has a girlfriend at the moment, and she's not the first. But my oldest never seems ready to settle down. Certainly not here." Jean appeared on the verge of saying more, then didn't. "I suppose there's nothing I can do except watch him leave again for New York when the time comes."

Kate patted her hand. "I wouldn't be thrilled to see Teddie ever leave Sweetheart Ranch." Which, remembering her talk with Meg, made Kate sound needy.

"You hope he'll take over the ranch. Just think. Maybe someday—once my children finally make me a grandmother—our little girl might marry your Teddie. I couldn't imagine a better match unless...never mind. They could combine Sweetheart with the WB. My, but we'd have a dynasty then."

"Dream on, Mom." Noah's voice came from the kitchen doorway. He held a steaming mug in one hand, his other braced high on the frame.

"It won't be a dream with Cody and Willow. Or Zach and Cass."

He saluted Jean with the mug. "I was going to talk to you about Wilkins, but I see you're busy." He glanced at Kate before he went into the other room again. "Going back to my side of the fence." And he was gone.

"What was that?" Jean asked, frowning.

"The reason I'm here." Kate stood. "I'd

better go make my apology. Thanks for the chat."

But Jean wouldn't let her escape that easily.

"Kate, after you've made your peace with Noah, bring Teddie next time." Her tone turned sly. "You both have a standing invitation to dinner, and perhaps you'll come more often. But don't rush off. Why not have a second cup of coffee with me before you apologize to Noah?"

Kate mumbled some excuse. There'd been a time when Jean had proffered constant invitations to spend an evening, a day, even a weekend at the WB for a sleepover with Willow when she and Kate were kids. Now Jean looked crestfallen.

"Then good luck. I wish someone would snatch that son of mine away from the woman he's been seeing in New York."

"That won't be me," Kate murmured, then, girding her loins against the scene that was to come with Noah, she started toward the front door. Jean reached out for yet another affectionate hug—or was that an apology of her own?

"In any case," she said, "come again. Don't be such a recluse."

AT THE BARN, Noah had kept one eye on the house while he argued with Wilkins. He hadn't intended to walk in on his mother and Kate. He'd only needed more coffee before he confronted the ranch foreman. Why was she here?

Noah wished he hadn't said what he did yesterday—today at the house either.

He tried to focus on the matter at hand. Noah had gotten a refresher course in Kansas winters during that first blizzard of the season, holed up in the Bluebird with Kate, and he was about to get another one soon. In fact, it had snowed most every day he'd been here, with a more severe storm brewing to the west now. Before nightfall the WB needed to prepare again. But then, so would Kate at Sweetheart Ranch. Not his problem, Noah told himself.

This morning—again—Wilkins had neglected to send someone out to clear ice from the tanks. In Noah's view, he was a poor manager, but the relationship between a rancher and his foreman could get tricky. Noah's father had fired, then hired people enough times during Noah's boyhood for him to learn that it wasn't always—like yesterday with Kate—a smooth road. In New York, he would have canned an employee like Wilkins for such disrespect.

Why should this be any different? The WB was a business, too, if not the one he'd chosen. He sneaked another glance at the house. Kate's truck was still parked there, but she hadn't appeared. Before she left, should he try to smooth things over when their quarrel hadn't been his fault? No, better stick to the matter at hand.

"Wilkins. You need to get ahead of this storm," he said, noting the man's slouch against the nearest stall, as if he wasn't even listening. Calvin Stern, however, had stopped raking the aisle floor, his ears alert. In other areas of the barn, several of the ranch hands were moving around. Probably eavesdropping too. "Tell Calvin to check those tanks. The boys should look over the herd before dark."

Wilkins didn't respond. Noah imagined he could see steam coming from his ears.

"Tomorrow I want these stalls properly cleaned. They always looked better than they have lately. Then that pile of horse manure outside needs to be moved before it's like the leaning tower of Pisa. Also, our inventory of medications is getting low."

Wilkins straightened. He took a step toward Noah. "Zach wants to assign chores around here like I'm still some green cowpoke, he can tell me. In the meantime, *Bodine*, take your laundry list of household duties—"

"I wouldn't have to tell you if you were doing your job."

"—and put it where the sun don't—"

"Wilkins, you're fired."

He snorted. "You can't fire me. And Zach's never had issue with the job I'm doing."

At the end of the aisle, his eyes wide, Calvin had frozen, still holding the rake. Noah could hear the other men in the tack and feed rooms. With an audience, Noah couldn't back down, or he'd have a mutiny on his hands. He'd gone to the house to talk to his mom about Wilkins, yet that wasn't one of her duties. For now, it was on him, and he'd made up his mind. For a long moment, he stood toe to toe with Zach's foreman.

Then he said, "Pack your things and get off this ranch by five o'clock."

"After you, again—like always," Wilkins muttered, but to Noah's relief, he turned his back, then stalked from the barn. Which left Noah alone with Calvin.

Noah believed in rewarding strong effort, giving people a chance to prove themselves. He liked to promote from within at J&B, which usually gained him an employee's loyalty. He wasn't sure about Calvin yet, or any of the other men who'd made it plain he was not the owner of the WB in their eyes and therefore had no authority. Maybe they'd only listened to Wilkins. Noah would soon find out, but it was time to really take charge of the WB.

"Calvin. What would you say to a generous raise in pay?"

"I wouldn't say no," Calvin mumbled. Unlike Wilkins, he was a hard worker. "Becca and I can use the extra money. The baby's growing, needing new things every day, it seems. And we're saving up to buy our own spread."

"Okay, then." He held out his hand. "You're the WB's new foreman."

They shook on the deal, and Calvin glanced toward the tack room, where someone had just dropped what sounded like a heavy saddle. "I should tell you those guys have more years in than I do."

But from all accounts, and according to Noah's mother, Calvin had grown up, especially since he'd been here. Taking on this new responsibility, in addition to the experience he'd already gained, could be the true making of him. Noah hoped.

"Then you'll need to convince them you're the boss."

Calvin beamed. "I won't let you down. You can count on me." He pulled his cell phone from his pocket. "Just gonna give Becca a quick call with the good news before I get the boys busy. I think we can beat this snow."

After Calvin wandered off, Noah looked down the aisle and out the open barn doors again in time to see Kate's truck barrel down the drive to the road.

If she'd come to see him, she'd changed her mind or gone home ahead of the storm.

He crossed his arms, stared down at his boots.

Maybe he shouldn't have made that crack about the fence.

Win some, lose some.

THAT EVENING KATE looked around the big living room at the McMann ranch. She had never felt truly a part of the Girls' Night Out group, and in fact, she'd joined more recently than some of the others, but she'd also felt guilty for putting her friends off so many times. And instead of making her apology to Noah earlier, she'd had that second cup of coffee with Jean—then chickened out. Here she was now, hovering in the doorway, holding the bottle of wine Lizzie had asked her to bring. Her palms were damp. As she'd told Noah's mother, social gatherings weren't her thing.

Lizzie spotted her just as Kate turned for the door, intending to drive home before the snow started. "Hey, you. No benchwarmers allowed. Come get in the game."

Kate didn't move. She and Gabe had readied Sweetheart Ranch, but what if they'd missed something in those preparations? Also, she didn't feel safe here. "I was just thinking I'd made a mistake in leaving my house."

"Everything okay?"

"Mostly, but…" She shrugged. "I had so much to do, I shouldn't have come."

"You mean working fourteen-hour days isn't enough? Don't you have a foreman?"

"Yes, but, Lizzie, I have nothing to contribute here. You're right, and so was Jean Bodine—I do spend all my time on the ranch, keeping it going—"

"And avoiding people who love you. Any

second now, someone's going to notice you with one foot out that door. I thought we'd already established that you don't enjoy being the object of public scrutiny any more than I once did." Lizzie frowned. "But a few of us have wondered if you're being snooty."

"What would I have to be snooty about?"

Lizzie didn't answer. Clara McMann had swept from the kitchen with a platter of food and, of course, she saw Kate standing there. "Come and get it, dear," she said, which was what Clara called everyone. A long-time widow whose land had sat barren for years, she'd gotten a new lease on life when Hadley Smith took over. He and Clara were now expanding the ranch and—along with Lizzie's husband, Dallas, who was Hadley's brother—making a profit again. It was good to see Clara looking so happy as she handed the plate to Lizzie.

Kate hugged Clara. "I feel like I'm intruding, it's been so long since I came to one of these get-togethers."

"Nonsense. Just plunge into the fray."

"Get ready," Lizzie added, "for a thousand questions. You're like the biggest, best-kept secret in Barren. There are those who keep track of the rare sightings of Kate Lancaster."

She winced. "I'm not that bad."

But Lizzie had a point. So had Jean that morning. They couldn't know how difficult it was for Kate to leave her safe space, to mingle, especially in such a large group, which seemed to keep growing. She didn't want to see any sympathetic glances from other women about Rob's loss or hear comments those like Bernice Caldwell—who was not a member of the group—might make about "poor little Teddie." Kate had a strong compulsion to remain on Sweetheart Ranch. To keep her little boy safe there too.

These women didn't know how dangerous the world could be. She certainly didn't want to be seen as a pathetic widow. The town's emotional charity case.

Kate preferred being labeled neurotic. And, in spite of Noah's advice, staying home.

Feeling trapped, she followed Clara and Lizzie deeper into the room and was suddenly surrounded by chattering friends, all wanting to know where she'd been hiding for so long. "Well, obviously, the ranch…" she said, trailing off when Olivia McCord rolled her eyes then folded Kate into another hug.

Despite her misgivings about being here, the evening seemed to pass by in a blur. Her friends' laughter was contagious, the talk stimulating, and so familiar they all but finished each other's sentences. Tonight, Kate had wine to drink ("just one glass because I'm driving"), delicious snacks to eat ("no more, Clara, or I'll have to roll home") and, above all, the good company of people she liked. People she'd pushed away for the past year.

For these few hours, she could forget reconciling the ranch accounts, worrying about Teddie—not that he was ever far from her mind—even her cowardice earlier about Noah. It wasn't until he was mentioned that she again regretted showing up.

"Of course, he won't stay here long," Olivia said.

"Right next door, though," Lizzie put in. *Traitor.* "I told Kate he has a lot to offer."

Her palms began to sweat again. "Yes, you did." She shifted on the sofa. "I'm still not listening."

"Why not?" Blossom Hunter spoke up. "There are a ton of good-looking men in this town, which is pretty amazing in itself for a place as small as Barren, but I have to say Noah Bodine tops the list. Except, of course, for my Logan."

Nell Ransom piped up. "I see your Logan and raise you my Cooper."

"Uh-oh." Lizzie grinned at Kate. "This could wind up in an all-out brawl, complete with hair pulling."

"Before that starts," Kate said, "my anxiety will drive me out of this house."

"This is no contest at all," Jenna Smith, one hand on her pregnant stomach, chimed in. "It's clear Hadley wins, hands down, even when I do admire the runners-up."

"Aren't you all terrible?" Clara, who must still feel sad for the loss of her own husband years ago, clucked her tongue. "I declare them all winners. They're my boys."

Kate had to laugh, even when her pulse kept thumping. Clara would adopt everyone.

Lizzie laid a hand on her forearm. "I didn't mean to start this. You can slap me now."

The air had filled with a dozen claims made in rising voices, but to Kate's relief, they soon became shared laughter, and no one left in a huff. By then, she'd thought she was safely out of range, but apparently not.

"By the way, I hear Noah looks even better than he did when he quit the WB—how long ago was that?"

Shadow Wilson pretended to ponder the

question. "Too long, if you ask me." She turned to Kate. "Would you really pass that up? According to the grapevine, in a short time, he's gotten pretty friendly with you at Sweetheart Ranch. Aren't you boarding a foal and mare for him? And from what I hear, Teddie thinks he walks on water."

"My, people have been busy." Kate cleared her throat. "Yes, I'm taking care of the colt, but that's where it ends. I've told Noah so."

"Ouch. What prompted that?"

"Not what you're thinking." *Going back to my side of the fence.*

"Lost opportunity," Olivia murmured from the other end of the sofa.

Kate tensed. "I'm not looking for another man. I had one." Her voice quavered. "Why can't you all understand? I don't want anyone else."

She had stunned them into silence. Or maybe they'd given up on her.

Still, her own words rang hollow. Had she pushed Noah away, too, as she had her friends, using Teddie as an excuse, to keep her heart safe? Noah hadn't suggested even being friends, so what was there to worry about? And yet she did.

Just maybe, intending to throw her friends and even Meg off track, she hadn't been honest with herself.

CHAPTER TWELVE

NOAH'S PROBLEM AT the moment wasn't last night's storm, which had dumped another eight inches on the WB, but a text message from Zach.

He walked the barn aisle the next morning, checking on horses on stall rest—a gelding with a wheezing cough, a couple of cow ponies with stone bruises. Noah stopped to pat a velvety nose, straighten a forelock. He'd always loved animals, the best part for him of being on a working ranch again. He made an exception for Midnight, the black that had thrown him. Still, they'd made their tentative peace, unlike Noah with Kate.

Having too much fun for Cass and me to come home, Zach had written. Willow heading for Savannah. East Coast honeymoon blowout. Carry on, pal.

As soon as his brother had heard about Willow and Cody's decision, Zach had obviously opted to stay wherever he was too.

Talk about punishment. Noah had tried to call him, but Zach hadn't answered. He'd also tried to reach Willow, whose only response to his message—Can't stay at WB much longer, what's your ETA now?—had been a curt I'll see you when I see you.

Still, he didn't mind ranch work as much as he had at first, or as a boy, maybe because Wilkins had cleared out. Calvin seemed to be adjusting to his new job, which left Noah a bit freer to focus on New York, where Brent wasn't happy with him. The London-branch launch continued to be frustrating. Or was that problem Noah's way of keeping clear of Kate, who was much closer next door than the company headquarters of J&B were in New York?

"Boss?" Calvin poked his head out of the tack room. "Soon as I finish here, I'm going to ride out to the far-west pasture. Snow knocked the gate down. If I don't fix it quick, we'll have Sweetheart Ranch stock over here." Calvin ambled into the aisle then hesitated. "Uh, Wilkins held me back, overruled any suggestions I made. Want to thank you for putting your trust in me."

"You're doing all right, Calvin. I appreciate it."

Most of all, he liked the fact that this new foreman—*Noah's* foreman, his mom had dubbed Calvin—didn't try to undercut him. As Calvin turned back toward the tack room, Noah said, "Second thought, think I'll ride with you."

"Sure, Boss."

Noah went down the aisle to choose a horse from the WB string. His sister's mare, Silver, seemed the wisest choice.

As he and Calvin rode on loose reins across the frozen ground, bridles jingling, they discussed plans for the rest of the winter. Noah wouldn't be here that long, but Calvin had good ideas about the WB.

They were loping near the property line and that gate when Noah spied Kate and Teddie riding toward them from the opposite side. She drew up, but Teddie kept coming.

"We're cowboys," he said. "Are you looking, like us, for strays?"

"No, our gate needs attention."

Kate hung back. "Don't bother these men, Teddie, they have work to do."

Instead, he nudged his pony closer to the fence between them and kept talking to Calvin.

Noah reined in Silver. "Kate, I'm holding to our bargain. You can't even say good morning?"

She briefly pressed her lips tight. "I have more to say than that."

Noah gazed at her for a long moment. Waiting her out. He could see her struggle to find the right words and wouldn't blame himself for letting her. The fence thing, like her accusation about Teddie and the gifted program, had hurt yet was only a sign of a broader issue.

"I, um, went to the WB yesterday, not to see Jean, although we had a nice talk, but to apologize. To you."

Teddie and Calvin had met at the downed gate and were examining it with great care. Kate glanced at them as if to reassure herself that Teddie was okay. Then the words rushed out. "I spoke harshly. I didn't mean to. That isn't like me, or wasn't until recently, and you said you understood, but before you fly off to New York again, which must be imminent, I do need to say I'm sorry. Very sorry. Teddie's well-being is important to me, but I didn't mean to imply that you were trying to…take him from me."

Noah didn't respond to the imminent part. "You didn't imply. You said it straight out.

Does this apology mean I have permission—until I leave, that is—to cross your boundary?" He didn't simply mean the fence.

"I didn't say that. I'm just grateful you realize the position I'm in with Teddie. And why." She refrained from saying, *You must since you're partly to blame.*

"But, Kate, if it makes him happy to talk with me now and then—to laugh when he's been grieving for so long, as you pointed out—I'm all for it."

He waited again, still angry, hoping for her agreement even when that might not be in his own best interest.

"He's happier, yes. As long as you don't put other ideas in his head," she finally said.

"What ideas?"

"You talked about New York—your environment—which is far from my favorite place in this world, just as the WB is for you, but as you're already aware, Teddie's mind is a sponge. His interests change every day. He wants to know everything. I won't have you spinning dreams for his future that don't include Sweetheart Ranch."

Noah shifted his reins from left to right hand. The gifted program was one thing, but how could she narrow her boy's entire world like that? And not feel guilty if he wanted something more? As Noah's father had tried to do with him? Noah had chafed under his relentless domination at the WB, had dreamed of other places, another life far from Kansas, until he'd had no other choice but to go seek it—and lose his father. Obviously, he hadn't made his point about Teddie the other day.

"Then, Kate, you might as well know. Yes, I would have been gone by now or on my way if it wasn't for Willow. She's doing a bit more traveling before she and Cody come back." He explained about their side trip to Savannah. "So I'll be here awhile longer after all. Maybe we can agree to let Teddie be the one to choose whatever interaction he'd like with me, let that happen organically and not worry about it. Maybe you could try to trust that I won't hurt him." As for Kate herself: "Maybe you and I could also connect somehow. Your choice there too."

When he'd first arrived in Kansas, Noah had wondered what to feel about Kate—if he had any right to feel anything at all. But that hadn't been the question to ask. Had he ever stopped wishing he hadn't lost her to his best friend? That answer was no.

Noah guessed he'd take whatever he could get from Kate. For the time he had.

She said, "You mean like…a truce?"

Forgiveness would be even better. "If that's what you want to call it."

She thought for a moment, then walked her horse closer and reached over the fence to shake Noah's hand. Teddie and Calvin were riding back toward them, Spencer's chunky legs working to keep up with the bigger gelding in the snow.

"Truce," she finally said.

Noah didn't believe for a second that meant anything beyond his few chats with Teddie whenever their paths happened to cross or not arguing with Kate. It sure didn't include Noah's stubborn feelings for her. On her part, she would never stop blaming him for Rob's death.

Noah wouldn't dare tell her how he felt.

SHE'D DONE IT. Clumsily, yet she'd apologized to Noah, which was becoming a habit.

"I'm proud of you," Meg told her as they prepared dinner that night. Teddie was upstairs playing a game on Kate's iPad, which he used more than she did. "I think it'll be good for Teddie to have Noah in his life."

"Temporarily," Kate said. On the way home, she had told him Noah was coming tomorrow to check on the WB's mare and Lancelot. Teddie had been super excited all afternoon. But what, exactly, had Noah meant about connecting with her too?

Although she couldn't deny her awareness of Noah—who was definitely attractive, as her friends had pointed out—that only made her feel disloyal. She'd had love—imperfect, tragic, as it turned out to be—then lost. And why assume he might be romantically interested in her?

Kate took silverware from a drawer, then set places at the table. She rooted around in another drawer for clean napkins. From upstairs, she could hear Teddie in his room. He'd finished his game, and Kate heard the thumping sound of his hobby horse being ridden.

What a pair she and Meg made. Mac hadn't called in the past few nights, and she'd seen Meg glance at the silent phone. She'd checked her messages just as often. Last night, while Kate was at the Girls Night Out meeting, she'd probably done so more frequently. Yet, even though she'd looked into the process of changing her name, Meg had still done nothing more about that. And she wasn't any more receptive to Kate's foreman—single, handsome—than she'd been before.

At which moment, Gabe himself rapped softly at the kitchen door, then stepped inside.

"Got a sec, Kate?"

"Of course," she said. Meg had turned to the stove and was stirring the vegetables with fast flicks of her wrist.

Gabe looked troubled. "I don't like how the foal looks tonight. Can you come see?"

Kate quickly shrugged into her parka. When she turned, she caught Gabe staring at Meg's back with a somber, intense expression, the look that told Kate he had a crush on her aunt. Kate said, "We may need to call the vet."

She hoped that wasn't the case. She'd have to phone Noah, then, too.

She opened the back door, then stepped outside into the chill night air but realized Gabe hadn't followed. He was still standing there, looking at Meg, whose spine was rigid. Her nape had turned an interesting shade of pink.

"Meg?" he said.

She didn't reply.

"Sorry to postpone your dinner."

He received her silence for an answer.

Finally, he spun on his boot heel, then stalked out onto the porch.

"I don't know why she was that rude," Kate said to ease the hurt she saw in his eyes as they crossed the yard, although she did know. Meg's silence was a reaction in itself.

"I do," was all Gabe said.

WHAT HAD HE meant earlier by "connect" with Kate? Noah silently scolded himself all through dinner until his mother finally put down her fork.

"I'm tired of that scowl, Noah. What is troubling you now tonight?"

"I'd rather not say." He wasn't about to admit how he still felt regarding Kate. Jean would never let him forget that. *She'd* get all sorts of ideas.

"Is it Margot?" Now it was Jean who frowned. "She called today, several times. Each time she sounded more irritated but wouldn't leave a message with me. Did you two have a quarrel?" Her voice had lifted at the end.

"Is that what you hope I'll say?"

She made a zipping motion across her lips,

then picked up her fork. "I think this chicken was a bit too old, don't you?"

"It's okay. A little tough."

"I wonder if Wilkins didn't kill an old rooster on his way out the door."

They briefly talked about the foreman's replacement. Noah said he was pleased with Calvin, and Jean agreed that he'd turned into a nice young man, in spite of his previous trouble with the law.

Noah finally ran out of things to talk about. "All right. If you must know, I had a discussion with Kate today. She's agreed to let her boy socialize a bit. She and I forged a tentative truce."

"About Rob?"

"Never that." He rolled his eyes. "Her mind's made up about me on that score. I can't change it."

"If you could—if you tried hard enough—maybe something better would come—"

"Mom, leave it alone, okay?" Noah cut into another piece of stringy chicken. And nearly choked on it. He took a swig of his beer. "You can hold on to that old dream for as long as you want." Apparently, so could he. "I'm just glad she's talking to me now. And that Teddie can too. I worry about him.

Kate has him locked down on that ranch like some prisoner. Why won't she loosen those reins a little?"

"She's afraid. For Teddie, for herself. Her mom left that ranch, remember, when Kate was scarcely older than her boy is now, then she lost her father—a decent man who'd raised her, loved her with all his heart—in that horrible tractor accident. I believe Rob's death affected her even more than it has Teddie. It will take time for her to heal enough to spread her wings."

"If she ever does."

His mom's gaze sharpened. "Your interest, even now, isn't only in Teddie's freedom."

"But that lockdown hurts him. If I can show Teddie something of the world, however small, feed his need for adventure, I think I should." No matter what Kate said. He'd have to be subtle but...

Jean looked thoughtful. "Your father and I saw that same need in you. I probably sensed your wanderlust, that desire for bigger things, long before you decided to leave the WB to Zach." She pushed her plate aside. "Sometimes I wish we hadn't put you in that program, even when it was necessary for you to blossom. We may well have lost you then."

"Aw, Mom." Noah reached for her hand. "You'll never lose me."

Jean blinked, but she didn't get to speak before Noah's cell rang. He pulled it from his pocket to check the screen. It was Kate. The brief call ruined the rest of his appetite. Noah pushed back his chair and stood. "The foal's in trouble." As he said the words, his phone rang again. "Margot," he said. "I better take this before I go."

Answering the call, he walked into the living room to get his jacket. "Hey. Mom said you phoned earlier."

"While you were doing your rancher thing."

"Yeah, I was." He suppressed a thought of Kate. Wondering about their connection, such as it was, he hadn't been fair to Margot. Their two-year relationship had moved into a more serious phase on her side, which he'd been trying to evade for too long. And he could hardly deny his feelings for Kate, which he'd recently acknowledged. But now wasn't time for the talk he needed to have with Margot.

She was speaking, but he'd missed part of what she'd said. "So—" she drew out the word "—I was here in dreary, rainy Manhattan this morning, thinking of you…"

He braced himself. "I'm sorry, Margot. I know I've been in Kansas longer than I should, and wait for it—there's more bad news. Willow and Cody are staying back east to see the sights in Savannah."

"Which means you're stuck there." She didn't sound as irritated as he'd expected.

"They have to come home soon. Their new house is being built, and their training business will ramp up in the spring. I shouldn't be here more than a couple of extra days—"

"Which makes me glad I decided to surprise you."

Noah blinked. "What?"

He heard a soft laugh. "I'm not in rainy New York, baby." Noah suppressed a flash of irritation at her habit of calling him that. "I hopped on a plane, and tonight I'm in Kansas."

"Kansas?" As if he'd never heard the word before. Noah was only half listening. He needed to get to Sweetheart Ranch. His mind was on the colt.

Margot's clearly wasn't. "As you said, it's freezing here, and in fact I'm on the porch right now. Please open the door."

CHAPTER THIRTEEN

KATE AND GABE MORGAN were in the stall with the sick foal when Noah arrived.

"I'm sorry to bring you out so late," she said with a glance at his worried face. "We have a call in to the vet, and he's on his way."

"What happened?"

Gabe explained, "I was doing a last stall check tonight when I noticed this guy was down—and not responding. Normally, he's at the door now when I make my evening rounds. I alerted Kate right away."

"We were hoping he was just slow to wake up," she said, fighting an urge to wring her hands, "but he's weak and has gotten weaker in the past few hours."

"I wish you had called me then."

"I'm sorry, Noah. I should have done that immediately."

He knew as well as she did, even considering his long absence from ranch life, that a newborn could go downhill very quickly and not survive. He probably also knew she'd hesitated to call him.

"Where's the mare?"

"In another stall and not particularly worried about her colt. Sad to say, that hasn't improved much, and my mare has been nursing him part of the time. Tonight, he isn't interested in her either. I can't say when he had milk last."

Noah hunkered down in the stall bedding and ran his hands over the foal. "I'd hoped we were out of the woods. Appears not. He feels way too warm."

"His fever has spiked since the first time we checked. That's when I called Doc Crane."

As she said that, a door slammed outside, and the man whom many people in town called Young Doctor Crane walked in. Boyish-looking indeed, he joined Noah in the stall. Kate and Gabe hovered in the aisle.

Doc Crane, whose dark hair had a serious cowlick, checked the colt's vital signs and took his temperature again. There was nothing boyish about his manner or the expression in his dark eyes, which were sharp and focused as he reported the figure on the thermometer.

"That's even higher than it has been," Kate murmured, more worried by the second.

"As you probably know, there are a number of health problems that concern us with these newborns." The doc straightened. "It's unfortunate that our boy here probably didn't get enough colostrum from his mama early on. I know you all tried to remedy that, and when I first saw him, he checked out healthy, but those antibodies are critical."

He made a more thorough examination of the colt, then looked at Kate. "You say he hasn't nursed in a while? He's pretty lethargic, doesn't have much interest in us—" He bent to look in Lancelot's mouth. "Ah. See this? His gums are spotted with little broken blood vessels. My best bet is we're looking at neonatal sepsis."

Kate groaned. "The most common cause of illness and death in foals, right? Sweetheart lost one last year."

"Well, let's not lose another." Doc rose from his crouch. "We'll need some blood work to confirm a diagnosis."

But the lab results would take time, and Kate wrung her hands. She couldn't think what else to do and avoided Noah's eyes until Doc Crane had drawn a sample, treated the colt as best he could without the lab report, given them instructions for supportive care in the meantime, then left to answer another call.

"I can sit up with Lancelot," Gabe offered.

Kate refused. "No, you go on—get some rest. I wouldn't sleep anyway."

She wasn't prepared for what Noah said next.

"I'm staying too." He stroked the colt's side. "Last thing I need, considering my prodigal son status, is to feel responsible for him dy…" He trailed off.

Quiet had descended over the now-chilly barn. Gabe went to the bunkhouse, then came back with blankets and water bottles. He arranged hay bales for them to sit on in the aisle outside the stall. "All set now?"

"All set," Kate agreed. "Thanks, Gabe."

"Call me if anything else happens."

"I will," she promised and, a moment later, was alone with Noah.

At least before the colt took ill, she'd been able to apologize for the other day. Sharing the night with Noah would be awkward enough without that between them.

Kate sat, then spread a blanket over her

legs. "Not exactly how you expected to spend your evening, either, is it?"

"All part of this temporary job." Sitting down on another bale, Noah frowned. "I'm pretty worried."

"So am I. Lancelot's helpless, dependent upon us to keep him safe."

"Like you with Teddie."

And if the colt failed to survive, her little boy would be devastated, but Kate didn't want to touch on that subject. She'd already taken a chance in agreeing to Teddie's relationship with Noah. "What would you have done tonight instead of bunking down in this barn?"

For a moment, he remained silent. "We have unexpected company at the WB. A friend of mine from New York," he said. "She turned up during dinner. My—uh—girlfriend, actually. I was already on my way to come here. I had to leave her with Mom."

Kate tried not to react. Of course he would have a woman in his life, and Jean had mentioned one. Noah was handsome, successful, and years ago he'd never lacked for female companionship. It was more surprising that he hadn't yet married, had a family of his own. "Noah, you don't need to stay. You should go home, be with her."

"I don't want to have to tell Zach I messed up again. No, I'd rather stay here. I'll make it up to her tomorrow. The WB isn't mine, but right now—it is my responsibility."

Kate couldn't keep from asking, "What's she like?"

"Who?"

"Your...friend." The word seemed to stick in Kate's throat. Not that she had any claim on him. He'd surprised her, that was all.

"Pretty, dark red hair, big brown eyes. She's a Realtor, sells penthouse condos and classic brownstones with eight-figure price tags to people in New York." He told her a little more about Margot, then noticed Kate shivering. "You're cold." He rearranged their hay bales together before he paired their blankets for more warmth and held them open for her to come closer.

Kate hesitated, but her teeth were beginning to chatter. "Th—thanks. I think."

It was either sit next to Noah with his greater size and body warmth among the stacked blankets or risk freezing to death. The barn temperature was comfortable enough for the horses, with their shaggy winter coats, and even for the foal wearing his own small stable blanket, but not for Kate.

Tentatively, she snuggled in against Noah's shoulder, thinking what different paths their lives had taken. *Maybe we can connect somehow too.* "Well, at least we won't get hypothermia." Kate absorbed his body heat and gradually stopped shaking. "We need to check Lancelot every half hour, though, alternating, if that's okay with you."

"That should work." After her first peek into the colt's stall, she hurried back to their makeshift nest. "He doing okay?" Noah asked.

"No change," she said. From the row of stalls on either side of the aisle, horses shifted, hooves thudding against soft bedding or a wall. One whickered, another answered, as if having their own Girls' Night Out meeting. Was it really possible for her to be…friends with Noah?

Kate's eyelids drooped. She was only dimly aware of him drawing her closer, wrapping his arms around her, telling her to rest. She inhaled his clean male scent, then felt his lips against her hair, a soft kiss at her temple. Too weary to object, Kate didn't pull away. Friends again, she told herself. And slept.

MARGOT MET NOAH at the WB's front door early the next morning. The foal had held its own all night, and Noah was hoping the lab work would indicate something less serious than the infection Doc Crane suspected.

In contrast to Noah's disheveled appearance, Margot looked fresh in a stylish wrap dress, with her makeup perfectly done. "You spent the whole night in that barn?"

"Sorry about that." Noah had rushed out the door last night as soon as Margot stepped into the house, exchanging only a few words before he ran for his truck. "If I'd known you were coming…" But that wouldn't have changed anything. The colt had been his priority then.

"I didn't want to spoil my surprise." The expensive scent she wore drifted through the air. "Your mother and I managed without you. Jean and I played cards, watched a movie until I couldn't keep my eyes open any longer. But I missed you." She walked with him into the dining room, where his mother had laid out a breakfast buffet on the sideboard. Normally they ate in the kitchen, Noah sometimes standing at the center island. "Do you know where I slept last night?" Margot asked.

Noah could guess. "Not in my room."

"Can you believe—your mother put me at the opposite end of the hall. The guest quarters are lovely, the bed comfortable, but it wasn't the same."

Noah fought a smile. "Mom's old-fashioned. I've never brought a woman to this house to stay overnight. It's Mr. and Mrs. only at the Bodine B and B, as far as she's concerned."

Margot arched an eyebrow. "She apparently made an exception for your brother."

"He and Cass are…" Noah wouldn't use the trigger word *engaged*. He didn't want Margot to start talking about a ring right now. Which only made him feel guiltier for leaning over in the night to kiss Kate, however chastely. He wasn't one to cheat on a woman or string her along. But had he? He'd already made up his mind about his relationship with Margot, admitted to his everlasting feelings for Kate, and he'd barely touched her last night. She hadn't responded. Instead, she'd fallen asleep. Noah finished weakly, "Zach and his girlfriend aren't here."

"Well," Margot said, "I must say I'm surprised to find the WB even more than I expected. So much land, and this house is bigger than I imagined."

"I'm glad you like it." Noah guided her to the buffet.

Jean swept into the room, nodded at Margot, then kissed Noah's cheek. "How's our baby horse doing? You look tired."

"Didn't sleep much." He wasn't about to mention spending the night with Kate there, often taking her turn, too, while she slept, being hyperaware of her closeness, the silkiness of her hair under his lips. "We're waiting for the vet to call with the lab report."

"You should eat, then rest. Calvin can run things here today. Maybe you shouldn't have trailered the foal to Kate's."

"Kate?" Margot echoed.

Noah glanced at his mother, then helped himself to the steaming scrambled eggs. Margot knew who Kate was. She'd heard about her through Rob. Noah added crisp bacon, a couple of his mom's flaky biscuits to his plate, then sat down. Jean poured his coffee, and Noah dug into his food. "I'll be all right after a hot shower."

Margot wrinkled her nose. "I knew I smelled…animals." She hadn't even asked about the colt.

"That's not uncommon on a ranch." His mom's smile looked too bright. "Margot, eat."

"I never have breakfast. Just coffee, please." She waited for Jean to pour.

"Goodness, you'd waste away on the WB. We eat hearty. We have to, but then I suppose living in the big city, you don't get much exercise."

"I belong to a fitness facility," Margot said.

"Hmm. Well, to each his own." She looked at Noah. "I prefer a natural look—especially in men. Nice, strong muscles that come from hard physical work."

"Mom."

"You're looking more fit than you did when you got here," she told him blandly.

Margot sipped her coffee. "What are our plans for today? After your shower, Noah."

"I'll need to get back to Sweetheart Ranch. Plus, the vet will call—soon, I hope." Guilt ran through him. "Maybe you and I can have dinner in town tonight." It was time for that conversation they needed to have, and at dinner he might find a way to gently broach the subject.

She sniffed. "You seem to be taking this whole temporary ranch thing too seriously. That horse is not your responsibility."

"I think it is."

Margot flinched. "Let me remind you. I

didn't fly halfway across the country to see you only to end up sitting here alone after all."

Noah watched his mom's phony smile broaden.

"You're not alone, Margot. We can shop while Noah's next door with that darling colt."

"Is there any real shopping here? On my drive through Barren in the taxi, I saw only a few stores, none that appealed."

"Then we'll go to Farrier. It's not far and a bigger town, even though Barren is our county seat. I'm sure you can find something there."

Noah doubted that. Margot wouldn't buy anything that wasn't from Saks or Bergdorf's or some designer boutique. During their first months together, she'd insisted on helping Noah buy a whole new wardrobe of European-style Armani suits.

Jean focused on her breakfast—a small serving of eggs, a single biscuit and orange juice. "Afterward, I'll drop you at—are you thinking the Bon Appetit, Noah?" She turned back to Margot. "The restaurant is Barren's version of fine dining."

"I'll see how the day goes," he said. "I'll give you ladies a call."

Noah decided his mother was pulling out all the stops. With another woman, that would mean a charm assault, but clearly his mom hadn't changed her mind about Margot. By the time she left, poor Margot might loathe everything about Stewart County.

Noah felt sorry for her. It was Margot's fault, though. She shouldn't have surprised him.

KATE HELD TIGHTLY to Teddie's hand as they walked into the barn and down the aisle. She was surprised to find Noah already there again, urging the colt to drink from a nursing bottle.

"Mr. Bodine! Hey!" Teddie had jumped onto the low cross board at the bottom of the stall door and went up on his tiptoes to peer into the stall. The foal's big brown eyes had the dull sheen of illness.

"At least the baby's on his feet," Kate said.

Noah looked at her. "With some coaxing. The vet's treatment last night may have helped a bit."

"Let's hope so. I haven't heard from Doc Crane yet."

"Me either," Noah said.

Teddie sent her a worried look. He hadn't let Kate rest until they came to see the colt, despite her misgivings. "Is Lancelot going to be okay, Mommy?"

"I hope so," she said again, ruffling his hair.

Satisfied, Teddie hopped down from his perch. "I'm going to see Spencer. He probably wants to go for a ride today. Maybe Mr. Bodine could come too."

"We'll see."

His mouth tightened. "Does that mean no?"

Noah couldn't hide his smile. "He's got you pegged."

"Teddie, we'll decide later."

"I already decided."

He scampered down the aisle before Kate could respond.

Noah laughed. "And I thought my mom had trouble back in the day with Zach and me. Looks like you'll be taking a trail ride today."

"We'll see," she repeated, then couldn't help laughing at herself.

Noah patted the colt, then, with the half-full bottle in his hand, left the stall. He stood close to her in the aisle. "You really think you're going to homeschool him?"

"He may teach me more than I teach him." But Kate didn't want to go there. She knew Noah's opinion of her choice, but that was not his concern. "You didn't have to come over. You should have stayed with your girlfriend. Gabe and I are here."

"In New York, I'm very hands on at J&B. Can't seem to break the habit."

She took a breath. "Noah, last night it wasn't wise of you to stay. You should have gone home. You and I will get along—connect—if we don't pick things apart or…complicate them."

She meant about Rob, of course, but also friendship with Noah. Kate was already kicking herself for not drawing away from him during the night, from that light touch of his lips to her temple, her hair. Being even closer together on those hay bales than they were now had not been a good idea. Maybe she should have frozen instead.

"I see." Noah frowned a little. "I thought you were asleep, which sounds bad and is no excuse. Do I need to say I'm sorry? You didn't stop me," he pointed out.

Dangerous territory. Kate moved toward the next stall. "I should have."

He sighed. "And yes, I know. There's Margot."

"Which—since you brought up your girlfriend—is the end of this conversation. I don't know why you did what you did last night, but it can't happen again."

Before Noah said anything, Teddie came flying down the aisle toward them.

"Can we take our ride now, Mommy?"

As if she'd never tried to squelch that idea. "I don't think so, honey." She could guess what was coming next.

"Why not? I want to—and I want Mr. Bodine to come with us." He ran over to Noah and wrapped his arms around his knees. "Please, Mommy, can he?"

"Teddie, I—" Noah began but her son cut him off.

"I'll keep you from falling off your horse this time."

Noah gave a shout of surprised laughter. "Now there's an offer that's hard to refuse."

He gazed at Kate who had to smile too. As long as the foal's condition didn't worsen, what harm could there be in taking her boy for a short ride? Gabe was here to keep an eye on the sick colt. Kate would also take her SAT phone with her. Noah tilted his head toward Teddie. "We did agree to let things happen organically."

Teddie looked up at him, then at her. "What's that mean?"

Kate said, "I guess it means we're going for that ride."

CHAPTER FOURTEEN

"At least I've had you to myself tonight," Margot said on the way home from the Bon Appetit. Noah had met her there for dinner after his mom dropped her off.

"Jack—the chef—puts on a good meal."

"The prime rib wasn't bad."

"The best Barren has to offer." Which Noah thought was pretty good.

But the T-bone he'd eaten weighed his stomach down like a rock. He'd spent the late morning, while Margot shopped with his mother, on that ride with Kate and Teddie, then grabbed a quick lunch at Sweetheart Ranch before going down to the barn again, where Lancelot had been much the same. Back at the WB, Noah had showered for the second time today, then barely made it into town by seven to meet Margot. She didn't like to be kept waiting. Tonight she was in one of her passive-aggressive moods, so Noah hadn't yet eased into their much-needed talk.

The restaurant had been crowded and Noah had realized he would risk making a scene.

Besides, he'd never been one for tough conversations, which that one certainly might be.

Margot breathed in the warm air. "This is an experience. I've never ridden in a truck before."

"Complete with the WB logo on the side. I'm glad we could forget the ranch for a while and enjoy dinner." He took a curve in the road a bit too fast. "Margot, I know this isn't the visit you expected to have, but I didn't count on having that sick foal to tend to either. The vet came back around five, which held me up. The colt's infection is just what he thought—neonatal sepsis."

"I have no idea what that means."

"Basically, an infection that can overwhelm a newborn. I'm praying it doesn't. Tomorrow he should be better, I hope." And Noah, who had a genuine affection for her and respected Margot, might find a better opportunity then for that talk. He mentioned several area sites they might visit on more neutral territory, assuming the colt didn't go downhill overnight. Doc Crane had started a more targeted antibiotic, and when Noah had left the ranch, Lancelot had been gingerly nursing again.

"I'll need to check the foal first thing in the morning. I'll take you to meet him, but after that, we should be good to go. He's pretty cute."

Margot sniffed. "I didn't bring suitable clothes for hanging around a barn."

Noah knew Margot was out of her comfort zone here, but the WB was still in his blood. Which surprised him, actually. By now, he was enjoying ranch work at times, even when reality—J&B and its problems—were still waiting for him in New York. There, he was truly in command, not merely stopping by, as he was at the WB, although his father wasn't around now to judge him. The greater success Noah craved was still far from Kansas. And yet… He tried to gentle his tone. "Then maybe you shouldn't have come."

She bristled. "What else could I do since you decided again to extend your stay—"

"I didn't, my sister did. And Zach—"

"Neither of them should expect you to spend one minute on that ranch."

"Margot—"

"You haven't been part of the WB for a long time. You always say you never really belonged there. Now, every time someone here *needs* you, including your next-door neighbor, you jump at the chance to help."

Noah swallowed. Had Margot really picked up on his feelings for Kate? "The colt at Sweetheart Ranch is the WB's. And I have a financial share in the ranch, so I can hardly walk away." Although he had once before. "I have a stake here emotionally too. This is still my family—and because of Willow's wedding, plus a lot more, I owe them. I happen to love my sister, my mother, my brother…"

"Even when *he* doesn't treat you well."

"He has his reasons." Noah was surprised to hear himself defend Zach, who'd stuck him with this extra job in the first place. "But, Margot, you didn't come all this way to fight with me." He didn't want to quarrel, either, yet this conversation, not the one he'd planned, was headed in that direction.

"No," she agreed. "Perhaps I came to stake my territory."

Noah felt as if he were stepping into a minefield. She was about to bring up the ring business, and his stomach turned over. "I've never liked being told what I should do, or when—one reason why I'm not running the WB full-time instead of Zach."

For a long moment, there was silence while Noah navigated the dark road. Then, although things were going downhill fast, he couldn't stop himself from saying, "Another thing that's been bothering me. I'm told you called Daphne at the office—"

"To ascertain your travel plans, yes, because you wouldn't tell me."

He spoke through gritted teeth. "I didn't know at that point."

She sighed. "Noah, what is going on with us?"

He clenched the steering wheel. *Say it*, but how without the right words ready? Here, too, like in the restaurant, she would be hurt, there would be tears, even shouting, and he might well run the truck off the road. He couldn't seem to speak.

Margot didn't have that problem. "All right, then let me be blunt. Your internal clock isn't ticking. I want a family, but I'll be thirty-five in April. I can't afford to spend another two years of my life wondering if we'll ever go any further than we are now."

His mouth pressed tight not to say the wrong thing, he turned in at the gates to the WB. Its

name and metal logo gleamed in the moon-
light, a reminder of where he'd come from, if
not where he'd gone. And Noah's heart seemed
to swell. Cowboy or not, this—like Sweetheart Ranch for Teddie—was Noah's birthright, even from a distance.

Margot kept going.

"Your mother and I looked in several jew-
elry stores this afternoon."

Noah dodged a pothole in the driveway.
This kept getting worse. Did she expect him
to propose while they were at the WB? He
felt like a heel.

He and Margot had rubbed along com-
panionably, sharing their common interests,
their urban lifestyle—if not an apartment
together—for long enough that Noah should
have made that formal commitment by now.
He didn't cheat and he had never strung a
woman along before either. He shouldn't start
now. And yet...

She wasn't the right woman for him. He
wasn't the right man for her. She deserved
someone who would love her as Margot
needed to be loved.

"Noah?"

The look in her eyes did him in. "This isn't
the place," he said, "to have this conversa-

tion. In a truck? We'll talk but not here." Not tonight. "I promise."

Yes, he was stalling. Hated himself for it, and she would feel humiliated for speaking so frankly then being rebuffed, but he'd find the words by tomorrow to tell her—somehow— that there would be no ring.

WITH BANDIT TROTTING after her, Meg rapped on the bunkhouse door. She'd had two choices tonight. Answer the ringing phone— if it did ring—and talk to Mac again or bring these blankets back to Gabe Morgan, as she'd promised Kate.

Blinking into the darkness, Gabe stared at her from the open doorway, his hair shining under the porch light, his eyes with that sober yet curious look. Arms crossed.

Meg thrust the blankets toward him, forcing Gabe to catch them, then turned away. "They're the ones you lent to Kate. She laundered them. You're welcome," she prompted him.

"Thanks," he said, his tone wry. He set the blankets on a bench just inside the door. "But why don't you come in for a minute? It's time we talked."

Adrenaline flashed through her. "About...?"

He waved a hand between them. "The silent treatment I keep getting." Bandit's tail swished back and forth like a fly swatter, his dark eyes bright. "The dog likes me," Gabe pointed out.

"Bandit likes all people."

She turned to peer around Gabe at the interior of the bunkhouse, curious in spite of herself to see how he lived in these job-related quarters. Was he messy like Mac or a neatnik like her? She stepped back. Why should she care? "I don't think that's a good idea."

"What? You don't feel safe inside with me?"

"I know little about you. I'm happy to keep it that way."

"Man, that's cold. I can't believe you and Kate are related."

She turned away but he lightly caught her elbow. Meg stared pointedly at their contact until he let go. "Wise decision," she said.

Instead of going back into the bunkhouse, Gabe closed his door, left the porch and walked beside her. "I'll see you home, then. I'm on my way to check that sick foal."

Meg picked up her pace, Bandit dancing at her heels. Overhead, the black sky was clear, sprinkled with stars, the air crisp and biting.

"No snow in the forecast," he said, as if determined to make idle conversation. "Kansas is pretty on a night like this. Pretty anytime, really. I don't even mind the wind or the dust, but then I was used to that."

In spite of herself, she asked the question. "You're not from here?"

"Texas born and bred. My dad's kind of in the oil business, but I always had a thing for horses, the outdoors. Ended up here."

"You're the opposite of Noah Bodine."

"Am I? From what I've seen, Noah's got more of the WB in him than he'd admit. He's good with the colt, has a nice touch."

"I've tried to tell Kate that he's not how she sees him."

"About her husband, you mean? I've heard some of that sad story."

And Meg shouldn't add to the gossip. "You won't hear any more from me."

In the darkness, Gabe laughed softly. "And here I thought we were getting started."

"On what?"

"That talk. How long are you going to stick your nose in the air whenever you see me?"

Her shoulder accidentally bumped his. Meg stepped away. "You want to know why I keep my distance? For one, you're foreman here and, as you said, I'm not Kate. I don't need to talk to you about this ranch or learn where you came from, and especially I don't need to know where you're going next. Men like you, cowhands or foremen, are usually transient, which I've seen before." Also pilots, she thought. "When I was a girl, I used to spend part of my summers with Kate and her dad, sometimes the better part of a year."

"Why?"

"Why not? I may be Kate's aunt, but we're also friends."

"She's younger than you."

"Not that much." She had to smile. "I liked being around Rob and Noah, too, who were more my age."

"That explains summers."

She sighed. "I'm a military brat. My parents were based at Fort Riley."

"Both of them, huh?"

"The family business." Meg's throat tightened. She remembered all the times before they'd left, packing their gear, and hers, the tense silence in their base house, the fresh uncertainty. Getting into the car in the middle of the night for the drive to Sweetheart. Saying goodbye again. Her ever-present fear. "They usually deployed separately, but when they went away at the same time, I stayed here with Kate and her dad."

"Your second home, then." Gabe looked up at the stars.

"It is." And even more so since she'd split from Mac. Her only home at the moment.

"I'd expect you to marry a guy with deep roots."

"A man who stayed in one place?" Meg winced. "Yet, go figure, I didn't. Something for a shrink to deal with someday, but for now all I can tell you is, I felt attracted to the glamour of his career." She told him a little about Mac's constant travel for a legacy airline, the exotic places he'd seen, but not about his neglect of their marriage or its sad demise after she lost the baby. Gabe already seemed to have deduced she was the next thing to an orphan. They were nearing the house now. "We've had our talk," she said. "Goodnight, Gabe."

"Meg." He kept pace with her. For several moments, he studied the sky again, and she listened to the soft lowing of cattle from the darkened pasture. "Reading between the lines—I can tell you've had a rough time. I imagine a stay-at-home guy would have worked better for you after being shuttled around as a kid."

She stiffened. Her fears hadn't been solely a reaction to being uprooted. "I'm not some pathetic lost soul. Don't feel sorry for me."

"I don't. But I think I understand." He didn't say why—part of the mystery of Gabe Morgan. He laid a hand on her shoulder. "You have nothing to worry about from me. You may even be right, that I'm here for the short-term." He paused. "In spite of all that, I like you. Can't help myself."

Meg eased away from his touch, which she should have done sooner. Why hadn't she walked away the instant she felt his hand on her?

"All I ask," he said, "is for you to stop being some kind of ice queen whenever I'm around. I've never hurt you…" He hesitated before adding, "Your ex did."

THE NEXT AFTERNOON, Kate drove back from town with a silent Teddie. She glanced at him again in the rearview mirror. At home, the colt had been doing better when they left for Teddie's annual physical at Barren's medical practice on Cottonwood Street. But obviously, he wasn't thinking of Lancelot now. "Are you okay, Bunny?"

"I don't like Doctor McCord."

Yet Teddie hadn't received any dreaded shots today, and Sawyer had reported he was in perfect health, hitting all his marks—exceeding, of course, in his mental development. There, he was off the charts. Kate still worried that Teddie had a big advantage over her, and Noah had made a sound point. How would she manage homeschooling when Teddie would probably bypass her, surely in a couple of years?

"Why do you say that? Doctor McCord is a friend, Teddie."

More silence, which she should have expected. She'd given the doctor permission to broach the subject of Rob's death with her son in private after the exam, but what exactly had Sawyer said?

"He talked to you, didn't he?" Kate recalled Sawyer's attempt to communicate with her when he and Teddie had come out of his office. He'd lifted his eyebrows and given her a slight shake of his head. "About Daddy."

Teddie pouted. "He doesn't know. He's not my friend."

Kate swung the truck off the road and into

the parking lot of the town's fast-food restaurant. "Bunny, I think you may be hungry or, as Aunt Meg says, 'hangry.'" He didn't smile. "Let's get a burger before we go home, all right? And discuss this?"

He folded his arms. "I'm not hangry."

"Teddie, then what did he say?"

"He said, 'This is between us men,' and I don't have to tell."

"Teddie Bear…"

"I'm not lying! He did say that, Mommy." The words burst from him. "He said Daddy is never coming back, that he can't because he…died. He's the liar, not me!"

So. Sawyer hadn't succeeded either. How many times in the past year had she tried to make Teddie understand about Rob? Less than a week ago, he had wept again in her arms. During their ride with Noah yesterday, had Teddie realized how much he missed his father? She had to try again. "Honey, we live on a ranch. Remember when Bandit's friend lost her puppy?"

"That was sad. I cried."

"Well, the same kind of thing can happen…to people. Even people we love."

"Not to my daddy." Teddie took a deep breath. "He lives in New York."

Kate said softly, "Yes, he did—and we missed him then. I know he always told you he'd be home someday. He thought he would keep his promise, Teddie." Rob had booked tickets to fly home that Christmas. He'd never made it. "But he can't."

"He's not a puppy. Daddies don't die."

Oh, dear God. After Rob's accident, Kate had bought half a dozen books with gentle explanations for what had happened to their family, and Teddie had rejected them all. One morning last week, Kate had walked into his room to make his bed and seen them in his wastebasket, ripped to shreds. That's when she'd called Sawyer to move up Teddie's physical exam, then asked him to intervene, hoping that a more neutral party might help.

With a sinking heart, Kate got out, opened the rear door, took Teddie from his car seat and leaned against the side of the truck, his rigid body held close to her. She smoothed a trembling hand over his silky hair. "Teddie Bear, we're not trying to make you unhappy. But you can't keep believing—"

"Yes, I can! Mr. Bodine lives in New York, too, and he's here now."

"That's different." She'd been afraid of this. Kate regretted taking that horseback ride yesterday but hadn't been able to say no. Just the light in Teddie's eyes had been enough for her to agree. Although she still didn't want Teddie to rely on Noah, how could she have refused to let him have those few moments of sheer happiness? As they'd trotted across the frozen fields, the sun shining, the sound of his laughter and the easy conversation he'd shared with Noah dancing through the air, her own heart had healed a little. But in retrospect, had that ride been wise? "You know Mr. Bodine is only visiting."

He wiggled out of her embrace. "Then he'll go back—and see Daddy."

Kate feared she'd been right. Teddie's surprising friendship with Noah made him feel closer to his father. As she'd suspected, Noah was in part a surrogate for Rob until Teddie believed he would be here again. Encouraging more "organic" rides or any other event might make things worse. Maybe she should choose another counselor for Teddie, though the first one hadn't worked.

He thought for a moment. "Why didn't they come together? He's Daddy's friend too."

Kate took his hand and buckled him back

into his car seat, even though Teddie could do that himself. Yes, he and Noah were also friends. But what if, once Noah left, he never returned? That might be good for Kate's peace of mind, but how would her son feel?

She had a sudden idea. Maybe, precisely because they were friends, this might work.

"Teddie. What if N—Mr. Bodine talked with you about Daddy? Would that be okay?"

"Maybe. We always talk," he said.

CHAPTER FIFTEEN

TEDDIE PEERED INTO the stall where Kate had been giving Lancelot a bottle of her own mare's milk. "Better and better every day, Mommy?"

"It seems so," Kate said as Bandit barked and a truck stopped outside. Her heart skipped a beat. She'd gotten used to Noah's daily trips from the WB to see the foal—and Teddie. Almost. This would be her chance to ask him about talking to her son.

But this morning, when Kate stepped out of the stall, he wasn't alone. He'd brought a woman with him.

Noah had mentioned his girlfriend. Who else could it be?

He helped her down from the truck's cab. She wore a full-length down coat, high-heeled boots that must have cost the earth and what looked to be a cashmere turtleneck with black pants. Her dark hair was stylishly cut. Everything about her said elegance and money.

Kate went to meet them, the empty bottle still in her hand. Her grubby appearance—hair that had dried on its own after a hasty shower, dirty jeans (she'd wrestled the colt into position) and her favorite parka with a stain—was a polar opposite. Kate had never particularly cared how she looked. Her daily work on the ranch didn't allow for vanity. Now, instead, she felt somehow…less than the woman who gingerly stepped through the mud into the barn and turned up her nose.

At Kate's side, Bandit growled low in his throat. Noah stepped around him.

To her surprise, he looked different this morning in a blue button-down shirt with a navy V-necked sweater, visible through his open shearling-lined jacket. His boots looked newly polished, although spotted with mud in places.

"Kate, this is Margot," he said. "Margot, meet Kate and Teddie."

"Hello," was all the woman said, her voice cool.

Teddie, who'd followed Kate and might normally start chattering away even with a stranger, said nothing. When Noah laid a hand on his head, Teddie slipped free, then resumed his perch on the stall door, talking to the colt. He hadn't greeted Noah, either, but Kate wouldn't reprimand him right now.

"Welcome to Sweetheart Ranch," she managed as Margot looked her over.

Noah raised his eyebrows. "As you know, Margot has been staying with us at the WB. I thought I'd bring her over, let her see where I've been spending time." It sounded as if he was apologizing, perhaps because he hadn't given Kate any warning of their visit.

She wasn't one to judge other people, but Margot wasn't winning any points with Kate, which seemed to be mutual.

Even Bandit had slunk over to plop down next to Teddie, who'd stopped just short of being rude. The dog gave Margot a baleful stare, then growled again.

Kate said, "Please, Margot, look around. We're not fancy here, but we do have some nice-looking horses." While Noah's girlfriend visited the animals, assuming he didn't go with her, Kate could ask him about Teddie. But Margot didn't move.

"I'm not a horse person," she murmured.

"Oh. Well, then, um…"

Noah's gaze caught Kate's, then slid away.

He looked disappointed, even embarrassed, as if he'd hoped Margot would keep an open mind. "I'll take a quick look at Lancelot, then we can go. I planned to do Monument Rocks today," he told Kate, "but Margot thinks that's too far for a day trip."

"I'm not an outdoor person," she said, glancing down at her muddy boots.

After the once-over she'd given Kate, Margot surveyed the barn from where she stood, taking in the stalls on either side of the aisle, flinching when one of the horses suddenly neighed, then sending Teddie and Bandit a dismissive look. Kate imagined Margot saying, *I'm not a kid person.*

Noah tried another suggestion. "So we'll drive to Topeka instead, see the state capitol, have dinner there."

"The city has some great restaurants," Kate murmured, although what did she know? Her last day off this ranch for a social event had been to attend that wedding in New York. Oh, and that one Girls' Night Out, which had been local. "Rob and I went to a good steakhouse near the capitol once, but I've forgotten the name." And that had been years ago. Margot must eat in fine restaurants every night.

"One meal at the Bon—what's the name?—was enough for me," Margot said.

"Bon Appetit." Noah sighed. "Kate was trying to be helpful." He turned toward the stall where Teddie was waiting. "Come see the foal. You may not like horses, but I guarantee you'll love this one."

"I'll just wait here, thanks."

Which left Kate with Margot and her own feeling of being a country bumpkin, poorly dressed, with no real experience of the outside world. She recalled Noah's remarks about New York; the restaurants; museums; the zoo, which Teddie would love. Was Noah right that she was crimping her child's sense of adventure? Perhaps she did need to think about that. Was she really keeping Teddie safe? Or limiting his development? She had no idea what to say to Margot, who drew back as if she feared touching Kate.

"I didn't realize how cold—primitive—a barn could be." Margot finally looked at her. "Is there some place warmer I could sit while Noah spends even more time here?"

"Why don't you go on up to the house, then? It's much cozier there. I'll give my aunt a quick call to tell her you're coming. Meg will have fresh coffee, I'm sure. My dog can show you the way."

Hearing his name, Bandit got up, his joints cracking. His tail hadn't wagged once since Noah arrived, but at least he didn't growl again. He trotted in front of Margot to the doors as Kate pulled out her phone to alert Meg she'd have company.

But wonder of wonders, Kate now had her chance to talk to Noah after all.

"SORRY ABOUT THAT." Noah dragged a hand through his hair. "I knew Margot wasn't especially fond of mud, barns or horses, but I thought we had reached an agreement. She'd stop here with me—and I'd take the rest of my day to show her the Kansas sights."

Kate slipped her cell back into her pocket. "Maybe you're not a Kansas-sights person."

Noah laughed, breaking the tension he'd felt since coming into the barn. Teddie climbed off the stall door, then ran over to him, wrapping his arms around Noah's knees. "Why is your girlfriend mean?"

At the moment, Noah couldn't disagree.

"Teddie." Kate didn't let her boy get away with that. "I need to speak with Mr. Bodine alone. I will talk to you at the house."

Teddie knew what she meant. He waited a few seconds too long before letting go of Noah. "Can we ride again after my time-out?"

Kate merely pointed toward the doors, then waited until Teddie had stomped his way across the yard, stepping in old piles of snow or puddles, mud splattering his jeans.

"He doesn't think he got a fair hearing," Noah said.

"No, but he's a child, not an adult."

"What's your excuse?" Noah grinned. "'Not a sights person?' I could tell from ten feet away that you and Margot aren't going to be best friends."

"I shouldn't have said what I did. I will scold myself later. Maybe we'll have to try again."

"If she has her way, we'll be on a plane tonight."

"Well, I can understand how she feels. I'm not a New York person."

"Keep going, Kate." But he was still smiling.

"Sorry, that was uncalled for too." And she did need to reexamine her prejudice against the Big Apple. If the city wasn't to her liking, that didn't mean she should turn Teddie off too.

Noah's smile faded. "I should have guessed what would happen. It's not as if Margot hasn't told me her views of the WB."

"In Manhattan, you probably get along fine."

"Yeah, we did, but lately..." He trailed off. "She seemed okay about meeting the colt until we actually left the truck." Or was it until she'd seen Kate? Margot had always been the jealous type. "We aren't off to a good start this morning, but then I haven't been very attentive lately either." Noah thought of confiding in Kate but only ran a hand over the back of his neck. Instead, he walked to the stall, opened the latch, then stepped inside. Lancelot trotted over to him. "Hey, buddy. How is he medically, Kate?"

"Doc Crane was here earlier. He's pleased with Lancelot's progress. I think we may actually make it through this."

Noah exchanged high fives with her. But did Kate realize she'd included Noah when she said "we"? Or had she meant herself and the vet? Noah let the foal nuzzle him as Kate went on with her report.

"He's emptying his bottles now—or actually nursing. Either way he's getting my mare's milk full-time. I'm afraid his mama is done with him. So I'll probably stable Lancelot with my mare and her filly."

"Then I might as well take the WB's mare home. Sure you can keep Lancelot awhile longer?"

"My pleasure. I've fallen pretty hard for this little guy."

Noah couldn't stop the thought. *And what if you'd ever fallen for me?* If, years ago, instead of Rob, he'd won Kate's heart. Where would they be now? In New York, at the WB or on Sweetheart Ranch? Would Rob still be alive? And why was he pondering all that when he couldn't tell Kate how he felt? He owed Margot that conversation first about their relationship.

She cleared her throat. "Noah, while I have the chance, and we're alone, I need to ask you something. Important."

"Okay. What is it?"

"As you know, the past year hasn't been good for Teddie—and me."

His insides knotted. Noah was already worried about Margot. Was Kate about to blast him again for the accident that had taken Rob's life? "Right," he said, "and I realize you think that's my fault, but—"

"This is about Teddie. He simply refuses to accept the truth. He still thinks Rob is coming home." She told him about her conversation with Teddie in the car after his doctor's appointment. "I've tried a thousand times and Sawyer tried to get through to him, but Teddie is adamant. Meg always says he's stubborn like me. He even asked me why you and Rob hadn't come here together from New York."

Noah's stomach tightened. "That's not good. He's such a bright kid, Kate, yet he's not mature enough to reason his way around something like this."

"While he understands that animals die, he insisted that daddies don't."

Noah glanced toward the colt's stall. "But he once told me that kids can have more than one daddy."

"If there's a divorce," she said. "He can understand that because some of his friends have parents who've split." Her gaze had clouded. "Do you see what I mean? I've considered a counselor again, but Teddie's not keen on the idea. I picked the wrong one soon after Rob passed, and he's reluctant to try another." She paused. "So, I wanted to ask, would you be willing to talk to him?"

"Kate, I don't think—"

"Teddie adores you. At first, I didn't feel that was the proper thing, but after the ride we took, our agreement to just let things happen, the friendship you've established with Teddie... You could be the best person to reach him."

"Me? I'm the guy who never made up with my own father. I don't have that kind of communication skill."

"I think you do."

"Kate, no, especially with a kid—your child. I wouldn't want to mess him up." And then, there was the blame she'd placed on him about Rob. What if he did damage Teddie? Not only would Noah never forgive himself, neither would Kate. "Teddie and I do have a nice friendship, one I never expected, and I'd like to keep that while I'm here."

"While you're here," she repeated, reminding Noah that he'd soon be gone.

He shook his head. Kate considered the friendship, like their truce, to be temporary. So how could she trust him with her son? "I'm honored to be asked, and I hate to disappoint you, but I'd better stick with no for my answer."

"Please. Just think about it, Noah."

That pleading look in her gorgeous gray eyes, his feelings for Kate, which he couldn't reveal, were almost enough to change his mind. He hated to let her down but...just as with Margot, what could he say?

"I'll let you know," he said.

"WHAT WAS THIS morning all about?" After returning that night to the ranch, Noah had taken Margot into the ranch office and shut the door. When they'd left Sweetheart Ranch, they'd taken their planned tour of the area, and Noah had held his tongue not to make the rest of the day unpleasant, but inside his mood hadn't improved. Nor had his resolve changed. He sat at the desk across from Margot's chair.

She toyed with the sash on her dress. Before they'd left town, she'd insisted they change clothes to sightsee and have dinner while they were out. "You knew before we went to that place that I'm not a—"

"Ranch person," he said for her. "I'm disappointed. I expected you to be civil to Kate and her boy."

"I was perfectly civil."

But Noah hadn't missed the undercurrents earlier and neither had Kate. Although he and Margot until now had usually enjoyed each other's company, and they did share common interests around business in New York, their mutual social circle and an initial attraction that had served them well, here they had little in common, including his new appreciation for the WB. "I get that you feel out of place in what must be an alien environment—"

"As it is for you." She gestured at his jeans and flannel shirt. "Maybe it's been fun for you to revisit the WB but—"

"You seem to think this is like some Disney World ride for me, but I haven't been 'playing cowboy.' The WB is a business, if in a different way, from J&B Cybersecurity. And the Lancasters have been neighbors for a long time—Kate's been doing me a favor with the colt."

Her gaze downcast, Margot fiddled again with the sash. "Is that all?"

"The least you could have done—" he began, then stopped. "What did you say?"

"Kate and her cute little boy seem to hold some fascination for you."

So Margot had indeed guessed how he felt

when Noah liked to think he had a firm hold on his unexpressed feelings for Kate. "Believe me, Sweetheart Ranch and Teddie are all she cares about." Which didn't exclude his interest. Noah swiveled the desk chair back and forth. "This time on the WB has been necessary. My mother takes care of the house, but she couldn't have managed the ranch too."

"Yet you're taking care of business with J&B—plus here. How fair is that?"

At first, he would have agreed with her. "Sometimes life's not fair." But Noah hadn't missed her mention of the company just now. Maybe this wasn't only about his decision to end their relationship as gently as possible. He took a deep breath. The right words or not, they had to come out. "Margot, I'm sorry about all this, sorrier than I can say, but we do need to talk."

"Yes, we do." She straightened her shoulders, retied the sash and met his gaze. "But may I start? I've been dying to tell you." Her eyes sparkled. "My father has an offer for you. He wants to buy J&B."

"It's not for sale."

Noah had been blindsided. And he'd

thought they were going to discuss their breakup.

"Please. Hear me out," Margot said. "I have his official offer upstairs in my bag, and the price is huge, rightfully so," she added. "You've made a tremendous success of the business, but why not cash out now? Take your profit—Brent will take his—and we'll be set for life."

We. Noah could envision Margot and her dad hashing out the details over a glass of wine from one of the many bottles in his cellar, which had an actual tasting room. Noah had once shared a glass of port with the man and cigars, both of which Noah disliked. He'd also gotten the message then. Margot's father expected to have control, but so far Noah had avoided any real clashes with him, for her sake.

"Margot, my own father wasn't an easy man." Quite an understatement. "Opinionated, stubborn about his ideas of how my life should go. When I left the WB, I became his biggest, eternal disappointment. You know that. No matter how much money I made, it would never have changed his mind. I won't let your father make my choices for me either."

"Don't be ridiculous. If you sell, you won't

have to work as hard. Daddy will give you a nice title in his company or, if you prefer, a board seat, certainly a corner office. You won't need to use it, though, unless you want to."

We'll be set for life.

Noah couldn't believe what he was hearing.

Margot tried to sweeten the pot. "We can spend more time together, travel if we want to—start our family."

He winced as fresh guilt flashed through him. Yet they'd never discussed having kids, and he didn't appreciate the notion that she might have been playing him ever since he'd opened the front door to find her standing on the porch. She'd acted as if their relationship was the sole reason she'd come, and he'd believed her. Noah felt betrayed. But that offer wasn't all. He sensed there was even more.

"What else?" he said.

"You'd also be getting what you wanted." Margot held his gaze. "Daddy hopes to acquire the Prentice start-up."

Noah's blood ran cold. "But Brent and I have been negotiating that. It's almost done."

"My father is closer to a deal."

"He's already been talking to them too?"

"He'll roll that company into J&B. You can manage them if you want—"

"Then he'll flip the combined businesses. Make himself an even bigger profit."

"If you want to jump ahead, put it that way…"

"What other way is there?" So that was Margot's hidden agenda, which his mother had suspected. "I give up the business Brent and I have sweated to build—sacrifice the greater upside that he and I would have by acquiring Prentice ourselves, plus the satisfaction we'd have in growing J&B, the profit we would get *someday* when we're ready to sell—and you get everything you've been asking for, thanks to Daddy."

Margot had turned pale. "It's more than time, Noah, for you to commit to our future. My father is only helping to clear the way."

Noah feared his head might explode. A few minutes ago, he might have agreed about a commitment. Even his mother had said he was dragging his feet. Now he knew his instincts had been right. "Then maybe he should also buy that ring you've been not-so-subtly hinting about. Forget that. I think we've talked enough." He didn't need the right words now. Margot had forced his hand.

"I'll make a reservation for you to fly to New York—alone."

"Wait, baby," she said. "Don't be like this."

"You didn't really think this would work, did you?"

Her chin went up. "I may have come on a bit too strong, but once you think about it, you'll see I'm right."

"I don't need to think." Noah stood, then walked over to the door. He didn't turn around. "We're not a good match, Margot. I'm sorry, but I'm done." He couldn't say it more plainly than that.

He heard her scrape back her chair and follow him into the hall. Her tone sounded incredulous. "You're breaking up with me?"

Noah kept walking. His second call would be to Brent. They needed to head off the Prentice takeover.

"Tell your father there will be no deal," he said over his shoulder.

CHAPTER SIXTEEN

THE NEXT MORNING, during another storm that had moved in overnight, Noah drove Margot to the airport in awkward silence. He'd known for months they weren't headed in the same direction relationship-wise and felt guilty for that. He wished he'd spoken sooner, but her betrayal still hurt. Noah had spent half the night on the phone with Brent, trying to circumvent the Prentice takeover by her father.

Now, having seen Margot off, Noah was back from Kansas City, and his truck plowed to a stop near the house at Sweetheart Ranch. Teddie flew out the door, wearing only a T-shirt and jeans. "Lookit all this snow! Do you know how to make a fort, Mr. Bodine?"

"I do," he said, feeling his spirits lift as he climbed down from the pickup.

Kate came out, holding Teddie's jacket. "Put this on before you freeze. 'Morning, Noah."

"Kate. Best kind of weather to build a fort." Noah's boots sank into a drift. "We got some good packing stuff last night. You game?"

"I... Yes." She sent him a look as if to ask if he'd decided about speaking to Teddie. But try to make a four-year-old understand that his father was never coming back? Because of his conversation with Margot, Noah hadn't had time to work that out—even to please Kate. Why not ease his tension by playing in the snow? He could think later.

Teddie was already at the kitchen door again. "I'm getting Aunt Meg. She can help us."

"Tell her to bundle up," Noah said. "We might even make a snowman."

In the barn, they convinced Gabe to join them, and the group set about making blocks for the fort, its design growing more elaborate by the minute. Noah knew Kate was waiting for his decision, but his final talk with Margot had been awkward enough.

As soon as he bent down to form another block, Kate pelted him in the back of the head with a snowball. Noah laughed. "Oh, you shouldn't have done that," he said, scooping up more snow.

And the fight was on. At first, Gabe and Meg held back while Kate, Teddie and Noah waged their snowball war. Then, Gabe dared to stick a handful of the cold, wet stuff down the neck of Meg's parka and she howled. "Why did you do that?"

When she faced him, though, her eyes were full of mischief. Who didn't love a snowball fight? Gabe laughed—and took off running. In the deep snow, Meg didn't get far chasing him before she went down. Gabe immediately ran back to her, his eyes somber. "You okay?"

"Fine." And grinning, she mashed a snowball into his face.

By the time they finished the fight—and building the fort and the snowman—everyone was out of breath from laughing. Noah had needed the release from the strain of ending a two-year relationship with hard feelings on both sides.

"Hot cocoa," Kate called out, moving toward the house. "I'll get a fire going."

Teddie didn't go with her. "I want to try out my fort."

Kate exchanged a look with Noah. "He must be cold, his snow pants are soaked…"

"I'll watch him. We won't be long."

They waited until Kate had gone through the kitchen door with only a brief glimpse behind her. Then Noah looked down, and Teddie was there, reaching for his hand. Inside the icy fort, they crawled along the tunnels, sat for a few moments in the main chamber before Noah finally led the way outside. They emerged encrusted with snow, but again Teddie didn't start for the house. The wintry sky looked hazy, and in the snow that came even harder, Teddie flopped down, sweeping his arms and legs back and forth to create an angel.

Noah watched him finish with a smile. "Your angel is magnificent."

"What's magni-fi-suh—"

"It means perfect. Beautiful. I know you like dragons and knights and cowboy books, but I never guessed you were an angel artist." And suddenly, Noah knew what his answer for Kate would be. Teddie's angel had been his creation but also organic like his suggestion to build a fort. He had touched on the subject himself first, and that was key to the message Noah would try to deliver now. Just let it happen. "Do you know much about angels—except how to make one?"

"I never made one before."

"Well, you did a fine job."

"I know there are angels in heaven," Teddie said.

Noah cleared his throat. "And sometimes, when people are old or sick, they become angels too."

Teddie looked skeptical. "In heaven?"

"Yeah, I think so. For instance, my dad—"

"The real Mr. Bodine? I knew him a little. He was kind of scary."

True, yet Noah still regretted the fact that he'd never reconciled with his father. Over the years, would Teddie's sorrow subside or grow until it threatened to consume him? Would he always feel the same loss Noah did to this day? He couldn't change that for himself, would never gain his dad's approval, but what if he could change the outcome for Teddie?

"My father could be scary," Noah agreed. "But when he was older and I was grown up, he…couldn't stay here any longer."

"Where did he go?"

Noah couldn't speak. He pointed at the sky. Snow sifted down around them, blanketed their already-snowy shoulders and began to fill in the angel shape Teddie had made.

His eyes were wide behind his glasses. "Did he fly a plane? By himself?"

Noah laid a hand on his head. "No, Teddie. He didn't. He…well, as folks say, like that puppy your mom reminded you about, my dad…got sick and couldn't get better. He passed away too." And on one level, despite their differences, Noah missed him.

"But people *don't*." Teddie looked wary now. "Did my mom tell you that?"

Noah wouldn't forget how smart the boy was. He really needed a therapist, a psychologist, not a temporary cowboy like Noah, who hoped he hadn't said the wrong thing. He wouldn't lie to Kate's son. "She mentioned it, yes."

Teddie's mouth set. "She's wrong. My daddy didn't go up to the sky. He's in New York."

"No, he isn't, Teddie." Noah's voice caught on the words. "I wish he was, because your dad was my best friend, and I miss him too—just like you do." His throat tightened. His vision blurred. "I miss him every day. I remember him every night."

"Do you cry?"

Noah swallowed hard. "Yeah, sometimes I do." He'd even cried in the past over Kate, who would never forgive him. "That's okay, you know. We, um, men can cry just like anyone else. It means you love him. You always will."

Teddie looked at him and broke Noah's heart, his tone hushed to ask, "He's never coming back?"

"No," was all he could say. Teddie deserved the raw truth. Noah only prayed that, no matter how painful the loss, Teddie could, at last, accept it. He prayed he hadn't ruined Kate's son and their fragile friendship.

Teddie threw himself against Noah there in the still-falling snow, wrapped his arms around Noah and cried. "It'll be okay," Noah said. "I promise." He wiped a tear from his eye too. He wondered that the droplet hadn't frozen on contact with his skin. He could feel Teddie begin to shiver. "We should go to the house," he began, but Teddie hadn't finished.

His voice sounded small. "Is my daddy an angel now?"

"Yes."

"Like your dad and the puppy?"

"Yes," he said, holding Teddie closer.

"A real one, not like the angel I made."

"For real," Noah assured him. "And you know what else?" He swallowed again. "He's watching over you right now. Even when we can't see him, he's always there. He'll be your guardian angel for the rest of your life."

"Mommy's angel too?"

"Your mommy's too," he all but whispered.

"And yours," Teddie added, nodding against Noah's coat. For another long moment, he stayed silent. Then he said, "Because he loves us all."

KATE HAD WONDERED what was taking Noah and Teddie so long until they came in the kitchen door and she saw their faces. Had something happened? "You're both blocks of ice, turning blue," she said. "Teddie Bear, get out of those wet clothes and into something warm."

Bandit danced around his legs. "My pajamas?"

"If you like—your robe and slippers too. We're having breakfast for dinner tonight."

"Yay! Eggs and bacon?"

The simple meal was one of his favorites, often made when Kate and Meg were too busy to cook or when Kate's spirits were low and her appetite gone.

She took a closer look at Noah. As he left

his sodden boots by the door, then hung up his wet parka, he appeared shaken, and for once, Teddie didn't keep jumping up and down or chattering about the snow fort they'd made. Without another word, he brushed past her to the hall, then up the stairs. Kate's heart was in her throat as her gaze met Noah's eyes. Obviously, he and her son had talked.

"Later," Noah said as if he didn't trust himself to tell her right now.

"Stay for dinner, then." From the look on his face, Kate wasn't sure she wanted to hear what he would have to say. Still, she needed to know. "You didn't spend as much time with the foal as you usually do, which can be done after we eat, and you need fresh clothes first too."

After Meg offered to finish cooking, Kate led Noah to the second floor then the spare room. If Noah hadn't reached Teddie, she didn't know what else to do. Try to find that new, more effective counselor, she supposed. Which wasn't Noah's fault.

"Thank you for giving Teddie such a nice day. Even Meg and Gabe enjoyed themselves."

Earlier, Kate had noticed the clear awareness between them, but, at least on Gabe's part, that wasn't new. They'd even spoken to each other without Meg's usual stiffness. At one point she'd seen him come closer to Meg, and for an instant, Kate had thought he might kiss her. Then Meg had lifted one hand and smashed the snowball into his face. Had she simply defused the moment? Or was there truly something there?

Kate opened the closet door. Inside, hung a few men's shirts and down vests. Unmoving, Noah stood behind her. She could hear his quiet, steady breathing. "These are Dad's things. I donated the rest long ago, but I couldn't let every piece of his clothing go."

"This isn't necessary, Kate. I should go home."

"No, please stay. I appreciate what you must have tried to do with Teddie. He's such a hard case, though. Maybe no one can get through to him."

Noah shifted his weight. Although they weren't touching, Kate could feel the cold emanating from him. "I think I did, actually," he said. "That kid of yours, the insights, the things that come out of his mouth…"

Kate's heartbeat quickened. "He talked about Rob?" She turned and found Noah standing too close. The pallor faded from his face as he told her what they'd discussed. When he reached the last, about Rob watching over all of them with love, she put a hand to her throat. "Oh, Noah."

"I couldn't speak after he said that until you and I got upstairs here. It's amazing what he does understand. We even talked about my dad, a little, which ironically seemed to help Teddie about Rob. I think he'll be okay—if not all at once."

Now it was Kate who felt shaken. Quick tears had welled in her eyes. "I can't thank you enough." Blindly, she pivoted again to rummage through the closet. He and Kate's father had been of a similar height, although Noah was a bit heavier, more muscled, which Kate had tried not to notice.

But this man, this budding tycoon whom she'd also tried to tar with the brush of her resentment about Rob, her blame, had been the person to finally show Teddie his way to the truth. How could she ever repay him?

"Kate." Noah's hand fell on her shoulder before he snatched it back.

She reached for a blue plaid flannel shirt. In those first days after Rob died, she'd taken one of his to bed with her, held it close and soaked it with tears until Meg had told her she was making things worse for herself. She needed to begin letting go. Kate had scooped up everything of Rob's in the master bedroom closet, then carried it all to the attic, wanting to dare Meg to object.

She turned once more, thrust the shirt at Noah then a down vest, but her dad's Wranglers looked too small for him. "I doubt these jeans will fit but…" Then she ran out of air and had to start over. "At least they're dry. You can change in here or the bathroom." She gestured at the adjoining space. "If you put your clothes in the hall, I'll stick them in the dryer for you."

But she soon learned it wasn't her dad he was thinking about. "Kate, he's always on my mind. Rob, I mean."

"Please," was all she said. *Don't.*

With a sigh, Noah took the clothes. And Kate stood there again like a statue.

He went into the bathroom, and she heard a rustle as he struggled to remove his clothes. She heard Teddie across and down the hall in his room, the patter of his slippers as he plodded downstairs. And still, she didn't move. Then Noah stripped off his white thermal undershirt. And through the half-open door before he reached to close it, she saw his bare back.

Kate froze. An angry, still-red scar angled from his left shoulder across his spine, then down the right side of his torso. Had the same attack that killed her husband grievously wounded Noah too? *Oh, dear God.* In an instant, she had pushed the door open.

"Not a pretty sight, is it?" he asked, meeting her shocked eyes in the mirror.

"I didn't know," she said. "I thought… But this is from that same night."

"Kate, it doesn't matter."

Yet, to her, it did. It mattered more than any words could say.

UNTIL HE HEARD her gasp, Noah thought Kate had gone downstairs. He wished she had, or he would never have taken off his shirt before he shut the door. Even his mother hadn't seen the grisly sight. Noah was already living on an edge. His talk with Teddie had gutted him, and her view of his wound had brought back that night in New York, the sudden attack from nowhere, the knife flashing, finding flesh…finding bone.

When she stepped closer now, slipped her arms around his waist from behind and pressed her cheek against his ruined back, he had to fight himself not to turn and run. "Kate," he said again, his body rigid.

"Your mother called, of course, the day after...this happened. She said you'd been hurt but didn't give me any details—because of Rob, so soon after he—people protected me, no one told me, but, Noah, you nearly died too..."

"I wasn't the one to worry about."

"But you were. And I...blamed you for not saving him."

He looked away. "You had every right."

"While you were bleeding too? Could you even stay conscious after a wound like that?"

"Until they loaded me in the ambulance. Then I'm told I passed out." Noah paused. "I kept waking up in the hospital, asking about him, then drifting off, but nobody would say how he was. It wasn't until a few days later I learned he was gone." Noah took a breath. "I would have given my life for him if I could. He had you and Teddie and your whole lives ahead of you. He loved you so much. In a few brief minutes, that guy took all that away, and I couldn't..."

"Of course you couldn't stop him. I was

wrong." Kate traced a finger over the long line of the scar. "Tell me more about this."

"I'd rather not."

"Please. I need to know."

Noah's voice quavered. "The guy got Rob first. Just exploded out of a short alley near the restaurant where we'd eaten dinner. We'd had a great time that night. Rob was more relaxed than he'd been in months. He said the pasta was the best he'd ever had, and we'd killed a good bottle of wine. Talked about the company, about you… We talked so long we closed the place. Who would have ever thought we'd take a few steps down a normally busy street in the middle of Manhattan and in those few seconds, it would be over for him? For the two of you—and Teddie without his dad?"

Kate waited for him to speak again, her finger retracing his scar.

Noah shivered. "I don't pretend to be a brave man. I had one chance to grab that knife—but missed. Rob was on the ground and I didn't think. I just moved. I was whipping off my belt to make a tourniquet when that jerk hit me from behind. The knife punctured my right lung. It was touch and go for a while, the doctors said, but here I am." He shook his head. "And Rob's not. I'll be sorry for that the rest of my life."

She'd once accused him of still being alive while Rob was dead. He heard her take a trembling breath. Then, without warning, like another, gentler assault, she pressed her lips to his spine. "Please don't feel guilty. It's me who's sorry. I had no right to blame you, to resent you for what that person did. You tried, Noah. You did try to save Rob. I'll never forget that."

Noah decided he must be crazy. But the warmth of her mouth on his sensitive skin—which reminded him every day of that attack, of Rob—was his undoing. Slowly, Noah eased away, then turned, and Kate was in his arms.

He'd lost her years ago to his best friend. He'd never told her how he felt. He wouldn't tell her now, even when it seemed she might forgive him after all. It was too much. Too soon, despite the years he'd spent alone or with other women, including Margot, who'd never quite measured up to Kate's standard for Noah.

In this one moment, she was his dream come true.

He held her gaze, speaking without words,

before he drew her closer, lowered his head and, for the first—and possibly last—time, kissed her.

CHAPTER SEVENTEEN

FOR ONE BRIEF SECOND, Kate couldn't react to his kiss. Noah had taken her by surprise, and her emotions were too fresh, too new to make sense of them just now. She knew only one thing: he hadn't left her husband lying on the pavement, bleeding to death. He'd nearly sacrificed his own life to help Rob. He'd cared about her and Teddie. He wasn't guilty.

Yet even those thoughts would have to wait for later.

Kate didn't pull away. She looped her arms around his neck and held on, opening to him as Noah deepened the kiss. She gave herself up to this unexpected moment, savored the sensation of his lips on hers, his strong arms holding her until, finally, Noah began to ease back. "I shouldn't have done that," he said.

She gazed up at him, remembering the press of her lips to the scar that must still pain him. It was she who should feel guilty.

Kate took a step backward. "You're right.

We shouldn't have. Noah, I'm a widow. A single mom, not someone like your friend Margot—with whom," Kate reminded him, "you're already in a relationship."

"We broke up. Last night."

Kate blinked. "Oh. I hope that had nothing to do with her visit to my barn. It was obvious she considered me to be some kind of threat."

"No, that had been coming for some time, really, and because she had an agenda I disagreed with, and…I didn't love her enough to make things work."

"But where does that leave me?" She shouldn't have initiated that kiss, even in sympathy. "I don't want you to assume I'm looking for…what? A quick fling until you leave the WB?" But, no. She'd also felt that zing of awareness with Noah that she'd thought she'd seen earlier in Meg with Gabe, and that did indeed complicate matters.

"I would never assume that, but I like you, Kate—I always have." Then Noah clamped his mouth shut as if he shouldn't say more. Neither should she, but she couldn't seem to stop herself.

"Even if I wanted to start something with you, how could that possibly end?"

His mouth tightened. "We don't need to figure everything out tonight."

"Maybe you don't, but I have Teddie to consider."

At that instant, he called up the stairs. "Mom! Mr. Bodine! We're eating."

"See what I mean?" But she had to laugh a little, and when Noah did, too, the crinkles at the corners of his eyes made him just too appealing. "It's hard to even get a moment to myself, much less for us to become...what?"

"Friends? We could start there again," he said with a winsome look that turned her heart. Kate had also entertained that notion before. "That's pretty simple, even basic, right? What do you say?"

A small voice called again, "Mom! Come on, I'm hungry!"

"Teddie, I'm on my way." She ran a light finger across Noah's cheek. "That is life at Sweetheart Ranch. My life anyway."

"Maybe, where you and I are concerned, you need to change things up a little." He nipped at her finger, then gave her a rueful look. "Ah, Kate."

He didn't have to say the rest. He knew that as soon as Willow came home, he would be free to leave. Kate and Teddie would stay on Sweetheart Ranch because she and Noah led opposite lives on different sides of the country. She was still an everyday cowgirl in jeans, and he was a cybersecurity expert in a three-piece suit, striding the concrete canyons of the city. She'd always known how different they were, but until today, blaming Noah had kept her safe.

Still. It had been more than a year since she'd been embraced by any male except Teddie—eighteen months, really, since Rob had left home, and on those few weekends when her husband had come back, they had quarreled. Bitterly, toward the end, and far from the ideal marriage she had wanted. The last time, one of them had uttered the word *divorce*.

Kate had spent the past year protecting herself and Teddie, but the warm gleam now in Noah's eyes told her clearly that he wanted more. What if she did too? What kind of longer-term arrangement could she and Noah work out? That didn't seem likely. She wanted to weep for him, for herself.

Sweetheart Ranch was her future, and Teddie's. Not a new relationship that might, in the end, hurt everyone.

"WELL, MY," NOAH'S mother said, looking way too pleased. "I never saw that coming."

Noah leaned against the kitchen door frame and stared at the floor. Jean had just mopped it, and the tile glistened in the sun coming through the skylight and the window above the sink. It hadn't taken long for him, because of Kate's reaction, to regret what he'd done yesterday in her bathroom—only a day after he'd ended things with Margot.

"Kissing her wasn't the wisest thing I ever did."

"And why not?"

He should have known what his mom's response would be, yet Noah hadn't been able to keep from telling her. Another error, perhaps, on his part. He hadn't thought beforehand; he'd blurted out the words.

"I know what I said—we should start with friendship, see where that led, but I can't make her any promises. I don't live here, Mom."

"Planes fly both east and west, you know. People have long-distance relationships all the time, and who knows, indeed, where that might lead? Situations change. So do people. Take you and Margot, for instance."

Noah had said much the same himself.

"Yeah, but Kate's not most people. She's planted at Sweetheart Ranch as if her feet are in cement." He couldn't see her pulling free, bending, going anywhere else, even entertaining the possibility of a future together.

"She's still grieving, Noah. So is little Teddie. But she didn't know the truth before. Now she does." Jean set the mop in the corner. "I've made no secret of my opinion that you and Kate would be grand together. Forget the difference in your lifestyles or where you both live. You complement each other. Yes, she's something of a recluse these days, but that could be temporary. Who knows? By this time next year, she could be flying with you to London—"

"Which reminds me. You need to renew your passport. As soon as we open J&B's branch there, you can see for yourself."

"It's a great city, but I'd rather you show Kate the sights. Can you imagine Teddie's joy at riding on the London Eye?"

Noah could envision exactly that, touring them around, eating in his favorite restaurant, taking the city's famous black cabs and red double-decker buses just for fun. Seeing Kate in his apartment, laughing as Teddie jabbed the buttons on Noah's private elevator. Having wine on the balcony with Kate after Teddie was in bed, holding hands as they took in the sparkling nighttime view. Kissing her again. Lots more.

His mom continued with her positive spin on the topic. "Kate's a fine person, warm-hearted, loyal—"

Inwardly, he groaned. "To her husband's memory most of all."

"—a wonderful mother. My grandchildren couldn't have a better one."

"I'll leave that coming generation to Willow and Cody."

His mother sent him an exasperated look. "Just when I've gotten my youngest married, Zach is engaged and you finally make a move with Kate, you dig in your heels. What am I going to do with you?" She hesitated. "The obstacles you mention are not fixed in stone. If you want to work things out with her, first convince her that being friends is only that initial step—then trust in fate. She has forgiven you, hasn't she? For something you weren't guilty of in the first place? The rest is minor."

"Is it? I carry the proof of that accident, Mom."

"Kate saw your scar, and that changed her view."

"She'd be seeing it every day if we did take our 'relationship' further."

She arched an eyebrow. "You didn't seem to feel that way yesterday."

"And I shouldn't have told you."

Jean crossed the kitchen to slip her arms around him. "Noah, the one thing that does really matter is your feelings for Kate. Maybe you should tell her, not focus on that kiss and let her think that's all it was."

"I don't think she's ready." If she ever would be.

"She might simply need a nudge."

But with his sister due home, the reminder that he'd always planned to leave here was sharp. Maybe he would do them both a favor if he tried to forget Kate. That thought hadn't left his mind before he rejected it. But if only they could have—what? He'd seen her reaction to his scar, felt her arms around him, her lips on his skin. Compassion, that's all it had likely been. An adjustment to her opinion of the accident and his role in Rob's death.

"Mom, you're dreaming again," he said at last.

"Am I? Or are you trying to wiggle out

of something that could be the best thing to ever happen to you?" She might have said: *As you did years ago when you left the WB*.

Noah couldn't answer that. He eased from her embrace, then left the kitchen, silently vowing to get back to business—his own future—instead.

Still, he felt a definite pang in the area where his heart should be.

But his mother was right about one thing: he should at least talk to Kate before he left.

"AND LOOK WHAT has already happened." Coffee mug in hand, after she had told Meg about the kiss she'd shared with Noah, Kate waited for her aunt's reaction. When that didn't come, she said, "I betrayed Rob's memory with the very man who took him from me." The words, said perhaps in self-protection, rang hollow. She'd seen his scar.

"You still believe that?"

Kate frowned. "Well, not after I heard the rest of the story. But I know I made the right decision to avoid any deeper connection with Noah."

"But Teddie likes him. I do too," Meg added.

Kate couldn't disagree. She liked him herself, more than she should.

Meg paused. "I think you're getting ahead of yourself. Noah asked you to be friends, not to marry him."

She had a point. Maybe it was only Kate who'd briefly imagined more.

"Our lives—mine and Teddie's—were completely upended when Rob was killed. Teddie hasn't processed that loss yet—"

"But he's starting to, Kate. Yesterday, Noah was a huge part of that."

She took a sip of her now-cold coffee. "I'm grateful, but I should have ended the kiss."

"Teddie needs a father, and you could use a man to shoulder some of the burden you've been carrying."

"I'm perfectly capable of running Sweetheart Ranch. I'm sure Noah can't wait to leave the WB again."

"How can you say that? Take the foal, which Noah could have left with you, then washed his hands of the whole business. Instead, he's been here every day when he could have sent the WB's foreman. Doesn't it occur to you that he came over to see you too? I cannot believe how dense you're being."

"No denser than you seem to be about Mac. Tell me. Do you or do you not keep one eye on your cell or the landline phone every night? When he doesn't call, you should see your face."

Meg looked forlorn. "That is absolutely false. But in case you didn't hear, he's planning to make good on his idle threat to come see me. I doubt he'll actually show up, but if he does, I will set him straight. More likely, he'll jet off to Cairo or Shanghai, instead."

"Mac's coming here? When?"

"He didn't say. All I got was, 'You should have answered your phone more often.' He blows in and out of my life—or did—whenever he pleases. See what I mean? If you'd been there when I...had my miscarriage, you'd understand. I will never go through something like that again, certainly not with a man whose first thought in the morning, his last at night, must still be about his next flight."

"I didn't know you were a mind reader."

"He wasn't even there!"

Kate paused with a sympathetic look. "I know how painful that was for you—"

"No, you don't. You can't. By then, there was nothing left—if there ever had been."

She took a breath. "That's how I still feel. About him."

"Do you? Then tell me I wasn't seeing things yesterday with you and Gabe. If what you say is true, you have a wide-open opportunity to make a new life for yourself." Her voice shook. "It's different for me. I need to stay focused on Sweetheart Ranch and Teddie. We've had too many losses. I can't think of anything beyond friendship with Noah—even that will only cause more heartbreak when he leaves."

"Is that so?"

"I don't have the same chance you could with Gabe or…Mac. If that were me, I'd throw my arms around Rob and try again."

"You have the chance," Meg murmured. "You just won't take it."

"My husband is dead! Yours is not."

"I mean with Noah. How long are you going to play the grieving widow? There's more out there, Kate, for you *and* Teddie."

Kate couldn't believe she'd said that. *The grieving widow.* "I'm not going anywhere," she said, "except down to the barn."

As she started toward the back door, she heard it open, then close again, and footsteps crossed the kitchen floor. Kate stopped and Bandit began to bark.

"Evening, ladies," said a rich male voice they both recognized. And, having kept his promise, Jonathan "Mac" McClaren stepped into the room.

CHAPTER EIGHTEEN

ALL AT ONCE, chaos had descended on the normally peaceful house.

"Bandit, stop," Meg sharply reprimanded the dog. He was jumping, wriggling, his tail going a mile a minute. "What are you doing here?" she asked Mac, certain her heart would burst from her chest.

"Just got back from Dubai. Told you I was coming."

"You didn't say when."

"Yes, I did. Guess you chose not to hear me."

How typical of him to put the blame on her, but Bandit didn't seem to share her opinion. Mac bent down to pat the dancing shepherd, then stood again. Meg continued to stare at her ex-husband. "I thought you'd finally given up."

"You hoped," he said with the smile that had once captured her heart, then shattered it into broken glass. Gently, he disengaged

Bandit from his chest, where the dog, up on his hind legs now, was pushing against him.

Meg couldn't help but note that solid wall of muscle. She had to give him credit: he kept himself in shape. In fact, he looked great, relaxed and well, except for his eyes. Now she could see regret and, worse, a bit of hope in their dark brown depths. "Some people know when to cut their losses," she said, sounding weaker than she'd planned.

He set down his duffel bag. "Maybe we're not a loss."

"Oh, but we were."

Kate, standing next to Meg, made a small noise. "Listen, guys. I'm, uh, going to check the horses. Teddie's already in the barn with Gabe. Give you some privacy to talk." She moved to hug Mac. "You can have the spare room."

"He's not staying here," Meg said. "He can find a motel. For one night."

"Nonsense." Kate tried to send her a look. "We have plenty of room."

Mac waited until Kate left before he spoke. "All right, you want to kick this off by rehashing the past, we will." He took her hand in his warm grasp. "I admit, we went through some rough times—my travel, the endless renovations on the house, those long separations…the baby," he added softly. "After that, things fell apart, but they can be mended."

She pulled away. "You always were a romantic. At marriage, however, you flunked."

"Meg, don't try to tell me you're blameless. You knew when we married that I'd be gone a lot. Too much at times, maybe, yeah, but other people make that work."

Reminded of her quarrel with Kate, Meg didn't respond. He had no idea how empty their half-finished house, in which Mac still lived, had felt whenever he was away. Or did he by now? She never wanted to feel that lonely again, that lost inside herself.

"I wanted to save whatever we still had then," he said, "but you packed up and left. How do you think I felt when I got that message on my phone?"

"Kate needed me. She'd just lost Rob—"

"Yes, she had, but you didn't come back," he insisted. "I'm still rattling around in that big house by myself. Everything I see— the new bathroom, the garden, your dream kitchen, our bed—is a reminder of what we could have kept together. You know what? Kate could have handled her loss, as dreadful as that was. She's a strong person." He thought for a moment. "Or did you think you could find the child we never had—here, in Teddie?"

Meg gasped, as she had when she first saw him in the doorway like a ghost from her previous life, the one that didn't suit her anymore. She needed to take Kate's advice, start that new life. "I like Sweetheart Ranch. I always did. Maybe my mistake was in thinking I could love Chicago."

"Love. me," he said, those two words sounding more like a question.

"Mac." Her heart twisted at the tone of his voice. In spite of his normally brash exterior, the way he had always overwhelmed her arguments, he did sound lost too.

He ran a hand over the nape of his neck. "Can we argue later? I got up at three this morning to catch the six a.m. flight from O'Hare. Right now, I feel like the worst case of jet lag ever." He had, after all, flown halfway around the world and back before he hopped another plane to see her.

"Am I supposed to feel sorry for you? Like always, you made your choice."

"Come on, Meg. Bend a little. It won't hurt—much."

She thought for a moment before she gave in. "Well, since you've come all this way—uninvited, I might add—it seems we do need to settle this, once and for all. We both need closure."

He shook his head, overhead light streaming through his dark hair. "How you can manage to turn this into some kind of business deal or another version of our divorce agreement beats me. But whatever," he said. "Is that your best and final?"

"Yes." She certainly wasn't about to renegotiate their broken marriage. It didn't exist.

He turned toward the stairs. "Then I'm going to try to get some sleep. I don't know if I'm in the desert or on the Kansas plains. If it's midnight or noon."

"Try noon," she said and couldn't suppress a half smile. "You know where the spare room is."

As soon as he hit the first step, her smile faded. She'd never intended to see him again, yet Meg could smell the familiar scent of his citrusy aftershave, the cold, fresh air from outdoors that clung to his coat, still feel the warmth of his touch, see the hurt in his eyes. She'd been afraid of this.

Maybe she wasn't that different from Kate—and her obvious confusion about Noah.

If Meg had moved on, at the moment, it didn't feel that way.

NOAH HAD FINISHED his chores for the day and was heading for the house at dinnertime when a quick toot of the horn had him stepping back out of the way. He didn't recognize the vehicle, which braked to a stop.

The driver's window rolled down. "Hey, Noah," Cody Jones called.

Noah's sister didn't say a word. From the passenger seat, Willow merely stared at him, as if she hadn't known Noah would be here. She sat, stone faced, when Cody got out of the car.

Tall and with wheat-blond hair, he stuck out a hand. "Glad to see you, man. Thanks for taking over while we were gone."

Noah thought of pointing out that he'd had little choice but didn't.

This was the moment he'd been waiting for. He should be turning cartwheels in his head. Instead, he folded his arms and watched Willow fuss with her bag, then finally emerge from the car. "Well," she said, looking him up and down, "if it isn't my wayward big brother."

Noah's gaze skimmed her from flowing blond hair to cornflower blue eyes. "You look good, kiddo." And happy. Her skin had a light tan, probably acquired on their cruise, and she glowed like the newlywed she was, deeply in love with her husband. In Noah's mind, their marriage seemed preordained, as if she and Cody had wed long ago before their painful breakup then reunion. "Have a nice time in Savannah?"

"And everywhere else," Cody put in, an arm slung around her shoulders. "I finally had to tell my girl we needed to get home."

"Not for your sake," she said to Noah.

Cody didn't react to her obvious displeasure. "Next week, if the ground isn't hard as rock, our builders should start on the new house."

"The barn too," Willow said, "but the outdoor ring will have to wait until spring."

"It's been a hard winter so far." Noah gestured at the snow on the ground. He heard a bellow from the pasture, where the WB's best bull made some protest. One of the horses whinnied in answer. "Mom tells me you two have already started your own training business."

That had been Willow's dream since she was indeed a kid. Cody's, too, he supposed. Their first bond had been over horses. "We've been using the WB's facilities so far." Cody glanced toward the house. "Zach here yet?"

"Haven't seen him since the day I arrived."

"Finally," Willow murmured.

Okay. This was his cue to apologize when Noah, who'd struggled to find the necessary words for Margot, didn't know how to start again. What he'd done to Willow was basically unforgivable. What could he say that might heal the breach between him and the baby sister he adored?

Noah would have preferred to do this with just the two of them here, but she obviously needed her husband's support.

"Willow, I'm sorry I missed out on the best day of your life. If I could, I'd turn back the clock, do it all different." He tried to gauge her expression but failed there too. Cody had pulled her closer, his lips against her hair.

Noah's voice cracked. "I should have been home to walk you down the aisle with Zach on your other side, but instead I was on a plane to London when you said your vows with Cody. With the time change, and the mess with the new branch office there, I only realized what the date was when your wedding was already over."

He heard tears in her voice. "You didn't even phone."

Later that night—or rather, the next morning—when he'd landed overseas, Noah had tried but failed to get a good-enough signal for the call, and when he tried again later, she hadn't answered. Perhaps she'd been on her flight to New York by then, but the damage had been done. Their few brief texts while she was on her honeymoon hadn't broken the ice.

"Tell me what I can do to make this better."

She rolled her eyes. "Really? You snap your fingers, and everything will be fine again? Noah, you *hurt* me."

"Believe me, I didn't mean to, and if it takes the rest of my life, I'll do anything—give anything—to make that up to you."

As a child, Willow had worshipped him, and whenever her world went wrong, she'd come to Noah, taking shelter in his arms from a breakup with her best friend or from their father's wrath. Now she leaned against Cody in silence.

"I know. I really am the prodigal son." Noah deserved whatever punishment she chose. "Let me have it, Willow. Give me your worst."

"Right now, I'd like to brain you with an iron skillet for missing my big show." She moved a little, glanced up at him, then down again. "That is, after I remember *my* manners. Thank you for the gifts you sent," she said stiffly. "You were too generous."

"Never that," he said. Noah had given them a full set of the sterling silver flatware pattern she'd chosen and a large check.

"It may be a while before I actually send out thank-you notes." Then she surprised him. "But after another whole year, my goodness, you're actually here again."

Cody laughed a little. "Man, you're in for it. I almost pity you." Then he sobered. "Just for the record, Noah, don't ever hurt her like that again."

Willow gazed at Cody, her love for him in her eyes. "That's my man." The tense set of her shoulders had relaxed, but she didn't smile. "You're not off the hook," she told

Noah, adding, as Cody had said, "Just for the record."

"I don't expect to be."

He also didn't expect what happened next. Willow suddenly moved, Cody's arm slipped from her shoulders and she slid into Noah's embrace as if she'd never left. "Welcome home."

He swallowed, hard. "I should be saying that to you." And he repeated those very words.

"I do love you, Noah," Willow murmured. "You big dummy."

While he was digesting that, grateful that she would save any further punishment for later, the front door opened, and with a glad cry, their mother charged down the porch steps, then flung herself at him and Willow in a three-way hug. Cody stood back, grinning.

Noah's sister was home. He was free to go.

Which didn't please him as much as he'd thought it would.

THE NEXT NIGHT, under a leaden sky that matched her spirits, Kate drove toward the WB. She couldn't say Noah's invitation had come as a surprise, but she hadn't expected to dread what was surely ahead and had been from the day he'd stepped off the plane in Kansas City.

Teddie drummed his legs against his car seat, looking out as she turned in at the gates. "Mommy, are we going to the WB?"

"We're having dinner with Mr. Bodine and his family." Kate hadn't told him earlier what the occasion was, or his excitement would have been off the charts before a big letdown.

"Yay!"

"Be on your best behavior, Bunny." There was no way to prepare him for what would happen later. Maybe she should have come alone, yet the invitation had included Teddie.

He made a face that Kate saw in her rearview mirror. "I hope I don't have to eat stuff like mushy peas or 'sparagus."

"You will eat what's put on your plate."

Teddie heaved a sigh. "Did you bring me a snack—I could eat in the barn."

"Maybe you could not."

Her smile was forced as she parked the truck. Tonight, she felt sure, would be goodbye. Willow was home, Noah had told her on the phone. There was no further reason for him to stay, and after they'd managed to make their peace over Rob's death, for her to want him to. Even to consider friendship again themselves. And she worried about Teddie. Better to keep things light and hope for the best.

They left the pickup and went up the porch steps. Noah answered the door, his smile looking as tight as Kate's had been.

He put a hand on her shoulder, and Kate had a flash memory of his touch in the spare room's bathroom, the taste of his mouth. Just friendship? "Come on in. Hope you brought ear plugs—things are noisy." He bent down to Teddie's level. "Hey, short stuff. You up for a nice steak?"

They exchanged a complex series of hand signals in greeting. "Did the cow live on the WB?" Teddie wanted to know.

Noah shot Kate a look that said, *Did I just make a mistake here?* "Yeah, it did. Finest beef in Kansas except for Sweetheart Ranch."

That didn't bother Teddie who was a ranch kid, as Kate had been—and after that she didn't have time to worry about anything else. Like honored guests, they were drawn into the circle of the Bodine family, plunged into the noisy atmosphere Noah had warned her about. She couldn't help but feel at home. Jean was famous for her hospitality, and dinner was delicious. So was dessert, and Teddie had two helpings of apple pie. Kate had little appetite.

The conversation later in the living room flowed, mostly about Willow and Cody's honeymoon. The newlyweds showed pictures of their side trips to Savannah, Charleston and Hilton Head, and Kate, without wanting to, envied their happiness.

"You're off to a great start," she told Willow. "That honeymoon, the new house, your business…"

"Pretty exciting. I keep pinching myself. How did I ever land this guy after all?" She sat close to Cody on the sofa, her head on his shoulder. They were holding hands.

Kate's first days with Rob had been idyllic, too, and she'd thought that was forever. Now, instead of wrestling with his father on the rug, Teddie was playing chess with Noah, their heads close together. She knew better than to wish for anything more.

"Booked my tickets to LaGuardia," he'd said in an aside during a rare quiet moment before dinner. "Leaving first thing tomorrow." Then he hadn't continued, as if he, too, was reluctant to have his interlude at the WB end.

He glanced up now from the game and caught Kate's eye. Her son had never played before but had quickly caught on to the strategy as he had once with Gabe about some video game. "Teddie, you're a tough opponent." The two shook hands, and Teddie crowed about his victory. Noah said, "Mom, there must be a reward of some kind for this boy—hot cocoa? With marshmallows?"

Jean rose to take Teddie's hand. "Come with me. I may have a cookie or two left."

Willow and Cody stood too. "Think we'll wander down to the barn, say goodnight to the horses. Those few that were here when we left on our honeymoon. I'm afraid they will have gotten lazy but with Zach away too they haven't had training." Their ploy seemed so obvious that Kate guessed Noah had asked for time alone with her earlier. Kate hugged Willow. She had missed her friend.

"It's good to have you home. Let's get together soon."

Willow looked astonished. Kate didn't often leave home to socialize. "Oh, and I imagine the Girls will be after me about the next meeting."

"Count on it, Willow."

Cody leaned down to kiss Kate's cheek. "Thanks for coming tonight."

"'Night, Cody. Congratulations again. You've got a great woman."

"Don't I know it." He and Willow went out the door, hand in hand, and Kate's throat tightened. She knew what Noah was going to say.

"Not much time left," he began, then moved to sit beside her on the sofa.

"You must be eager to get back to your business. The real one, I mean."

His gaze held hers. "Hasn't been a hardship, though, here at the WB."

Kate attempted another smile. "What am I hearing? A cowboy after all?"

"Not really but being back here has shown me what I've missed." He reached for her hand. "Kate, that includes you, and about that friendship... I can't leave without telling you what else I already feel." He paused. "I wouldn't be honest if I didn't let you know that I've had...feelings for you for a long time. Before you even started seeing Rob. Way back you were too young for me to do anything about that, and later, because he and I were friends, I sure couldn't poach on his territory. So I let that go—you—and I wish I hadn't."

"Don't say any more, Noah."

"I have to. I think…we could actually make this thing work. See where it goes beyond friendship if—when—the time is right."

"I can hardly say I don't care about you, too, after that kiss we shared. But I never imagined how you felt…and I did marry Rob. You'd already moved east then while our lives remained here."

He said it for her: "Until I made him that offer he didn't refuse." She had forgiven him for the attack but not for that.

"Yes, and nothing was ever the same between Rob and me."

"I'm sorry, Kate, but he grabbed that chance with both hands and didn't regret his choice." Noah hesitated. "He wasn't happy at Sweetheart Ranch. Surely you knew that."

"I didn't know."

"Or didn't want to admit you did?" Noah pushed on. "The money worries I mentioned before were only part of that. By nature, Rob wasn't a cowboy any more than I am."

She withdrew her hand from his. "He certainly gave a good impression of one."

"He did a good job, but he'd grown up in town, and he stayed on that ranch for you until—for his own well-being, his future and your family's—he couldn't stay any longer."

"That's untrue."

"Is it? Think. Why else would he change his whole life from country to city? That was an enormous shift. His greatest regret was that you refused to join him in New York, to bring Teddie there. That tore Rob apart. In fact, the night of the attack, we touched on his quitting because he couldn't see any way to keep you otherwise."

A chill ran down Kate's spine. "I hope you're not saying it's my fault he left for New York. I was blindsided by his decision. I needed time to adjust—to decide— and when I did, I couldn't make that move. Goodness, if I needed proof that my life is here, there's that wedding I attended in Manhattan. I couldn't wait to get back to Sweetheart Ranch."

"Which you haven't left since. I don't think it's that simple." He held her gaze. "Kate, you can't hide there forever. There's a larger world—"

"Your world. Look what that did to Rob."

His eyes darkened. "Look at Teddie now.

You're doing him a disservice by holding him back from those bigger adventures we talked about. Someday he won't thank you for that. He won't be four years old forever."

Kate went rigid. "I accused you once of co-opting my son. It seems I wasn't wrong. You're trying to do that now."

"I'm not. But I do care about him. I care about you. What are you so afraid of?"

That was easy, but she wasn't about to share. Rob's death, she'd vowed, would be the last tragedy in their lives. She couldn't risk Teddie's safety, her own peace or either of their hearts. "I'm not willing to gamble on Teddie's security."

"How does our relationship affect that?"

Kate waved one hand. "Your 'larger' life isn't ours. You'll keep on flying to London, or wherever, just like Meg's ex does, expanding your business with J&B, but we belong here—and this is where we'll stay. I can't see any other path, Noah."

"I didn't ask you to move to New York." *Not yet.* "But in the meantime—"

Teddie burst back into the room with Jean. "Mom! I had six marshmallows in my hot chocolate! Big ones!"

She could barely respond except to hold

him close. "He'll probably be up all night," she told Jean.

Noah's mother glanced between Kate and Noah. Her expression clearly said, *Is something wrong?*

Kate looked around for their jackets. "It's going to snow again. Nothing new, but I was just telling Noah I'd like to get home before the storm moves in." With that small lie, she made her quick goodbyes, blinked as Teddie hugged Jean, then turned toward the door with his hand in hers. Noah was right behind them.

"I'll walk you out." At her truck, Teddie climbed into his car seat, his attention focused on the complex series of restraints. "Kate, we haven't finished—"

"I'm afraid we have."

He waited while she checked the seat, as she always did. "Before you go, I need to speak to him. I wouldn't want to leave tomorrow without letting Teddie know."

"When we get home, I can tell him." *After you're out of his life.*

"I think that should come from me. He trusts me and that's important."

Kate had to admire Noah. Not every man would be as sensitive to a child's needs. If he didn't say the words himself, Teddie might resent him. Surely, no matter who told him, he would grieve. She'd always known that.

"All right, then. Please keep it simple."

She stepped back while Noah spoke quietly to Teddie. She watched her son's face begin to crumple, watched Noah lean in over the car seat to awkwardly embrace him. Teddie gripped Noah's shoulders. When Noah pulled away, he looked broken, as he had the night they'd talked about angels. His voice was tight. "See you soon, short stuff."

As Noah gently closed the door, Teddie was crying. "You can't go!"

Kate had no words. She merely shook her head at Noah, who did the same.

"I made things worse, didn't I?"

"No, you were right, Noah. He did need to hear that from you." She watched her breath frost in the cold air and huddled deeper into her parka. More snow was coming, all right. She should thank him for all he'd done, for his kindness to Teddie, for the way he'd treated her. She couldn't speak. With her throat shut, Teddie still sobbing and maternal guilt twisting her insides, she got into the truck and drove off.

"He doesn't have to go, Mommy!" Teddie wailed. "I won't let him!"

"Yes, he does, Bunny. I'm sorry too."

In her rearview mirror Noah watched them until she reached the gate and turned toward Sweetheart Ranch.

CHAPTER NINETEEN

IN THE MIDDLE of the night, Noah jolted awake. He'd only been dozing, wishing he hadn't made Teddie cry, but someone was pounding now on the WB's door downstairs. His heart racing, he jumped out of bed, fumbled into his clothes, then ran down the steps. His mother, wearing a fleecy robe, followed after him. "What's happened, Noah?"

"I don't know. No good news comes at two a.m."

Expecting to see the sheriff—had something happened to Cass and Zach?—he flung open the door. Instead, Kate stood there, wild eyed, her face bluish-white in the overhead porch light. Snow sifted down on her shoulders. "Noah, is Teddie with you?"

"No."

Her face fell. "I went to check on him, and his bed was empty. I looked all over the house, but he wasn't anywhere." She gulped in a breath. "I—I didn't know where else to turn."

"I'm glad you chose me." Noah drew her inside. She was trembling, not merely from the cold. Jean hugged her, then rushed toward the kitchen to put on a pot of coffee. No one was going to sleep until Teddie was found.

"Earlier, when I put him to bed, he was still crying. I sat with him until I thought he'd finally fallen asleep. Then a few minutes ago…" Kate couldn't go on. "I prayed he might be here—although how would he cross our land by himself in this storm?— but obviously he's not."

"He can't have gone far." Noah called up the stairs. "Cody! Willow! Get up. We need you down here."

Cody was already standing on the landing. He took in Kate's panicked face. "I heard," he said, buttoning his shirt. "I'll fire up the Gators. Willow's getting dressed."

Noah glanced at his mother, who'd come back into the room. "There are five of us," he said, "but we need more. Mom, you'll stay to help coordinate the search. Call down to the bunkhouse. Calvin's not here but you can rouse the other hands." He turned to Cody. "Forget the Gators. Have you looked outside?

We're supposed to get another foot of snow tonight." And there was still plenty on the ground from previous storms.

Kate's teeth chattered. "The road's nearly impassable. I slid down our drive and then on yours, so the trucks may not be much help either."

"Then we'll ride horseback."

Jean said, "I'll tell the boys to saddle up."

Minutes later, they all rode out of the barn-yard, shoulders hunched against the icy wind and driving snow. "This is worse than the time we got caught in that first blizzard," Noah shouted to Kate, who, on Willow's horse Silver, was probably wishing she'd brought her own more familiar mare. "We'll find him, Kate."

She drew up beside him as Cody unlatched the gate into the near pasture. Willow had taken the four-wheel drive, hoping to cover the distance on the snow-covered road be-tween their two ranches, then, if necessary, head into town. What if Teddie tried to reach his friend Seth's house there? Cody on Diva, his paint mustang, and four other cowboys on horses from the ranch string had set off to make a grid search of the WB. Riding Zach's stallion Midnight, Noah went with Kate toward Sweetheart Ranch.

They rode close together, legs occasionally brushing. The wind howled. The snow came down horizontally into their faces, like that day in the rental car.

"I probably checked him half a dozen times tonight," Kate said. "I knew how upset he was. I should have guessed he'd do something like this—run away."

But being unhappy didn't necessarily lead to leaving home. Except, maybe, in Noah's case too many years ago. He had a flashback of his last argument with his dad, then packing his bags. *I'll show you.* "Was it because of what I said?"

Kate shook her head. "Teddie didn't blame you. He blamed me. He said I'd made you leave—like I did Rob."

"Ah, Kate. He's a kid. Teddie has his own logic, but he couldn't mean that."

They picked their way across the frozen ground, unable to see ten feet beyond their flashlight beams. Her voice fell and Noah strained to hear her next words. "He said—he'd never see you again either."

His gut tightened. Teddie had obviously come to view him as a stand-in father. He was afraid that, like Rob, Noah would never come back. "I should have found a better way to assure him that I'll see him again." Though he and Kate hadn't settled that for themselves.

She gave a dry sob. "He thinks you're going to…die too."

Noah leaned over to brush tears from her cheeks. "Don't cry. You'll freeze."

Noah's face already felt stiff. His heavy parka didn't quite keep out the worsening cold, and even Midnight's hide shivered under Noah. He wouldn't say this to Kate, but how much longer could a small boy survive in this? Where could he have gone? And how? Certainly not on foot. He wouldn't make it from his house to the road before hypothermia set in.

"Kate, did you see prints around the barn?"

"Footprints?"

"Hoofprints," he suggested. "Was his pony in its stall?"

"I didn't think to check on Spencer. I should have. I left Meg at the house in case Teddie came home and just jumped in my truck."

"Then our best bet is he's with that pony."

A quick call to Gabe on Kate's SAT phone

confirmed Noah's theory. Spencer was missing too. They were almost to the boundary fence a bit later when Noah spied a tiny figure on horseback in the distance.

"There!" he yelled, and then, "Teddie!"

It couldn't be anyone else.

As he called out, Noah saw the little boy shift in the saddle, then fall sideways. He tumbled off the pony into the deepening snow. Noah expected Spencer to turn tail and run for the warmer barn, but he didn't. The gelding stood over Teddie as if to shelter him, nudging him with his nose. The two had obviously jumped the fence from Kate's side, successfully this time, even without a gap to shoot for.

"Teddie!" Kate kept shouting as she spurred Silver into an awkward gait as fast as the mare could travel in this snow.

Noah followed on Midnight, the stallion fighting the bit, but Noah stayed in the saddle. Kate reached her boy first, slid off the horse, then gathered Teddie into her arms. She laid her cheek against his head and wept harder than she had before.

"Bunny, you scared me...scared both of us."

"It's dark out here," Teddie said, shaking

all over. Ice crusted his jacket and hood, his mittens and even his eyelashes.

"Where on earth were you going, Teddie Bear?"

"To see N-N—Mr. Bo-dine."

Noah dismounted beside her. "Let's get him home, Kate. And call his doctor."

"What if Sawyer can't get through? And the clinic's closed. We'd have to take him to Farrier General—"

"Sawyer will try. In the meantime, we need to get Teddie's core temperature up."

She didn't seem to hear anything he said. She wouldn't let go of Teddie, even when Noah tried to pry him from her. "Let me carry him. Midnight's bigger, stronger than the horse you're on."

Kate wouldn't agree. Finally, not to waste time, he lifted Teddie into her arms on Silver, and Noah remounted Midnight with Spencer trailing behind to the house at Sweetheart Ranch. There, Noah carried Teddie inside, where Meg took over, murmuring soft reassurances that everything would be all right. A man Noah didn't recognize stood behind her.

But any introductions could wait for later. Noah left Kate and Teddie to be cared for, took the Bodine horses to the barn; cooled, then put them in empty stalls; blanketed them with the spares he found and filled water buckets. No one was riding any more tonight. He'd worry about getting home later.

He stopped to visit briefly with Lancelot. The colt looked stronger and had gained some weight, which he was glad to see before he left town. Then he pulled out his cell phone to call the WB. "Teddie's safe," he reported. "Mom, let the others know, okay? He's home now."

"Thank heaven. Willow's here already. The road was empty. The hands are riding in as we speak to get warm and regroup. I'll tell them the good news." Her voice quavered. "I'm glad you found that little imp. Give him a kiss from me."

"I will." And one from Noah too.

He hung up, then went back to the house, poured himself a mug of the hot coffee Meg had prepared. She informed him that Sawyer McCord was on his way. Then Noah went upstairs to make sure Teddie was all right.

About Kate, he wasn't certain.

Tonight—Teddie's escape—had pulled her out of her safe space. Frightened her.

He didn't suppose she would leave it again.

As HE'D DONE when Lancelot was sick, Noah didn't leave Sweetheart Ranch until dawn. He'd sat with Kate by Teddie's bed, talking softly to him. He'd assured the boy he would come back again to Kansas—unlike poor Rob—and that their friendship would endure. To Kate, he hadn't said much at all.

Yet Noah had an extra day to make his case with her. His plane was probably boarding right now in Kansas City. He was still thinking what to say when he finally reached the WB's barn. Noah had driven home with Calvin, who'd picked him up in one of the ranch trucks, apologizing because he hadn't been there last night to help. The rig behind carried Silver and Midnight. By now, the snow reached a man's knees and would have been cold, hard going, if not impossible, on the way home even for the tough WB cow ponies. The pickup slid up to the barn doors.

"What a night," Willow's voice said when Noah walked in. She poked her head out of the first stall, a pitchfork in hand. "Cody went back to bed, but I keep thinking what might have happened to Kate's little boy out there in the dark, the storm."

"Me too."

"How is he, Noah?"

"Bundled under half a dozen blankets, snuggled up with his mom. Sawyer couldn't believe he'd ridden Spencer out in the storm, but by the time he arrived, that warm bath and some blankets, another hot cocoa had helped to warm Teddie. Sawyer said he'll be all right." Once he'd unloaded Midnight and led him to his stall, he said, "Thanks for helping, Willow. I appreciate it."

"I didn't do it for you."

He almost sighed. As she turned away, he took the pitchfork from her. "Listen, I can't leave today after all—I need to rebook my flight—but I'll be out of your way tomorrow, no more reminders that I skipped your wedding. Before I go, how can I at least try to heal the rift between us?" Not that his attempt to do the same with Kate and their relationship had worked. That was still up in the air too.

"I think you said everything before, Noah."

"I didn't say this." He held her gaze, remembering all the years when she was little, then growing, and finally an adult. "You're the best sister a guy could ever have, and I hate seeing such distance in your eyes. Especially because I caused it. I'm sorry," he said again. "I wouldn't have spoiled your beautiful wedding for anything—"

"Except that sudden flight to London."

"Wish I could have missed that plane." He did sigh. "The launch of our new branch office has been nothing but one mess after another, and before I knew it, instead of flying to Kansas, I was on my way to the UK to put out yet another fire. By then, I was exhausted—so was Brent—and I barely knew what day it was, or I would have handled that crisis differently, not gone at all." Or was he so fixated on making a success of J&B that he'd made the wrong choice? "I would have been here instead, but at least next week the new branch will be official, which opens up the whole European market. Things should settle down."

"My brother, the captain of industry."

He shook his head. "Not quite. Please forgive me, Willow." He cupped her face in both hands. "I promise, I'll never miss another big occasion in your life and Cody's."

"What about the small ones?"

He couldn't lie. "I'll do my best there too."

"What's the catch—I have to name my firstborn after you?"

He smiled a little. "Well, middle name, maybe."

Willow snickered. "You really are a wheeler-dealer. How could I forget? When I was a kid, you always bartered with me over chores. Conned me, really, into mucking stalls for you with a promise to buy me a new saddle or take me to Disney World."

"Worked, didn't it?"

"Yes, but I'm no longer that little girl. I'm onto you, big brother." She actually snorted. "I'm a much better negotiator now."

Noah saw his chance to shift the conversation a bit from his own shortcomings. "I'm really proud of you. I'm sure your training business will take off like a rocket come spring, and Cody's a great partner. I'm also glad you'll be living on the WB as Mom gets older."

"So will Zach and Cass, probably."

Noah wasn't sure of that. Zach's resentment of Noah was a factor; he just might decide to leave the ranch permanently to get back at him. And where was he at the moment? No one had heard from him. "If so, Mom will be in her glory—grandkids running around everywhere."

"Let's not get ahead of things," Willow

murmured, but with a blush. "Cody and I have enough to do this first year." She covered Noah's hands with hers, and with their banter about the WB, he'd felt a shift in the break between them.

"I love you, Willow," he murmured, "with all my heart."

She cleared her throat. "That's what family does. We love each other—even you."

"Even me," he said, kissing her forehead. His father being the exception about Noah.

After a moment, Willow drew back. "Now. Since you're still here, and I no longer feel like taking a skillet or riding crop to you, let's get these stalls cleaned."

Noah grinned. "At your service."

"I'll let you do the hard work."

THAT EVENING KATE read Teddie his favorite book, *Janie Wants to Be a Cowgirl*, then tucked him into bed with an extra kiss. She'd given him so many in the past twenty-four hours Teddie was now scrunching up his face beforehand, saying, "Ewww," but Kate couldn't resist. Having him safe and well at home was a huge blessing. As she went down the stairs, she hoped she wouldn't have nightmares as she had last night—or what was left of it once she'd finally fallen asleep.

Tonight at least, she was especially grateful to be in her warm house, her little family sheltered from the last of the storm that would blow out by morning. Snow lay in drifts everywhere on Sweetheart Ranch, and Gabe would need to plow again tomorrow. She felt another pang of loss. Had Noah's plane left on time that morning?

A quick rap at the front door made her pause on the last step, and Noah's face suddenly appeared in the window. Kate did a classic double take.

"Noah. I thought we'd said goodbye." That was, before Teddie ran away.

"I changed my flight till tomorrow." He stomped his boots on the entryway mat. His serious hazel eyes met hers. "Can we talk?"

Kate looked around. In the family room, Meg and Mac were watching a movie together—miracle of all miracles—so Kate led the way to the more formal living room. "Teddie would be glad to see you again—" which was a huge understatement "—but he's sound asleep."

"Maybe before I leave, I'll go up. I won't wake him. But I came to see you." Noah dropped onto a chair, rested his forearms on his spread knees. He stared down at his linked hands. "I've managed to convince Willow that I'm not the worst brother in the world. I thought I'd take another shot with you."

Kate sat on the sofa. She began, "Noah, I was more than grateful for your help last night but—"

"Thank heaven we found Teddie, but I can't just let this go—us, I mean. I know I'll be in New York and you're here. That's a given, but my mother's right. That's not enough reason to call this off."

"Why wouldn't Jean say that? Above all, she misses you. She wants her family together. If that were Teddie, I would too."

Noah glanced at her. "Maybe that's the point. Aren't you curious to see where *we* might go? And I don't mean New York."

She knew what he meant. He must remember their kisses too.

"With luck," he said, "we have most of our lives ahead of us. Why keep burying yourself here at Sweetheart Ranch? Rob wouldn't want you to do that."

"Why?" she echoed. "Because we don't want the same things. We never will." She abruptly rose from the sofa. His unexpected visit was too painful. "I think you'd better go."

His eyes darkened. "Because I came too close to the truth?" Noah stood. He captured her fingers, tucked their joined hands against his chest. "When that man attacked Rob—slashed me too—without warning, we were fighting for our lives. Maybe I should never have offered Rob that job. If I hadn't, yes, he might still be alive. But would he, really?"

"I don't know what you mean."

"I've told you he wasn't happy here. He wanted desperately to get off this ranch. He wanted more for himself, for you and Teddie."

"That job—that company you're so proud of—took my husband, his father, from us! For the last six months of his life, we endured a wretched separation that damaged our marriage, perhaps for good. I still wish I'd had a chance to find some solution..."

"So do I—with my own father—but sometimes that's not possible. Maybe it's time you faced up to your decisions, not his. I was with Rob for those six months. He didn't feel he had any other choice. Cattle prices were down, a hailstorm had damaged the crops...

he owed creditors, loans that Rob couldn't pay."

"Is that supposed to be a revelation? I learned very young that times can be difficult, but situations change."

"Exactly," Noah said.

"We're doing okay now. If Rob hadn't run off to New York, he would have seen that for himself."

"But he didn't."

"And you have no right to judge me—a man who abandoned his family and the WB. I wonder if that wasn't your plan for Rob too."

Noah ran a hand over his hair. "My *plan*, if there was one, was only to help improve Rob's *situation* and, I hoped, yours and Teddie's too. Just like I tried to help with his schooling. I liked the thought of us all being there in New York, friends again, and I've told you what I feel, Kate, what I've always felt so…yeah, from a personal standpoint, I also liked the idea of having *you* nearby."

Stricken, Kate merely stared at him.

She never knew what she might have managed to say, but she didn't have to. Teddie must have heard their voices. He clattered down the stairs, into the room and flung himself in Noah's arms.

"You didn't go!" He buried his face in Noah's chest.

Over Teddie's head, Noah's gaze held hers. Kate saw a world of hurt there, far worse than the day she'd first accused him of co-opting her child's affections. She saw the love he had for Teddie, for her—a love, not simply friendship, that she'd never known was there.

He stroked Teddie's hair. "Guess I've already said too much."

He lifted Teddie and carried him toward the stairs, then up to his room. Kate didn't follow. She stood there, rooted to the living room carpet, unable to make out their quiet conversation, only the low rumble of Noah's voice and Teddie's happy, high-pitched chatter. She couldn't possibly take these last moments from them. Teddie, if not Kate, had been given a reprieve.

But had Noah been right? Had she tried to tie Rob down, as he'd accused her of doing with Teddie? What if she could leave the ranch? What if she and Teddie actually took a vacation to see some sights, as Willow and Cody had on their honeymoon? She wouldn't go as far as South Carolina or Florida, but

Teddie would have an adventure when the very notion still made her stomach turn. Or, what if she showed him the city Noah loved, even for a weekend like the one she'd spent at her college roommate's wedding? That hadn't killed her.

It was a long time before Noah came downstairs. He didn't meet her eyes as he said, "I'll call him from New York."

He didn't mention Kate. This—not last night—was to be the real goodbye, then.

"I wish…there was another way," she murmured.

Noah didn't answer that. He opened the front door.

The wind swept in, tossing his hair and whipping strands of Kate's hair around her until she couldn't see. Blindly, she reached out, her hand grazing Noah's arm. "Have a safe flight tomorrow." Before she'd taken a single step from Sweetheart Ranch except in her thoughts, she'd already closed off her options with Noah but couldn't seem to speak.

For another moment, he looked deeply into her eyes. "I wanted you near me," he said in a low voice she could barely hear, "even when I knew I could never have you for myself."

Oddly, as she watched him leave, it seemed as if the world was ending all over again.

And it was her fault.

CHAPTER TWENTY

NOAH CRAMMED ANOTHER pile of papers into his briefcase. Swearing silently, he checked his watch. He was running late, as usual. His flight to London would leave within the hour—or as soon as his driver reached Teterboro Airport, where the company jet was ready to go.

"Daphne," he yelled. "Where's the new Prentice contract?"

He and Brent had finally managed to bypass Margot's father and seal the deal for the acquisition of the start-up company, which would be completed while Noah was in the UK. The branch-office launch would happen tomorrow, and his bags—one containing his tux—were waiting in the outer room.

"First thing you packed," she called back, then appeared in the doorway. "You've asked me twice. Change of plan, Noah. You're not leaving for another half hour. There's someone here to see you."

For an instant, Noah hoped his unexpected visitor might be Kate. He'd been by turn humiliated, embarrassed and miserable since he'd left Sweetheart Ranch a week ago. He couldn't believe he'd put his feelings on the line then or how much he still missed her. And Teddie. Yet she didn't appear. Instead, his brother walked into the office. "What the— What are you doing here?" Noah asked.

Zach didn't wait for an invitation before he dropped onto one of the leather chairs in front of Noah's desk. "Nice seeing you too," he muttered.

"No, but I mean…you're supposed to be at the WB." According to their mother, Zach had returned to the ranch the day after Noah left.

"Maybe I got used to traveling. Ever since Cass and I got home, I've had this itch to hit the road again—or, in this case, take to the skies today."

Noah glanced toward the anteroom, where Daphne sat. He didn't have time to play guessing games. "Why are you really here, Zach?"

He lifted a finger. "Number one, I wanted

to ask you in person. This isn't much notice, but will you be my best man?"

Was he kidding? They hadn't said five civil words to each other in recent memory.

"Zach, I—"

"Just say yes. I already talked to your secretary."

"Administrative assistant." Daphne loved her title.

"Anyway. She'll switch things around in your schedule. I'm getting married again."

Noah had known Zach was engaged. "But you haven't yet—"

His brother raised his left hand, the one with a new silver band on his fourth finger. "In the Bahamas."

"You went out of the country?" Noah had envisioned them driving around the US like Willow and Cody. Zach hated flying as much as Kate did, yet it seemed he must have a passport.

"Man, what a place. Once we reached Atlantis, Cass thought it was the most romantic spot she could imagine. So, we got hitched. Right on the beach. At sunset."

"Mom didn't know?" She hadn't told Noah. "She must have had a fit. You actually deprived her of another big wedding?"

"Bigger than Willow's." He groaned. "Can you imagine living on the WB another six months while she and Cass planned our event? Mom already told me after Willow's wedding that she'd pull out even more stops the next time now that she has experience. You weren't there," he reminded Noah with an arched eyebrow, "when those two tore the ranch apart. I couldn't go through that again."

"Wow," was all Noah could think to say.

"Yeah. So now, to placate Mom, I'm told we have to have a second ceremony—to make things official, at least in her mind. She promised it will be a small, simple wedding. And reception. I can only hope."

"Man, I don't envy you."

Zach wasn't smiling. "You don't? What I hear, you had your chance and blew it."

"What are you talking about?"

A pair of fingers rose this time. "Number two. Kate Lancaster."

His pulse thudded. It wasn't Noah who'd ruined that. "She made her choice—again—and I have none, except to honor her decision."

"In plain English, how could you let that woman go?"

"It was quite the reverse." Noah hadn't talked to anyone about her. He'd spent the past week holed up in this office, working until midnight not to have a pity party at home alone with a bottle of single malt scotch. "I already humbled myself, laid it all out, and you know what she said?" He didn't wait for Zach to respond. Noah was angry now, another emotion he didn't need. "'Have a safe flight.'"

Zach gazed out the wall of windows at Noah's view of Central Park and the rain. "You let that stand?"

"Don't lecture me. I'm the oldest, not you."

"Well, you obviously need a talking to. Cass used to give me a hard time. I gave her one, too, but in the end—" he grinned "—I never thought I could be this happy. You really gave up with Kate? Mom says she's never seen two people who belong together more—except me and Cass, of course, or Willow and Cody." The eyebrow lifted again. "She also tells me you're crazy about Kate's kid and you've wasted enough time. Instant family, my man. Why pass that up?"

"I couldn't convince her to try, even to take things slow."

Zach stretched out his legs. "Maybe you

didn't try hard enough. You always did take off whenever things got rough."

Noah felt heat rise on the back of his neck. "If you mean my leaving the WB years ago, you know why. I wanted a different life, Zach."

"Sure." He waved that same hand at Noah's well-appointed office. "But you also wanted to get away from Dad. Just making my point."

"I don't need your point. That's all history."

"Is it? That why you rarely come home now, even when he's not there?"

Noah flinched. "When I was a kid, about Teddie Lancaster's age, I was intimidated by Dad's loud voice, his overbearing manner, his constant disapproval, which only got worse over time. He went easy on you because you were younger, but he had all those expectations of me for the WB."

"I know that. So what? You're not a kid now."

"I still remember the night I left…home. He took me into the ranch office, ranted and raved about my 'betrayal,' as he put it. I'd never stood up to him before, and I have to say it felt good to hold my ground—until he delivered his ultimatum." Noah took a breath. "'Leave now—and you're no son of mine.'"

"Ouch. Nobody else has forgotten that, either, but that was a long time ago. He still left you your share of the WB," Zach pointed out.

Noah couldn't argue with that. Living in New York, working his tail off here to succeed, he'd been surprised by the inheritance he'd eventually received, but he'd never planned to return, certainly not to take over the ranch. Never considered what his father had done, including Noah in his will. *It's time you earned it*, Zach had told him.

"I don't come home because I have a business to run—like you with the WB."

Zach gazed at his boots. "Yet all you remember is how unhappy you were there. Am I right? I'm grateful you managed the spread while Cass and I were gone and, yeah, you did a good job, but didn't you feel even a glimmer of satisfaction then?"

"I didn't…mind it as much as I thought I would, okay?"

"Especially staying next door to Kate, huh?"

"Drop it," Noah murmured. "Though I suppose that might suit your purpose to have me take over permanently. Maybe Cass misses LA, planning big social events there, and the ranch is too confining for her. Maybe you'd rather live in the city too."

Zach looked aghast. "No, I wouldn't."

"Come on. You didn't mind taking over the WB yourself?"

"Nope. How many times do I have to tell you that?"

Surprised, Noah wondered if he'd ever been listening. He glanced at his watch. "I've always thought you blamed me for leaving you holding the bag."

Zach suddenly grinned. "Are you completely nuts? I get up every morning thanking the lord for my good fortune. Cass loves it there too. Frankly, I was glad when you left."

"Then why—"

"Do I give *you* such a hard time? One thing, it's fun."

Noah hid a faint smile. That was Zach, and this unexpected conversation seemed like old times again between brothers, like that first night before Zach had left the WB to take a vacation—and get married. Noah searched his desk drawer for his favorite pen. He'd use it to sign the Prentice deal tomorrow. Kind of a good luck charm, because for the past week, he'd been expecting that to go sour too. "Knock yourself out," he said at last.

"Well, I've said my piece." Zach stood. "I'm holding you up, and I'm meeting Cass at the Guggenheim. We're in New York for a few days before heading back. The drizzle here is a nice change from the snow we've had all winter."

"Part of which you missed. I'm sure there's more to come." Noah walked him to the door. "Are we okay, then?"

"Why not?" Which sounded like a foregone conclusion for Zach. "I think I've ridden you hard enough for now. Remember what I said, though, about you and Kate. I know she's a real homebody, but then so was I. Is this fancy office, your title on the door, the luxury apartment Mom told me about, what you really want? I'd even give up the WB for Cass, if that's what it took to be with her." In the doorway, he slung an arm around Noah's neck. "You won't do better than Kate, you old dog." He held up more fingers on his free hand. "By the way, and this is number three, I never resented you for leaving the WB." His voice dropped lower. "I resented you because I've missed my big brother."

Noah swallowed hard. "I've missed you, too, Zach."

"Then hop on that fancy plane of yours, hotshot, and be there—this time—for our wedding." He laughed. "Guess who's one of Cass's bridesmaids?"

AFTER ZACH LEFT, Noah sank into his desk chair again. Considering their reunion, he wished he could spend time with his brother and Cass while they were in the city, but London was calling. He added a few things to his briefcase, then closed it. In the anteroom, Daphne kept clearing her throat, as if to remind him the car was waiting downstairs. Time to go.

But had Zach been right? Had Noah left the WB years ago merely to make his own way in the world? Or did he always leave whenever things got tough? Even Wilkins had pointed that out.

True, their father had not been an easy man. From the time he was five years old, Noah had been trained to take over the WB, when all along Zach had probably wanted the job. Finally, of course, Noah had rebelled against those expectations, the narrow restrictions placed upon him. All it had taken then was that one explosive argument to create the break that had lasted with his father until he died. Similar to Kate and Rob's separation, Noah had never been able to work out their relationship.

He did remember those unhappy times at the WB, but lately, even with his dad no longer there, he hadn't gone home when the rest of his family needed him, Willow's wedding being the best example.

Were his dad's ultimatum and Noah's last words to him all there was to remember? *I'll show you.* They'd both displayed hot tempers then, but at other, better times, he'd taken Noah as a kid fishing or camping on the far pastureland with Zach, and the three of them had cooked over a fire, then slept under the stars. His dad, in a sleeping bag between them, had even told his boys ghost stories, terrifying them, then making them laugh at themselves. Despite their longtime rift, his dad's death had affected Noah deeply, perhaps more than he'd realized until now.

He'd felt a glimmer of that when he talked with Teddie about Rob. About angels.

Noah had never been able to win his father's approval, and he couldn't change that. Yes, he'd made a success of himself, and with J&B doing well plus the Prentice acquisition's promise, the future looked even brighter. And yet…

When he'd left Kansas, determined to prove himself, he hadn't stopped loving his father. Because of his disapproval during Noah's boyhood, maybe he'd stopped loving himself.

For years Noah had focused solely on business, yet J&B was only part of life. If not, and that was the same accusation he'd leveled at Kate about Sweetheart Ranch, he would never have let her know how he still felt about her. He wouldn't have taken to Teddie as he did. He'd missed out on something after all—having a family. He loved that little kid, loved her too.

His next thought felt like a blow to the head. He hadn't wanted the WB, a life that could have been spent with her and, now, Teddie. Instead, as Zach had said, he'd run off to New York, to his faster-paced lifestyle, to the few women who'd never seemed as right as Kate did for him. No wonder he'd never married, and to be honest, he wasn't that happy alone. Was it possible his business, like Sweetheart Ranch for her, had been his own safe haven?

Maybe Noah had been hiding out too.

And what if—the notion seemed like a burst of sunshine after another Kansas blizzard—Kate needed him now just as he'd always needed her?

TEDDIE RACED THROUGH the house again, steps ahead of Meg. This morning, Kate had gone to town, and Meg suspected she'd made her escape to avoid another meltdown from her son. "Hey, sweetie. Hold up."

Teddie picked up his pace. "I don't have to do what you say!"

"Oh, yes, you do, young man," Meg called in her best imitation of Kate's mom voice. "Stop or I'll have to send you to your room."

Teddie's defiance would have astonished her—he was usually an obedient child, at least with her—but in the week since Noah had left, he'd become a pint-size monster. Worse yet, he could outthink Meg, who often felt out of her depth. He'd been off his kitchen chair and running through the downstairs rooms before she could blink. She wished she'd told Kate no about babysitting today.

"Problem?" Mac had wandered into the room, yawning. He wasn't an early riser.

Meg gritted her teeth. Since he'd shown

up a week ago, she'd been avoiding him as much as possible, not ready to negotiate that closure to their broken marriage. "I guess I wasn't cut out to be a nanny." Or, apparently, a mother, another issue she and Mac had never discussed.

He grinned as Teddie sped past again, pieces of the brownie he'd been told to eat at the table flying everywhere. "Let me try."

Meg said, "I doubt you can do better."

"Watch me."

She had to hand it to him. Mac was faster than she was, stronger, too, and in another circuit of the main floor, he snagged Teddie with one arm—Meg had long ago stopped being able to carry him—then tickled him until he was giggling so hard the rest of the brownie fell from his mouth.

Meg groaned. Now she'd have to mop the floor. And why was Mac still here? He should have been flying to Paris or Hong Kong by now, wherever his current route might be. She didn't want to remember their movie night together, the warmth of him next to her if not touching, the laughter they'd shared over the rom-com they'd watched. Her choice, because she'd hoped he wouldn't last five minutes before leaving the room. Kate, the traitor, hadn't joined them as a buffer, the role she'd been reluctantly playing since Mac first walked into the house.

"You give?" Mac raised one hand to tickle Teddie again. "If not, I'll have to call on Mr. Grabby Fingers—and you don't want him. He's a fiend at tickling little boys."

Teddie roared with laughter. "I'm not afraid of Mr. Grabby." He wriggled to get down. As soon as Mac set him on his feet, Teddie darted off. "Can't catch me!"

Meg watched him veer off toward the kitchen. "Mac, he's headed outside."

They would never catch him then. Teddie had a million hiding places on the ranch, or he might run to the barn to crouch in Spencer's stall unseen. Since the night he'd run away in the blizzard, he'd been grounded, but at the moment he wasn't obeying any rules.

If Kate got home and Teddie wasn't here, she would be terrified, and Meg would be in trouble. She and Kate weren't exactly best buddies since their quarrel about Noah. And Mac.

"Hurry," she shouted as the back door slammed. Then Meg heard a scramble on the steps followed by a loud "oof." Mac entered the kitchen again with Teddie squirming between him and Gabe Morgan.

"Thought I'd ask if Kate's offer of lunch was still open," Gabe said, holding fast to Teddie's arm. "Didn't expect to run into this escapee."

"You're a lifesaver," Meg said. "Thanks, Gabe."

"No problem."

He and Mac had met the first day after he arrived, and Gabe looked him over again now. Mac returned the stare, the air suddenly full of testosterone. "Maybe you'd rather eat your lunch at the barn," her ex drawled.

"Mac," she said in a chiding tone.

Teddie struggled until Gabe released his arm. Seeing an opportunity, he was about to take off again, possibly for the front door, when Meg blocked his way.

"Go to your room, Teddie. Now."

His mouth turned down. "Are you going to tell my mom?"

"Yes, and she won't like hearing how you've misbehaved."

"I don't care! You're mean!" He stormed past her to the stairs.

Meg waited until he'd slammed his bedroom door, then turned to Mac. "I appreciate your help, but I can manage from here." With Kate gone, she would have to make Gabe's lunch.

Mac stared at Gabe. "You should go. Meg and I have important things to talk about."

She opened her mouth to respond, but Gabe met her eyes. He'd never said or done anything specific to make her think he had a real interest in her, but in that moment, she saw resignation in his gaze. "He's right," Gabe said, then opened the door. "Tell Kate thanks, but I need to go into town anyway. I'll eat lunch at the café."

Mac watched him go, the door shutting softly behind him. "I've been meaning to ask. What is he to you?"

"Kate's foreman. Period. I can't believe you were that rude."

"Seems like a nice enough guy, but you're more than Kate's aunt to him."

"And what is that to *you*?" Meg blew a wisp of hair from her face. "Why are you hanging around? I realize we haven't talked—"

"Gee, I noticed there never seems to be a good time. You're better than Teddie as an escape artist. Until we do talk, I'm not budging."

"You still have a job, right?"

"I took a short leave of absence so you and I could iron things out."

Meg couldn't quite believe he was serious. Mac loved to fly; he'd never switched his schedule for her before.

"The new and improved Jonathan Mc-Claren," he murmured.

"Mac, I'm flattered that you came all this way, that you want to somehow patch things up. But I'm not interested." Although he could be a dear at times. He'd been good with Teddie. Mac would have made a great father.

His tone was flat. "You aren't."

"I've made a life for myself here."

"Have you?"

The start of one anyway. "I'm a big help to Kate with Teddie."

"Great work this morning," he pointed out.

"I know, but he's been awful ever since Noah went to New York."

"Because he and Kate couldn't 'work things out.' Which, as I'm sure you're about to tell me, is none of my business." He gestured between them. "You and I, however, are."

"I don't know what you want from me."

"Exactly," he said. "Same goes. Now we're getting somewhere."

"Mac, I won't change my mind. I'm happy here."

"You were happy enough in Chicago until you suddenly seemed to notice I wasn't there half the time. You were okay until…the baby. So what else is it, Meg?"

He had her there. "Something I haven't wanted to confront, I suppose." She needed to be honest with him, with herself. "Mac, you always…remind me of my parents. I know, that's neurotic and at first, I thought— hoped—I could get over the worry I felt every time you left home, that constant fear of something terrible happening—"

"That is neurotic."

Meg couldn't disagree. "I mean, you *fly* in a metal tube tens of thousands of feet up in the air. So many things can go wrong, and I can't help how I feel. When I was a kid, I always had that fear of watching my mom or dad, sometimes both of them at once, leave me behind—" she felt a band of steel around her ribs "—not knowing if I'd ever see them again."

His voice gentled. "They were army people, Meg. Warriors. I'm a commercial pilot in an industry with an excellent safety record. Flying is far safer than driving a car—banal statistic, I know, but it's true."

"I still worry. And after Rob was killed—"

"Not in a plane."

"—I went a bit crazy. Don't you see? Even in a different manner, Kate's loss could become my loss too."

Mac came closer. "Rob was walking down the street, and a minute later, he was dead. Safety's an illusion, him being a prime example." His eyes held that same warmth and understanding she'd first fallen in love with, the look that seemed to tell her everything would be all right forever. "Sweetheart, I never realized you had such fear. Which must mean you care about me, a little." He hesitated. "Listen. If you want me to, I'll…resign, give up flying for the airline. I can always teach. Because what I don't want to give up—the divorce made me see what I *can't* lose—is you."

Tears filled Meg's eyes. "You're serious."

"I'd do anything to have you back." He cracked a smile. "Even beat that guy Gabe to a pulp if I have to."

"That won't be necessary. There's nothing between us."

"Not that he wouldn't like there to be."

"You men," she said, blinking. "Mac, I don't need you to sacrifice what you love—flying, I mean. That's a part of you that I fell for, but in the end—"

"It's not the end, Meg. Please."

"We were over when—as you bluntly mentioned—the baby died. That was real, not in my imagination, and if we'd had any chance before, after that we didn't. Not only were you not there when it happened, you came home, then left again as soon as you could."

"I had to. I was on the schedule."

Meg scoffed. "See what I mean? The airline would have given you compassionate leave, I'm sure. Did you even ask?"

"I don't remember. All I do remember is you shutting me out. I couldn't reach you, Meg. You turned away, grieved without me. You don't think I heard you crying? Saw the shattered look in your eyes every time I tried to approach you?"

"You had your priorities. See above."

"We're talking about our *baby*. You don't think that unborn child was my priority too? That you weren't?"

"No," she murmured. There. He wanted

to discuss everything that had gone wrong? Finally, she'd said it.

Mac let out a breath. "Meg, I wanted to be there for you. I wanted to hold you."

"Instead, you packed and left. As you always did."

"Yeah, but you want to know why? Not only because I couldn't comfort you." His gaze looked blurry. His voice sounded husky. "I didn't know how to comfort myself, okay? I'm not the kind of guy to wear my heart on my sleeve, and I couldn't watch what was happening to us. That was an excuse, I know that now, but I felt...somehow I'd failed you but didn't know how to make anything better. And you wouldn't let me try." He paused again. "What happened to us—not only to you—was terrible, and I hope that never happens again, but I'm miserable without you. We could try to have another baby—not to replace the child we lost, that's not possible, but to go on...together. I want you back. I love you, Meg." He shook his head. "I don't know what else to say."

"You still do love me? After all the grief I've given you?"

He cradled her face in his hands. "You have—and yes, I still do. Love you."

How many times had Meg wished her parents would leave the army? That their family could stay intact, always? And actually, it had. Her parents had both survived, retired from the military with full pensions. Her fears had seemed valid once, but she'd been a girl, not a woman then, and now, Mac had just handed her his heart.

What else could she do? He was right. She did care about him. Meg moved deeper into his embrace, raised her mouth to his and felt she was truly home. Sweetheart Ranch would always hold a special place in her heart, but her place was with Mac. The only man she'd ever wanted, the man she loved.

He was right about that too. There were no guarantees—except for that.

CHAPTER TWENTY-ONE

KATE CAME BACK from town to find her aunt and Mac locked in an embrace, and it seemed apparent they'd been that way for some time. Meg looked radiant.

"We're staying—or rather, getting back—together," she announced. "I'm not going to change my name after all. I never took that next step after I looked into the process—which should have told me something."

Kate hugged her but felt her spirits sink. She already missed her aunt and best friend. "That means you'll be leaving for Chicago." It must be the week for people to leave.

Meg rattled on, oblivious to Kate's mixed feelings. "Temporarily. Mac will begin flying out of Charlotte in the spring. Cutting back on his schedule. A nice change, don't you think?" Her eyes sparkled like the brilliance of her engagement ring, which along with her wedding band was now on her finger again. "Kate, I do hate to leave you—but we'll be house hunting there soon. Can you just see me in a gorgeous Southern-style home with gobs of crown molding?"

"Sounds lovely."

Mac said, "In the meantime, we need to get our house in Chicago ready for market."

"I'm not looking forward to that," Meg said, "but I'm so excited!"

"Obviously." Kate hugged her again, then Mac. "I'm happy for you both. I didn't really want to lose my favorite uncle-in-law."

Mac grinned. "You won't lose either of us. The welcome mat in North Carolina will always be out." He must see, though, that Kate was fighting tears. "We'll put a swing set in the backyard, how's that? Or one of those elaborate climbing things, for Teddie."

"And maybe one of our own." Meg grinned. "We're going to try for a baby again."

"Oh, Meg. You're both so dear to me. I'm glad things worked out." But the words had sounded choked, and Kate's throat tightened.

Meg's glowing smile faded. "You'll be all right?"

"Of course. You've been a tremendous help. With Teddie too."

"Speaking of... He's been banished to his room." Meg explained the flying circuit of the house, the brownie crumbs everywhere. "Including, I'm afraid, the carpet in the living room. I cleaned as well as I could on the first pass—"

"Don't worry about it. I'll talk to Teddie. I can't believe how badly he's behaved all week. He's not himself."

"But you do know why."

"Yes," Kate admitted. She felt that way herself.

"You know the solution."

"Meg, we've been over this—"

"And you haven't yet called Noah to straighten out your own relationship." She turned in Mac's arms to give him another kiss. "If we can do it, anyone can."

Kate wasn't sure she agreed. She'd made herself clear before Noah left. She hadn't heard from him since. "I don't see how."

Meg slipped from Mac's embrace, then set her hands upon Kate's shoulders. "Call him. Make Noah happy—and yourself. Teddie too," she added. "Or, are you really going to hole up here at Sweetheart Ranch forever— fine as it is—living on memories of Rob, your mother's abandonment, your dad's accident? All of that took people you loved from you, but there's something else for you, waiting.

That doesn't mean betraying Rob's memory. Don't you think he'd want you to make a new life?"

"Without him," Kate murmured, yet her thoughts didn't focus now on Rob. She envisioned Noah's face, his expression when they'd said goodbye. Maybe it was indeed Kate who'd made things impossible between them. *I wanted you near me, even when I knew I could never have you.* Had she been clinging, as Meg said as well, to the past? To her own sorrow over Rob, her guilt? Maybe they never would have reconciled but divorced then gone their separate ways except for his court-mandated time with Teddie. She would never know.

"Noah was right, wasn't he? He told me Rob was no cowboy, that he wanted off this ranch, but I pressured him to stay."

"Because that seemed safer for you."

"I was wrong, Meg. I would have had Rob stay even when he was unhappy." She'd tried to force him to make a choice that wasn't right for him, protected herself, as she always did, for fear of losing again. But that's exactly what did happen. She'd lost the last six months of his life too. "What kind of love is that? We were great together once, but sadly that's over now."

And at last, Kate knew. Like Meg, she had to begin to truly live again. Not only for Teddie's sake but for hers too—perhaps the best way to honor Rob's memory. Kate had thought once, briefly, of taking her son on a weekend trip or a real vacation, but her imaginary plans had now changed.

"I'm not calling Noah." Kate paused for another moment, as if perched on the edge of a high cliff. She didn't know if there would be a bottom, but she jumped anyway. "I'm flying," she said, "to New York."

TWO NIGHTS LATER, not quite knowing where he was, Noah landed again in Kansas City. With a sense of déjà vu, he rented a car, then drove toward Sweetheart Ranch. He was here early for his brother's second wedding next week but had other personal business to tend to first. At least it wasn't snowing, the roads were clear—and this time, he didn't dread seeing his family. But he had no idea how to approach Kate, as he had so casually in the airport before getting snowbound together in that first blizzard.

He felt so jet-lagged after his turn-around

trip to London and the late-night celebration for the branch-office launch—smashing success!—before his flight back he could hardly see. He was knocking at her front door before the right words came to him. As usual.

Meg answered and her eyes brightened. "Noah."

"Is Kate home?"

"Kate's always home. Or she has been. Come in." Meg called up the stairs, "You have an important visitor," then vanished into the family room, where Noah could hear obvious sounds of some musical movie from the TV. Bollywood, it sounded like.

Kate came down the stairs, a dress hanger over one arm and a sweater draped around her neck. Her dark hair looked mussed. Her gaze shot to his, and she froze. "Oh. Noah. I was just packing."

"Sorry to interrupt," he began, but he wondered if he'd heard right. Travel? Where could she be going? Kate laid the clothes on a small chair in the entryway. Noah couldn't read her expression. "Teddie asleep?"

"Yes. I hope." She arched an eyebrow. "He's been a madman—"

"Ever since I left?" But her answer to the question he'd blurted out might not be the one he wanted. "Kate, I know we didn't part on the best of terms. I know you thought that was goodbye—me back to New York, you staying here—"

"Wait. I think we need some privacy for this." She turned, then led him to the opposite side of the house from the entry and family room. She indicated a seat in the more formal living room, but Noah remained standing. He shrugged out of his overcoat, flung it over a chair, then shoved both hands in his pants pockets. Kate seemed to feel awkward too.

"You, um, look the same," she murmured, eyeing his three-piece suit, "as you did when I met you in the airport that day."

"No jeans and flannel shirt tonight. I was in London."

Kate hadn't taken a seat, either, as if she didn't expect him to stay long. Or was thinking of tossing him out. This wasn't how he'd envisioned their heart-to-heart talk. Had he really expected her to throw herself in his arms? "Oh, London," she said. "You mean for the branch office?"

"Yeah. Everything went well there, but I've spent most of the past couple of days on a plane. A quick in and out of the U.K.—" His voice dropped low, his tone pleading. "Because of you. Kate. I didn't finish saying what I need to the last time I saw you. I *love* you. I think I've always loved you, and I'm through trying to hide that even from myself."

She half smiled. "I thought I was the one who hid."

"In a different way." Noah didn't care now that he didn't have the perfect words. He spoke from the heart. "I might not convince you this minute to give us a real chance, but if I have to commute between Manhattan and Barren every weekend, every holiday, every vacation I have, hell, every personal day or when I'm running a raging fever—I won't give up. No matter what, I'll be here. I'll wear you down until you can't say no."

Her eyes softened. "That sounds drastic. What if you don't have to convince me?"

Noah blinked. "You mean—"

"Why do you think I was packing? Where do you think I was going?"

Not to New York, surely not. Kate hated the city. She'd gone there once—for that wedding—but hadn't changed her mind. She'd told him so. Still, hope burst in his chest like a flower opening up.

"You were coming to see me?" Noah shook his head. If that was true, and he prayed it was, he'd made this wretched trip halfway across the world and back without needing to. Noah took a tentative step toward her, and Kate took another, then they were in each other's arms.

"I don't need to pack now. You came to see me first," Kate said.

"Plus, I wouldn't dare skip my brother's wedding next week. I understand you're a bridesmaid."

"And you're his best man."

"I kind of make a habit of that," he said, remembering her wedding to Rob. Now, it was his turn with Kate to make a life together, if not right now, then soon. "After Zach and Cass are married again, I'm staying for a while, making time for us. You and me. And about the WB…after this winter, I realized it's still my home."

"You big…cowboy," she murmured, then raised her face to his. "I love you too."

Noah kissed her, and to his vast relief, Kate didn't hesitate. She kissed him back.

WELL, KATE THOUGHT. At least Noah would be a part-time cowboy. The next morning—after they'd talked half the night and he'd finally slept at Sweetheart Ranch, and they'd seen Meg and Mac off for Chicago with teary goodbyes and promises to see each other soon—he and Kate went down to the barn with Teddie, where Bandit, who'd come with them, scampered off to inspect some interesting smell outside.

Kate was still smiling. Seeing Teddie's face that morning when Noah appeared in the kitchen for breakfast had been the perfect cap to a perfect yesterday.

He and Noah headed straight for Lancelot's stall, as if they'd never been apart. Teddie jumped up and down until Noah gently reminded him to be quiet around horses.

Then he gave her a pointed look. "What do you think, Kate? After this colt's weaned, which won't be for a while, he'd be ready to go back to the WB—"

"No," Teddie said emphatically, being careful to lower his voice.

"Or," Noah said, pausing, "maybe you'd rather keep him."

Teddie's eyes widened. "Here? For good?"

"I'll ask Zach for official permission, but I'm sure he'll agree." Noah's brother, he'd told her, didn't object to much of anything these days. Kate was glad the two had reunited as brothers.

"Thank you, N—Mr. Bodine!"

He laughed. "I think you can call me Noah." Teddie hugged him, then dashed over to fling his arms around Lancelot's neck. "And after all, you did name him. In my book that means you own him. Okay with you, Kate?"

"Okay," she agreed.

"Then I'll have two horses!"

"Yes, you will, and someday this whole place will be yours," Kate said.

Teddie was no longer listening. He was over the moon about the foal but also because Noah would be a true part of his life now. When Teddie had had enough time with his new colt, he dashed off to chase one of the barn cats, then Noah turned to her.

Hands clasped, they walked outside to stand in the bright sun that bounced off the snow. They gazed at the land around them, their eyes tracking Teddie's whereabouts. "I know we're not ready to make this official—I've promised you can take all the time you need—but we should at least hash out the where of it that can get us there. You're not about to give up Sweetheart Ranch—I wouldn't want you to—and I'm in too deep with the business right now to think of selling out. Considering the fact that you were already packing last night, will you consider spending some time in New York now and then? I think Teddie would like the city, which is full of those 'adventures' he can have. There's even horseback riding."

"In Manhattan? I didn't know that."

"There's a rental operation in Central Park." He paused. "Can you see yourself there, Kate? A little?"

She didn't hesitate. "I've shut myself away on Sweetheart Ranch for far too long. Maybe I'd like some adventure too."

Noah broke into a grin. "Who are you? What have you done with the woman I love?"

"She's already changing. My mother leaving years ago, my dad flipping his tractor, even Rob… Bad things happen sometimes, horrific things, but we have to go on. Instead, as you said, I walled myself in. Teddie too."

Noah gazed up at the blue sky. "When I left the WB long ago, I didn't intend to come back—except for the occasional family thing. My dad and I were done at that point. I wish we'd had a second chance, but we didn't. My fault as much as his."

"Like me with Rob."

"Yeah, but you know what? I did miss the WB. I've done a lot of thinking about that the past few days. My leaving then—Zach said I ran off—was just that. I didn't know how to reach Dad, how to make things right except to knuckle under and do what he wanted— take over the WB. He sure couldn't reach me. So I ran from the ranch, and from him." He shook his head. "No, from myself too. It wasn't only the ranch I was escaping. It was his judgment, but in my head that has followed me everywhere. I took refuge in the business, just like you did here, from the pain."

"Then I guess we both need to change."

"I can't prove myself to Dad now, but I can stop running from those unhappy feelings. He did love me as he could. He left me part of the WB, a sign maybe, his hope that one day I'd come home, and—I felt this when I talked to Teddie about angels—I think Dad's watching over me too." Noah swallowed. "From now on, I can be a better brother, a better son to my mom. Prove myself not to him, but to myself. Maintain a better balance in my life—our lives."

Blinking, Kate twined her arms around his neck. "Speaking of mothers, remember when you told me that Teddie needs more mental stimulation? Instead, I wanted to keep him here, safe and protected, but that's not always possible, is it? I could never homeschool him, Noah." She'd seen him beat Noah at chess when Teddie had never played before. "So I'm thinking maybe that gifted program in Farrier might be right for him. The one you went to?"

"It's a great program. I'm pretty sure we can get him in. Don't worry about the cost."

We, he'd said, and *our lives*. Kate liked the sound of that. It would mean driving Teddie to school every day, but they were already making decisions together. It seemed absolutely right that this should be one of the first.

"We can do this, Kate. I'll spend as much time as I can here, working as I did remotely from the WB. Helping Zach and you too. When I need to be back in the city, you can come with me—as my wife, I'm hoping, one of these days. Who knows? Maybe you'll even want to get a passport."

Kate grinned. At last she would venture forth into Noah's bigger world, not as scary a proposition as it would once have been, and she teased him. "I can't wait. To see New York, I mean."

He laughed again. "Yes, you can. But I'm really glad you're willing to try."

Kate moved closer and felt the strong, steady beat of his heart, the softer echo of hers. After a long moment when she couldn't trust her voice, she lifted her face to his, and they kissed, then went back for another. From a few yards away, she heard Teddie make a sound of disgust. Bandit barked, and she and Noah drew apart, laughing.

Years ago, he had made his escape to the city. Kate had hunkered down on Sweetheart Ranch. But if she had lost so much in her life, look now at what she had gained. Maybe she and Noah had both missed the point before. If the bad things in life couldn't be avoided, or hidden from, then neither should the good.

From now on, and always, Noah would be her safe haven.

And Kate would be his refuge.

* * * * *

Get 4 FREE REWARDS!

We'll send you 2 FREE Books plus 2 FREE Mystery Gifts.

Love Inspired books feature uplifting stories where faith helps guide you through life's challenges and discover the promise of a new beginning.

FREE Value Over $20

Get 4 FREE REWARDS!

We'll send you 2 FREE Books <u>plus</u> 2 FREE Mystery Gifts.

Love Inspired Suspense books showcase how courage and optimism unite in stories of faith and love in the face of danger.

FREE
Value Over
$20

YES! Please send me 2 FREE Love Inspired Suspense novels and my 2 FREE mystery gifts (gifts are worth about $10 retail). After receiving them, if I don't wish to receive any more books, I can return the shipping statement marked "cancel." If I don't cancel, I will receive 6 brand-new novels every month and be billed just $5.24 each for the regular-print edition or $5.99 each for the larger-print edition in the U.S., or $5.74 each for the regular-print edition or $6.24 each for the larger-print edition in Canada. That's a savings of at least 13% off the cover price. It's quite a bargain! Shipping and handling is just 50¢ per book in the U.S. and $1.25 per book in Canada.* I understand that accepting the 2 free books and gifts places me under no obligation to buy anything. I can always return a shipment and cancel at any time. The free books and gifts are mine to keep no matter what I decide.

Choose one: ☐ **Love Inspired Suspense**
Regular-Print
(153/353 IDN GNWN)

☐ **Love Inspired Suspense**
Larger-Print
(107/307 IDN GNWN)

Name (please print)

Address   Apt. #

City   State/Province   Zip/Postal Code

Email: Please check this box ☐ if you would like to receive newsletters and promotional emails from Harlequin Enterprises ULC and its affiliates. You can unsubscribe anytime.

Mail to the **Harlequin Reader Service:**
IN U.S.A.: P.O. Box 1341, Buffalo, NY 14240-8531
IN CANADA: P.O. Box 603, Fort Erie, Ontario L2A 5X3

Want to try 2 free books from another series! Call 1-800-873-8635 or visit www.ReaderService.com.

LIS21R

HARLEQUIN SELECTS COLLECTION

From Robyn Carr to RaeAnne Thayne to Linda Lael Miller and Sherryl Woods we promise (actually, GUARANTEE!) each author in the Harlequin Selects collection has seen their name on the *New York Times* or *USA TODAY* bestseller lists!

YES! Please send me the **Harlequin Selects Collection**. This collection begins with 3 FREE books and 2 FREE gifts in the first shipment. Along with my 3 free books, I'll also get 4 more books from the Harlequin Selects Collection, which I may either return and owe nothing or keep for the low price of $24.14 U.S./$28.82 CAN. each plus $2.99 U.S./$7.49 CAN. for shipping and handling per shipment*.If I decide to continue, I will get 6 or 7 more books (about once a month for 7 months) but will only need to pay for 4. That means 2 or 3 books in every shipment will be FREE! If I decide to keep the entire collection, I'll have paid for only 32 books because 19 were FREE! I understand that accepting the 3 free books and gifts places me under no obligation to buy anything. I can always return a shipment and cancel at any time. My free books and gifts are mine to keep no matter what I decide.

☐ 262 HCN 5576   ☐ 462 HCN 5576

Name (please print)

Address   Apt. #

City   State/Province   Zip/Postal Code

Mail to the **Harlequin Reader Service:**
IN U.S.A.: P.O. Box 1341, Buffalo, NY 14240-8531
IN CANADA: P.O. Box 603, Fort Erie, Ontario L2A 5X3

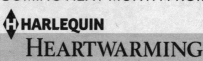
#387 THE RANCHER'S UNEXPECTED TWINS
Jade Valley, Wyoming • by Trish Milburn

Dean Wheeler is willing to marry Sunny Breckinridge and be a dad to her orphaned niece and nephew to own the ranch he loves. But is risking his heart in a pretend marriage part of the bargain?

#388 FALLING FOR THE LAWMAN
Heroes of Shelter Creek • by Claire McEwen

Gracie Long is impulsive and bends the rules. Deputy Adam Sears follows a strict moral code. As they work together to track poachers, Gracie starts to wonder if she can have a future with someone so different.

#389 THE TEXAS SEAL'S SURPRISE
Three Springs, Texas • by Cari Lynn Webb

Former Navy SEAL Wes Tanner loves his rescue horses—and they need his help. When pregnant Abby James arrives in town, seeking a fresh start, she lends a hand...but can she save Wes, too?

#390 THE REBEL COWBOY'S BABY
The Cowboys of Garrison, Texas
by Sasha Summers

When Brooke Young and Audy Briscoe become guardians of their best friends' baby, they have to set aside their rocky past to give baby Joy the family she's lost. But falling for each other wasn't part of the plan...

HWCNM0821

Visit
ReaderService.com
Today!

As a valued member of the Harlequin Reader Service, you'll find these benefits and more at ReaderService.com:

- Try 2 free books from any series
- Access risk-free special offers
- View your account history & manage payments
- Browse the latest Bonus Bucks catalog